P9-CEO-506

MURDER IN MAYFAIR

Murder in Mayfair

An Atlas Catesby Mystery

D. M. Quincy

NEW YORK

This is a work of fiction. All of the names, characters, organizations, places, and events portrayed in this novel are either products of the author's imagination or used fictitiously. Any resemblance to real or actual events, locales, or persons, living or dead, is entirely coincidental.

Published in the United States by Crooked Lane Books, an imprint of The Quick Brown Fox & Company LLC.

Crooked Lane Books and its logo are trademarks of The Quick Brown Fox & Company LLC.

Library of Congress Catalog-in-Publication data available upon request.

ISBN (hardcover): 978-1-68331-225-3
ISBN (ePub): 978-1-68331-226-0
ISBN (Kindle): 978-1-68331-227-7
ISBN (ePDF): 978-1-68331-228-4

Cover design by Lori Palmer
Book design by Jennifer Canzone

Printed in the United States.

www.crookedlanebooks.com

Crooked Lane Books
34 West 27th St., 10th Floor
New York, NY 10001

First edition: July 2017

10 9 8 7 6 5 4 3 2 1

To my mother and father, for giving me everything worth having

CHAPTER ONE

Had his mount not lost its shoe on the return journey to London, Atlas Catesby would not have been in a position to purchase another man's wife.

He'd left the ornery stallion he'd borrowed from his friend, Gabriel Young, the Earl of Charlton, in the care of the inn ostler and removed to the inn, a ramshackle affair with a curious overhanging upper floor. He and Charlton had just taken their seats in the rustic parlor when a commotion kicked up in the yard. The harsh bellow of a man was interrupted by the agitated voice of a woman.

Charlton looked in the direction of the yard. "I wonder what all the clatter is about."

"It's none of our concern." Atlas sipped his too-sweet ale and tried to ignore the rumpus, the lingering discomfort in his left foot reminding him he had enough problems of his own. "We're just passing through. Leave local matters to the locals."

"How can you drink from that?" A mild look of disgust marred Charlton's face, a visage most ladies of London's haute *ton* found tremendously appealing. The earl's own pewter tankard remained untouched. "Lord only knows where it's been."

"I'm thirsty. Besides, I've encountered worse."

"It does not surprise," Charlton said with a haughty lift of his amber brow, "that your treks to primitive lands have accustomed you to filthy conditions that are incompatible with good health."

"On the contrary." Atlas bottomed out his tankard. "Getting out of England is precisely what keeps my health and sanity intact. It is being stuck here indefinitely that tests my nerves." His broken left foot, which had yet to heal properly, had kept him grounded in gloomy England for far too long. How he longed for the warm sun and sweet breezes of the Mediterranean.

The publican's wife approached and set two earthenware plates of mutton on the scarred table with a clank. She straightened, hands on her hips, and peered out of the taproom's sashed windows. A crowd composed of what appeared to be mostly ostlers, postboys, and passing travelers had gathered in the yard, but the object of their interest remained hidden from view.

"He's a mean one, that Varvick." She was a thick-featured woman with a lived-in face who spoke with a harsh accent. Atlas detected a Germanic lilt to her words. "There's no telling vat he'll do next. Selling her like she's cattle."

Atlas, who had minimal interest in gossip and even less in the goings-on of a small village he'd never visited before, kept his attention on slicing his meat, which proved surprisingly rich and delicate, considering their shabby surroundings.

"I beg your pardon?" Charlton sat up straighter, perky with interest, which prompted Atlas to suppress a groan. Next to the finer things in life, his sybaritic friend loved nothing more than a good on-dit—unlike Atlas, who was still recovering and wished to reach London as expediently as possible, hopefully with no further interruptions along the journey. "What's this you say about someone being sold?" Charlton asked the woman.

"That Mr. Varvick, he calls himself gentry, but he behaves no better than a common cutpurse in St. Giles." The publican's wife leaned closer. "Selling his vife like a lamb to the slaughter. He's already ruined her by parading her in the yard with a noose around her neck."

Atlas looked up from his plate. "A what?"

"A halter," she said. "He's auctioning her off to the highest bidder. There's no telling vere that poor gel vill end up."

"I say!" Charlton stared at her, obviously aghast. "Do you mean to tell us that people still sell their wives in this day and age?"

She harrumphed. "Not decent folk."

Outrage seared Atlas's chest. "Surely she has family who will put a stop to this farce."

"I couldn't say." She lifted one shoulder. "Nobody knows Mrs. Varvick's people or vere she come from. The mister, he spends most of his time in London, and he just showed up vith her one day, and that vas that." She wiped her hands on her apron. "Can I get you anything else?"

"No, our thanks to you, madam." A charming smile touched Charlton's lips. As the publican's wife shuffled back to the kitchen, the earl turned to Atlas. "Selling one's wife. Can you imagine?" He cut a small slice of mutton. "The humbler classes defy understanding. Although"—he paused thoughtfully with a forked bite of mutton suspended in the air—"perhaps I would feel differently if I knew what it was like to be leg-shackled."

Atlas dragged a heavy hand down over his mouth and chin. "Such humiliation is not to be borne."

Charlton's fair brows inched upward. "My good man—"

Atlas's chair screeched across the sanded, stone-flagged floor as he came to his feet, his mutton and throbbing foot all but forgotten. "Especially for a woman without a family's protection."

Charlton groaned. "Not again. Do sit down, Atlas," he implored. "I beg of you. For all we know, this has all been prearranged, and she has a lover who will bid for her, and they'll go off happily together."

"And if she doesn't?" Atlas fixed him with a cold stare. "You comprehend as well as I the hellish prospect she faces."

"Oh, very well." With a dramatic sigh, Charlton rose and tossed his fork aside to follow Atlas out the door. "She could very well have the face and form of a troll, and no harm *of that manner* will come to her."

They stepped outside into the courtyard and weaved their way through the crowd of onlookers. The interminable downpour that had dogged their journey from Bath had left the yard sodden and reeking of mud, damp hay, and horse dung. The rain had eased, giving way to a gray and overcast afternoon, but the moisture in the air remained thick enough to wring water from it.

"I'll give you a shilling," called a long-faced man with an eager grin as they passed him. "Is she a good shag? Do we get a chance to sample the goods before we buy her?"

When they reached the front of the crowd, the object of the idiot's effrontery came into view, and she was far from the boisterous fishwife Atlas had expected. This woman stood straight-spined with her head lifted. Dark hair framed perfect cheekbones and refined features set against ivory skin. Defiance glittered in her amber-brown eyes as she stared straight ahead, giving no indication she'd registered any of the jeers. She carried herself like a queen surveying her subjects rather than a woman facing great degradation.

"She's a spirited wench who doesn't know her place," said the man standing next to her, a proprietary air emanating from his stocky form. He possessed a shock of thick gray hair and appeared to be at least two decades older than the young woman. His clothing and deportment lent him the appearance of a country squire, but the thick rope clutched in one beefy hand marred that impression. Atlas took some satisfaction in the sight of the noose at the other end of the rope mired in mud on the ground rather than wrapped around the woman's neck.

"She's always been high in the instep, that one," whispered a gravelly voiced woman who'd nudged up behind Atlas and Charlton.

"Her new master must take a firm hand with her," said the man, presumably her husband, although the bastard clearly didn't have a clue as to the proper treatment of one's wife.

"I'll pay twenty pence for the pleasure," called a raspy, laconic voice with a slippery lilt. Atlas turned to get a look at the bidder, a hook-nosed man who appeared to be past his middle years, somewhere in his early sixties, gray at the temples and bald on top, wearing clothing that hung loosely on an emaciated form.

"Mr. Briney makes a generous offer." The auctioneer's face brightened. "But I fear I can't take less than twenty-five for such a comely wench."

"Twenty-five it is then." Briney made a provocative humming sound in his throat, his eager gaze fastened on the woman. "Mrs. Warwick looks infinitely worth the price."

Murmurs of disapproval swept through the crowd. Atlas's stomach clenched at the thought of this vulture laying his hands on a respectable woman. The object of Briney's interest showed no reaction, but her delicate complexion betrayed her, and her color heightened, a blush of pink appearing on her angled cheeks. He also noticed that her hands, clasped together demurely in front of her, were white with strain.

"No decent man would do such a thing," a woman standing behind them said.

"It's not as if Mr. Briney there is going to marry her," her companion answered. "Even if he could."

"She's still as married as I am, even if he sells her," came the reply.

"A shame," said her companion. "And she being a respectable woman and all."

"At least she was before this."

Atlas had had enough. He started forward, but Charlton placed a staying hand on his shoulder. "As you say, let us leave local affairs to the locals."

"This is not a local affair," he spoke through clenched teeth. "This is a matter of decency and honor, and well you know it."

Charlton sighed. "You cannot save every woman in distress."

"No," he said under his breath. "But I can attempt to save this one. Thirty pounds!" he called out, even though he could ill afford to part with the funds.

A collective gasp sounded from the crowd. And even Mrs. Warwick turned to look at him with a wary expression on her pale face.

"Sold!" Her bastard of a husband spoke in a heated rush, as though worried Atlas might change his mind. "Hand over the thirty pounds and the wench is yours."

"I'll require a bill of sale before any blunt changes hands." The words were brisk. He wanted documentation that showed her to be as free and clear of the bastard as possible, but Mrs. Warwick didn't appear to appreciate the gesture. Resentment simmered in her vibrant eyes.

"Of course, of course," her husband said hurriedly. "I shall bring it to you tomorrow."

"I shan't be here on the morrow. Later today, if you please."

"As you say." Warwick turned to his wife. "Come along, Lilliana." She stared icy daggers at the man but still turned to follow him.

Atlas stepped forward. "The lady remains with me."

The husband swung around, a suspicious gleam in his eye. "You haven't paid for her yet."

"We will remain in the taproom in full view until such time that you return." She was far safer with him than with her husband, who'd just whored her out to the highest bidder.

"No," she said suddenly. "I wish to return home with my husband." Atlas stared at her. It was the first time he'd heard her voice, and the clipped, upper-class tones shocked him. This was no country lass.

"There you have it," said Warwick. "She prefers to stay with me until the sale is final."

Atlas blinked. How could she possibly prefer the company of such an obviously vile man?

"You have my word as a gentleman that I will not harm you," he said to her in an attempt to reassure the woman that she would be safe under his protection.

She looked him in the eye, determination etched on her face, a slightly deprecating tone creeping into her words. "I go with my husband."

He should let her go—after all, the woman's welfare really was none of his affair—but he couldn't risk letting the bastard sell her to the highest bidder along the road or to the hollow-cheeked, falcon-featured Briney, who watched their ongoing interaction with undisguised interest.

He turned to Warwick. "If the lady leaves the yard, the deal is off." He examined his fingernails in a show of disinterest. "The choice is yours."

He heard her outraged intake of breath. "Godfrey"—she clutched her husband's arm, for the first time betraying a fissure in her granite composure—"please let me come back to the house. I beg of you."

Warwick regarded her with open disdain. "I am done with you. You will never be allowed to darken my door again."

"I'll hold my tongue." She bit her bottom lip, tears swimming in her vivid eyes. Atlas could not quite make out their color—golden-brown certainly, but with a certain coppery glow to them. "I'll never say another word about it. I swear it."

"It is too late for that," the husband said coldly before turning to Atlas. "I shall return presently."

She did not watch him walk away but instead stood there, still and quiet, as though trying to withstand a horrible pain rippling through her body. Perhaps she found a hellish husband preferable to the unknown vagaries of a stranger. Atlas felt a twinge of conscience for having a hand in her distress. Soon enough, he would make certain she understood he meant her no harm.

"Mrs. Warwick, it is damp out here in the yard," he said gently. "Please allow me to escort you within." She didn't look at him, didn't even acknowledge that he'd spoken. "Mrs. Warwick?"

She turned on her heel and marched into the tavern without a backward glance. He followed, and Charlton fell in step beside him.

"Excellent work," his friend said. "You've succeeded in buying her. Now what are you going to do with her?"

Atlas shook his head. "Damned if I know."

Chapter Two

As he escorted her to a tavern table, Atlas could not help but notice that they were the focus of extreme curiosity—he and this woman he knew nothing about.

People who had just moments ago treated him with the deference due a gentleman now regarded him with open suspicion and even outright contempt. They no doubt thought she was at his mercy, but he—who saw how she wore her poise and dignity like armor—knew better.

Although Charlton joined them at their table, the publican's wife seemed to save her seething, disapproving looks for Atlas, especially when he asked her to bring food and drink for the woman he had just purchased for thirty pounds.

Good Lord. He had no idea what to do with her. He planned to be aboard his cousin George's thirty-two-gun frigate when it departed London in a matter of weeks. He was inclined to return this woman to her people before he sailed. But in order to do so, he had to find out who she was.

"Allow me to introduce myself—"

She leveled a frigid gaze at him. "If you even think to lay a hand on me, I will gut you in your sleep." She spoke in precise, cut-glass tones. "You'll never know another moment's peace in this lifetime."

Charlton burst out laughing and slammed a hand on the table. "By God, I like this woman." Mirth still quivering on his lips, he said to her, "Rest assured, madam, you could not find yourself in better hands. My friend here makes a habit of rescuing damsels in distress."

Atlas bristled at his friend's words. "As I was saying, I am Atlas Catesby, lately of London. My companion here is Gabriel Young, the Earl of Charlton, also of London, as well as Charlton Abbey in Hampshire."

Surprise lit her face at the mention of Charlton's title, but she did not seem impressed, which was unusual. His friend's lofty title and fine-boned good looks normally provoked swoons of admiration from the opposite sex.

"It is a pleasure to make your acquaintance," Charlton said.

"Although we deeply regret the circumstances under which we do so," Atlas added.

She studied him for a moment. "Is your given name really Atlas?"

He dipped his chin. "It is."

"And do you also have a brother named Menoetius?"

A startled laugh escaped his throat. "I do not." Her knowledge of the Greeks surprised him. More evidence she hadn't been born and bred in the country.

Charlton darted a confused look between the two of them. "Who is this Menoetius fellow?"

"The brother of Atlas," he answered, keeping his attention focused on Mrs. Warwick. She held herself very still, sitting at the edge of her seat, her posture excellent. With her even, delicate features, she could be considered handsome, but Mrs. Warwick was not a beauty, even though she carried herself with the confidence and bearing of a diamond of the first water.

He couldn't make any sense of it. How had such a proud woman of obvious good breeding come to be married to a blunderbuss like Warwick?

"I have three elder brothers," he told her, "and they are called Apollo, Hermes, and Jason."

One side of her mouth quirked up, revealing a sense of humor buried deep beneath that marble reserve. "Are you quite serious? Have you any sisters?"

He paused. "Yes."

"And?" She raised a queenly brow. "What are their names?"

"Thea and . . ."—he swallowed against the tightening in his throat—"Phoebe."

"Your parents must have been great fans of Greek mythology."

"My father was."

"And your mother?"

"Was a great fan of my father."

"A rarity in marriage, to be sure."

"I haven't had the pleasure, so I wouldn't be in a position to know."

She blinked and looked away. "Well, I have. As you've had the misfortune to witness."

He leaned forward, eager to understand this enigma of a woman. "One can only assume that your marriage was unhappy, and your husband has obviously treated you in a disgraceful manner, yet you were eager to return home with the blackguard."

"Yes." She said it simply, as though she didn't owe him any explanation, which of course she didn't, but he couldn't help being damned curious.

He sat back. "I don't intend to cause you any harm."

Those bright sherry-colored eyes came back to him. "Then release me."

"You are not a prisoner. However, I do feel duty bound to return you to the protection of your family."

"I have no family."

"Everyone has family," he said. "Although at times we might prefer not to claim them."

She rose. "I would like to go and refresh myself." As courtesy dictated, the men stood as well.

She didn't wait for permission. They watched her walk up to the publican's wife and exchange a few words before a chambermaid led her out of the taproom.

Regaining his seat, Charlton's gaze lingered after them. "What do you think the chances are of her climbing out the window and vanishing into the wilds of England?"

Atlas sat as well and sipped his saccharine ale. "She's too proud for that. If Artemis chooses to part company with us, I'd wager my mount that she'll sail out the front door and vanquish anyone who steps in her path."

"Artemis?" Charlton's golden brows lifted. "Dare I ask which goddess she is?"

"The daughter of Zeus. Aloof, courageous, and confident"—Atlas's mouth quirked—"and so protective of her virginity that when a hunter threatened her purity, she turned him into a stag and set fifty dogs upon him."

"That seems apt." A devilish gleam shone in Charlton's eyes. "She might not be a virgin, but I can definitely see Mrs. Warwick setting wild beasts upon you."

* * *

Atlas set Mrs. Warwick's valise on the floor of the chamber he'd taken for the night. "I regret it is not the most comfortable accommodation, but fortunately it's just for the one night."

She stood by the window, looking out, her slender form perfectly erect. "And where do you plan to sleep?"

"With Charlton. The inn only had two available beds." He stifled a sigh. "If you were better acquainted with the earl, you would understand just how great an inconvenience that is."

"I did not ask for your help."

He tapped down a twinge of impatience. It had been a long day, and his foot had been throbbing for hours. By the time her husband had returned with the bill of sale, their journey had been delayed long enough to require that they stay the night. "Nonetheless, you have it. Forgive me if I did not wish to see you ravaged by your former neighbor, who looked most keen to pay for the pleasure."

"I would have managed him." She turned from the window. "Is it true what your friend said?"

"In regards to what?"

"Do you make a habit of saving females who are in trouble?"

The air in his lungs iced. "No." He turned to go, thinking of the time he had failed miserably in that endeavor. "We leave for

London in the morning. If it is convenient, please be ready to go down to break our fast at the seven o'clock hour."

"None of this is convenient."

He was too tired to spar with her. "I thought you might be agreeable to staying with my sister Thea in London until you make arrangements for your future. Perhaps we can discuss it further in the morning."

"Yes," she said, surprising him by not objecting to his plans for her. "Let us talk on the morrow."

He returned to his musty bedchamber to find Charlton sniffing the counterpane. "They clearly don't make a habit of washing the bedclothes. How many other travelers do you think have slept on these?"

Atlas shrugged out of his jacket and sat to tug off his boots. "Considering the look of this place, I would venture to guess dozens."

Charlton shuddered. "That's what I was afraid of. We'll be crawling with bedbugs and lice by the morning."

"It is more than likely." Yawning, Atlas arranged his greatcoat over the bedclothes and reclined on his side of the bed.

Charlton watched him. "You are sleeping in your clothes?"

He closed his eyes. "So it appears."

"That's very uncivilized."

"Quite," he agreed before drifting off to sleep.

* * *

By morning, she was gone.

"What do you mean gone?" Atlas demanded of Mrs. Wenzel, the publican's wife. "Where did she go?"

He and Charlton had come down to breakfast at the appointed time. When Mrs. Warwick had not appeared by seven thirty, he'd asked the chambermaid to go and look in on her. That's when the publican's wife had shared the news of Mrs. Warwick's early departure.

"Likely back home." She wiped down the scarred bar with a soiled rag. "That'd be my guess."

Frustration bubbled in his chest. "Mr. Warwick treated her abominably. Why would she return to him?"

Mrs. Wenzel didn't answer. She didn't appear to think any more highly of him, a man who had purchased a woman, than the husband who had sold her.

"Bitte, meine Frau." He switched to her native tongue, thinking it might make her more amenable. He had a natural talent for languages, which his travels had greatly enhanced. "I just want to help her."

Her expression lightened. *"Sie sprechen Deutsch?"*

"*Ja*," he answered in the affirmative. "I have had the good fortune to visit Bavaria."

"She hasn't gone home to the husband." Mrs. Wenzel was instantly more talkative, seeming to enjoy speaking to someone in the language of her childhood. "But to her boys."

He frowned. "What boys?"

"Two children she has."

Atlas's mouth dropped open. Outrage simmered within him. It was even worse than he'd first thought. He switched to English to make certain he'd understood her correctly. "Are you saying that reprobate sold away the mother of his children?"

"Children? Mrs. Warwick has children?" Charlton, who'd watched their exchange with open curiosity, shook his head. "I don't believe I've ever encountered a more vile man."

"How did she leave?" Atlas asked Mrs. Wenzel in German.

She lined up pewter mugs behind the bar, readying them for the day's use. "One of the ostlers give her a ride in the wagon."

"Has he returned?"

"Jasper?" She nodded. "*Ja*, he's likely out in the stables."

After thanking her, he strode out to the stables with Charlton trailing. "You speak German too?" the earl asked. "I say, how many languages have you mastered?"

Atlas didn't break his stride. "Six, give or take."

"Goodness." Charlton hastened his step until the two men were walking side by side. "Where are we going? What did the *fräulein* say?"

"To the stable. She said the ostler gave Mrs. Warwick a ride this morning."

"Maybe you should leave her be," the earl said. "You cannot hope to part a mother from her children."

"I did not part them. That bastard Warwick did."

"For some unfathomable reason, some females become very attached to the sniffling, noisy little nuisances they push out of their bodies." Charlton sidestepped a muddy puddle. "My sister Emma is unaccountably besotted with her new babe, and all it does is eat, sleep, and produce malodorous messes."

Atlas shot his friend a sidelong glance. "You do realize that you're expected to sire an heir to carry on the exalted Charlton line."

"The act of begetting an heir, I do not mind in the least." The earl flashed a mischievous grin. "Fortunately, there is a nursery where the little nuisance can be housed until he's sent away to school."

"What a heartwarming view of fatherhood." They rounded the stable door and soon located Jasper, the young man who'd driven Mrs. Warwick home. He was a tall, strapping lad with sandy-colored hair and inquisitive eyes blinking in a narrow face.

"I didn't take her directly to the house," he said, twisting his cap in his hands.

Impatience rippled through Atlas. "Where then?"

"She asked to be set down a ways from the house. She said she didn't want to wake the household. That she would enter quietly."

Atlas swore under his breath. "Saddle my mount immediately."

While Jasper went to ready Thunder, the black stallion Atlas had borrowed from Charlton, the earl gave him a quizzical look. "What has got a bee in your beaver hat now?"

"I fear she intends to take the children."

"Can she do that?"

"By law, no." He walked over to the stall to help Jasper saddle his mount. There was no time to waste. "However, I doubt Mrs. Warwick would allow so minor a thing as the law to get in her way." After getting directions to the house—an old rectory—from Jasper, he led his mount out of the stables.

Charlton walked alongside. "What precisely do you plan to do besides riding to the damsel's rescue on your black steed?"

"Warwick likely knew his wife would never leave the children." He swung up onto Thunder. The nasty-tempered animal pranced restlessly, his neck swaying left and then right as if assessing his chances of getting a good bite out of his rider's thigh. Atlas kept a firm hand on the reins. The last thing he needed was another injury. "I think it's a trap. I only pray I'm not too late."

Charlton watch him wrestle the animal under control. "Why don't you take my gelding? I don't know why you insist on this stallion. You and he are too alike—stubborn and foul tempered—to get on with each other."

"Nonsense." Atlas guided the reluctant mount toward the lane. "We're going to be great friends."

About ten minutes later, the modest property came into view. The old rectory, with its tan stone exterior and two tall columns on either side of the front door, was tidy, well kept, and far nicer than Atlas had expected. From the looks of the house—comfortable but not too large—and its surrounding property, Warwick didn't appear in need of the thirty pounds he'd earned from selling his wife.

Atlas's attention went from the house to the group of people standing in the front yard: that bastard Warwick, another man dressed in country clothes that differentiated him from the servants, and two men flanking a defiant Lilliana Warwick.

Chapter Three

"You should have known better than to steal my sons." Triumph gleamed in Warwick's eyes.

"They're my children," his wife snapped, her slender shoulders proud and unbowed. "I can hardly steal what is mine."

"By law, you have no rights to them now that I've cast you out."

One of the two men flanking Mrs. Warwick, a short, square-shaped toad, gripped her arm in a proprietary manner that made Atlas's neck burn. "Come along now, Mrs. Warwick."

"Unhand me, you addlepated fool." Trying to twist free of his grasp, Mrs. Warwick stared frantically up at the house. Atlas surmised that her children must be within.

"Surely there is no need for this." The man dressed in country clothes, who had a passing resemblance to Godfrey Warwick, stepped toward them with a calming, outstretched hand. "Let us settle this in a civilized manner."

"Always playing the saint." Godfrey's words dripped with sarcasm. "It's done, John. Move aside."

The square-shaped man holding Mrs. Warwick's arm interrupted them. "I am the magistrate, and this is an official matter. I'm afraid Mrs. Warwick must retire to the local gaol."

Atlas's patience ran out. "I will thank you to take your hands off my property." The words—low, dark, and controlled—held an unmistakable note of warning. The attention of everyone in the yard swung in Atlas's direction, the players in this sordid scene finally taking notice of the interloper standing by the front gate.

The man called John ran an imperious gaze over him. "And who might you be?"

"I could ask the same of you," Atlas replied coldly. He had the size advantage over all of these men. And at well over six feet, he wasn't opposed to using his bulky frame to encourage people to oblige him.

"This is John Warwick," Mrs. Warwick explained, "my brother in marriage."

"What do you mean by saying Lilliana is your property?" John looked away from Mrs. Warwick and back to Atlas. "She is my brother's wife."

"No longer," Atlas replied. "He sold her to me for thirty pounds. She is under my protection now."

John inhaled sharply. "How dare you, sir? I should call you out for casting aspersions on this house and this family's good name."

Atlas's lips curled into an icy, closemouthed smile. "This scapegrace didn't seem to have a care for your good name when he put a collar around Mrs. Warwick's neck and sold her like cattle on market day."

"It's true, John," she said. "Godfrey wasn't content to just cast me out. He had to make my humiliation complete by selling me to the highest bidder."

The color leached from John's complexion. He turned to his brother, the shock etched on his face seeming genuine enough. "Is that true?"

"Yes, it's true," Godfrey returned impatiently. "If you hadn't been so busy tending to your wife, you might have heard the news. Everyone else in the county has."

"Tending to his wife?" Mrs. Warwick looked in askance at John. "Why? Is Verity unwell?"

A shadow crossed the man's face. "A stomach ailment. She's suffering terribly."

"I am so sorry," she said to him. "If there is anything I can do—"

"Enough of this." The magistrate's self-important voice brimmed with impatience. "I'll be locking Mrs. Warwick up until it's decided what is to be done with her."

Atlas stepped into the man's path. "She goes nowhere but with me." From his pocket, he withdrew the bill of sale Godfrey had presented to him yesterday. "I have proof of ownership in my possession."

Her husband balked. "You should have kept a tighter leash on your property, sir. Sadly, you did not, and she attempted to steal my children, thereby breaking the law."

Ignoring Godfrey, Atlas stared intently, aggressively, down at the magistrate. "As I said, she goes with me. I take full responsibility for her."

The magistrate darted a concerned glance at Godfrey before tilting his head back to peer into Atlas's face as the larger man towered over him. "If I release her into your care, you must maintain control of her."

"Now see here, Felix." Godfrey's face reddened. "You cannot allow her to go free."

"But she is not free," his friend stuttered. "Mr. uh . . ."

"Catesby," Atlas said.

"Yes, Mr. Catesby will be in charge of her."

Atlas spoke to Mrs. Warwick. "Shall we go?"

"I cannot leave," she whispered, her eyes shiny with emotion. "My children."

Godfrey smirked. "They are not your children. In the eyes of the law, they are mine and only mine."

"Either you leave with Mr. Catesby," said Felix Bole, the magistrate, "or I take you into my custody until such time as it is determined whether you will stand trial for attempting to abduct Mr. Warwick's children."

She clenched her fists at her sides, her trim body taut with tension. "They are the children of my body. My own flesh and blood. It is ghastly to separate a mother from her children."

John Warwick regarded his brother with a combination of disbelief and disgust. "Surely an accommodation can be made for Lilliana to see the boys."

Godfrey ignored him. "The gaol or your new master," he said to his wife. "Those are your choices."

Atlas strode to her side, taking great pains not to limp on his aching left foot. "I will help you find a way," he murmured with quiet resolve. "I give you my word. Come away with me now. At the moment, there is nothing you can do here."

She stood very still, not acknowledging that he'd spoken. Atlas's chest constricted at the distress he registered in her face.

"Come." Atlas put a hand to her elbow. "All will be well."

He saw the moment she realized her situation was hopeless because she didn't resist when he took her arm and led her away from her children.

* * *

Once they settled into the hired carriage, Mrs. Warwick in the front-facing seat with Atlas and Charlton sitting across from her, an unbearable fatigue seemed to come over her. Her face pale, she laid her head against the worn squabs and closed her eyes.

She did not open them again until they reached London, when the stench of dung and waste fermenting in the Thames filled the carriage. Outside, the clacking of hooves against the pavement, the shouts of the costermongers, and the sales cry of a far-off milkmaid—"Milko!"—filtered through the air. Directly above them, a light patter sounded on the roof.

She blinked and straightened. "Is it raining?"

"This is London," Charlton said. "When isn't it raining?"

"I fell asleep." She peered out the window at the muddy streets and the people rushing by, huddled under their umbrellas. "How could I have fallen asleep?"

"You were no doubt exhausted after the ordeal of the past twenty-four hours," Atlas said. "Did you sleep at all last night?"

She shook her head, weariness etched in the aristocratic lines of her face. "He'll keep them from me. He knows it's the greatest punishment he could inflict upon me."

Atlas did not ask to whom she referred. "I know of a well-regarded barrister. I thought we might go and see him on the morrow."

"The law will not help me. It was designed by men to be to their advantage."

He could not disagree with her assessment. "Nonetheless, I thought you might like to learn exactly what your options are."

Neither of them bothered to mention divorce, which was prohibitively expensive and next to impossible, particularly for someone like her who had neither influence nor funds at her disposal. "As I mentioned previously," he continued, "I thought I would take you to my sister Thea's home. I think you'll find her very congenial company."

She studied his face, and Atlas wondered what she saw. Unlike Charlton, he was not a particularly handsome man. The angles of his face were too sharply defined, and his nose a tad too strong, to be considered appealing.

"Why are you troubling yourself on my account?" she asked.

"It is the decent thing to do. How old are your children?"

"Peter is seven, and Robin is almost five." She inhaled a shaky breath, and he saw the toll the unfortunate events of the last twenty-four hours had taken on her.

"Are you certain there is no family—a cousin, a family friend—upon whom you wish to call?"

"No," she said quietly. "I have no one." And then quieter still, "At least no one who will still have me."

Atlas's sister lived on Great Russell Street in Bloomsbury, near the British Museum, in a Restoration-style house with arched sashed windows. Like most of the neighborhood, the mellow brick mansion must have been very grand once, but the passage of time had reduced it to a state of elegant shabbiness.

They went up the one step leading to the glossy black front door and stood beneath the flat canopy resting on two columns that framed the front entrance. Mrs. Warwick was looking up, studying the picturesque fanlight topping the doorcase, when the door creaked open. Fletcher, Thea's ancient butler, greeted them and, after having Atlas repeat Mrs. Warwick's name twice, shuffled across the worn parquet floors, showing them to a door near the back of the house.

"Madam," the butler said, announcing her visitors. "Lord Charlton, Mr. Atlas Catesby, and . . . erm . . . a guest." It did not surprise Atlas in the least that the old servant had already forgotten Mrs. Warwick's name. Thea had attempted to pension Fletcher off more than once, but the man wouldn't hear of it.

They found his sister hard at work at a round breakfast table littered with books and papers, her hair its usual unruly mass of dark curls. She held up a staying hand while she scribbled a sequence of numeric figures on a sheet of paper. The butler retreated while Atlas and Charlton stood by quietly, quite used to this sort of greeting, until Thea punctuated her last numeral with great flourish and threw the pencil down.

She looked up, her face brightening. "Atlas, what an unexpected surprise." Her interested gaze swept over them and landed on Mrs. Warwick. "And you've brought a guest. How lovely."

"I hope we aren't interrupting," Atlas said.

"Not at all." She came to her feet and shook out the skirts of her black muslin gown. "I could use a reprieve from work. I'm translating a volume of classical mechanics."

"To what purpose?" Charlton asked.

"In the interests of learning, of course." Thea closed one of the notebooks on the cluttered table. "If one can translate the geometric study of classical mechanics to one based solely on calculus, imagine the broader range of problems that could present themselves."

Atlas leaned toward Mrs. Warwick. "Thea is a mathematician," he murmured. "Do not be alarmed if you cannot understand a word she says. I never can."

Thea turned to her brother with a nod toward the lady beside him. "Won't you introduce us?"

Atlas dipped his chin. "Mrs. Thea Palmer, allow me to introduce Mrs. Lilliana Warwick."

"How delightful of you to visit." Thea's smile was genuine and unaffected. "I do hope you'll call me Thea, Mrs. Warwick. Mrs. Palmer sounds like my husband's mother."

"Gladly," Mrs. Warwick said. "If you will consent to call me Lilliana."

"I should be pleased to. Now that that's settled, let us adjourn to the upstairs sitting room, where we'll be ever so much more comfortable." They followed her into the front hall and up a marble staircase until they came to an unfussy but comfortable-looking room decorated in pale silks.

"Now," Thea said in a no-nonsense manner after they'd settled in and tea had been served, "why don't you tell me why you are here?"

"Dear Thea is never one to mince words," said Charlton with an indulgent smile, his azure gaze lingering on their hostess.

Atlas stretched his long legs out in front of him, which was a relief after the cramped carriage ride. "Mrs. Warwick finds herself in need of accommodation."

"Then of course she must stay here," Thea answered promptly.

Mrs. Warwick gazed down at the teacup she held in her lap. "I wouldn't want to be an inconvenience to you."

"Nonsense." Thea's words were crisp. "I shall be glad of the company."

"Thea does occasionally pull herself away from her sums only to find herself mostly alone in this great mausoleum," Charlton said from where he'd comfortably settled his elegant form in a plush silk chair.

"Besides," their hostess continued as if Charlton had not spoken, "I suspect you have quite an interesting tale to tell as to how my brother came to bring you here."

Atlas tensed. "Thea, Mrs. Warwick has been through an ordeal that she likely prefers not to discuss."

"No, it's quite all right." Mrs. Warwick took a deep breath. "Mrs. Palmer . . . Thea . . . has every right to know the truth of it."

Her hostess regarded her with sincere interest. "And precisely what is this truth?"

Mrs. Warwick kept her voice even. "That if you give me shelter, you will be harboring a woman of the lowest reputation."

"Goodness." Thea's chocolate-colored eyes widened. "How intriguing."

Atlas shifted, his face heating. "There is no need—"

"Yes there is," Mrs. Warwick interrupted him. "If I am to stay with your sister, she deserves to know I will bring dishonor to her house. That is the truth, and I cannot take advantage of her kindness by remaining here under false pretenses. I am sorry if I have shocked you, Mrs. Palmer, by speaking plainly."

"No need to worry about that." Charlton sipped his tea. "Very little shocks our Thea. Unless she were to somehow puzzle out that two plus two does not equal four."

"Actually, two plus two does not always equal four," Thea bristled, her impatience with the earl plain for all to see. "The answer depends on the measurement scale you use."

Charlton's golden brows rose, but Thea had already dismissed him and turned her full attention back to Mrs. Warwick. "You do not strike me as a dishonorable woman."

"Nor is she," Atlas said.

"Mr. Catesby is very gallant, but our acquaintance has been a short one," Mrs. Warwick said. "He does not know me."

"Atlas is always gallant." Thea sipped her tea. "He is also an excellent judge of character."

"He was especially chivalrous in this instance." Mrs. Warwick carefully placed her tea on the teak side table at her elbow before forcing the words out. "He purchased me from my husband to prevent my being violated by another buyer."

Thea gasped. "Your husband *sold* you?"

"Now see here, Thea." Atlas leaned forward, his words forceful. "Surely Mrs. Warwick has endured enough humiliation without being called upon to recount the dreadful episode."

"Of course." Thea held Mrs. Warwick's gaze. "Although she has nothing to feel ashamed of. The sole personage who has acted dishonorably is the cad of a husband who pledged to protect her and instead exposed her to serious harm and abasement."

Something akin to gratitude flashed in Mrs. Warwick's eyes. "I am fortunate Mr. Catesby came to my rescue, but I do not wish to impose any further on either of you."

"Nonsense. You are very welcome to stay here. In fact, I must insist upon it." Thea spoke with a finality that suggested she considered the subject closed. Scooting forward, she reached for the teapot. "Now, can I offer anyone more tea?"

Chapter Four

An uneasy tension emanated from Mrs. Warwick as she stared out the window of Thea's outdated coach. The appointment with Mr. Barrow, the solicitor, had not gone well. The laws of England viewed Mrs. Warwick as her husband's chattel. She had no rights at all to the children.

"There must be a way in which to forge an agreement with Mr. Warwick," Atlas said, wincing when the carriage hit a bump. His sister's conveyance was reasonably well sprung, considering its advanced age, but even the slightest upset jarred his aching left foot. The trip to Bath had done little to ease his discomfort.

"Any such agreement would be null and void." She turned from the window to look at him, the sun's rays casting shadows across her face. She looked very well in a muslin day gown that, while not in the first stare of fashion, was elegantly worn and appeared to be well made. "You heard what Mr. Barrow said. Legally, I do not even exist as a person independent of my husband. The moment we married, we became one person, and that person is my husband. It would be as if Godfrey had signed a contract with himself."

Atlas could not help but admire her self-possession. She'd remained poised and unruffled throughout the meeting, even managing a bit of grim humor after learning that if she amassed significant debt or committed murder, her husband would be held responsible because, in the eyes of the law, she did not exist apart from him.

Perhaps I should do away with Mr. Warwick, she'd said dryly. Since we are legally one person, I imagine the law would view that as suicide.

"Are you certain your family cannot come to your assistance?" Atlas asked.

"Yes, quite certain." She betrayed no emotion except for the way she fisted the lap of her skirts in clenched hands—hands that he observed were smooth, delicate, and finely made. They were the unblemished hands of a lady, evidence that Warwick had not forced her to do manual labor in his household. "I have no family to speak of. Except for my boys."

"Barrow did say the courts can compel Mr. Warwick to support you if you have no other means of subsistence."

"What about my children? They will be missing me. We've never been parted before, not even for one evening."

"Perhaps there is another way." Atlas leaned forward, his mind working. "Mr. Warwick is a man who appears to be very much attached to his purse. Perhaps in lieu of providing financial support, he would agree to an arrangement which allows you to visit the children."

Mrs. Warwick's intelligent eyes narrowed. She appeared to ponder his suggestion. "It is possible. Godfrey might well prefer to be parted from his children for a few hours rather than from a few shillings on a regular basis."

"I'll have a note delivered to Buckinghamshire immediately," he said, heartened by the possibility of having found a resolution to her problem. "We shall see if I can negotiate a reasonable visitation schedule for you to see the children."

"No, not Buckinghamshire. Today is Monday. He'll be at the shop."

"What shop?"

"He maintains a haberdashery on Wigmore near Bond Street."

A shopkeeper? Atlas had taken Warwick for a minor country squire, not a merchant. "But I thought you lived in the country."

"The children and I do live in Slough, in the county of Buckinghamshire, but Godfrey keeps chambers above the shop and comes out to the country house from Saturday to Monday."

"That's an unusual vocation for a country squire."

"But a necessary one because Godfrey's older brother, John, inherited the family's country house," she said. "Godfrey had to make his own way. He acquired the house a few years before we married with earnings from the haberdashery."

A new image of Warwick began to take shape in Atlas's head. Prosperous merchants often imitated their social betters by purchasing country boxes to improve their sense of consequence and position in society. A different approach to negotiating with the blackguard began to take shape in his mind.

"No need to send a note then. I'll go and see Warwick myself."

* * *

The haberdashery was situated just a street away from the bachelor's quarters Atlas kept above a tobacconist's shop on Bond Street, so he walked over the next morning to pay Warwick a visit.

The tidy shop sat on a busy commercial street frequented by some of London's wealthiest denizens. A glazed black door dissected two handsome bowed windows above which a gilded sign in dignified type trumpeted the name "Warwick & Sons."

Inside, the man in question stood behind a mahogany counter with brass-accented drawers that dominated the orderly space. An orange-haired clerk in spectacles cut muslin for two well-dressed lady customers while Warwick looked on with a critical eye.

Fabric, thread, tape, bindings, ribbons, buttons, and other trimmings were displayed on oak shelving units and behind the counter, on the shelves of a fitted wall unit that also contained a series of small drawers. The space rivaled some of the best shops on Bond Street, and Atlas could well imagine the enterprise being profitable enough for Warwick to afford a country box.

He stood quietly just inside the door until Warwick caught his eye. His face impassive, Warwick left the ladies in the care of his clerk and came over.

"Mr. Catesby," he said, "to what do I owe this visit? I understood any business between us to be concluded."

"You understood wrong." Atlas drew off his hat, walked past Warwick to one of the shelves, and picked up a brass button, examining it. "Our business is far from over."

Warwick followed him. "I'm afraid I don't take your meaning."

"There is something rather significant you neglected to share about Mrs. Warwick."

Warwick leaned forward and lowered his voice. "If you think to get your money back because you've now experienced firsthand what a cold, unbiddable bitch my wife is, I fear it is too late for that. You have a bill of sale, and the transaction is complete."

Atlas's neck burned. "I should quash you beneath my heel like the insect you are, to speak of your own wife in such a manner."

"Such devotion to my dear Lilliana." Warwick gave him a thoughtful look. "Could it be you've managed to find fire where I've only found ice? If so, you have my felicitations. I found lying in my wife's bed to be as warm and welcoming as swimming in the Thames in January."

Atlas clenched his fists. It required all his self-control to keep from wrapping his hands around Warwick's thick neck and squeezing that salacious smirk off his face. "You neglected to mention that Mrs. Warwick has two young sons who are in need of their mother."

"They need their father, and that is who they have." Beneath a facile surface, the man seethed with anger. "They are my children and only mine in the eyes of the law."

Atlas tamped down his temper. "All children need a mother's love and care. I've come to arrange an equitable agreement that allows Mrs. Warwick to see the children on a regular basis."

Dark amusement twisted Warwick's blunt features. "She certainly must have thawed a great deal to bring you under her influence so easily. But I fear I cannot accommodate you."

Atlas did not miss Warwick's indecent insinuation. He was just about to plant his fist in Warwick's smug face when the two customers at the counter concluded their business and turned to leave, packages in hand. Warwick hastened to open the front door for them. "Lady Clarissa, Lady Jane, thank you. I do hope to see you again soon." Just outside the door, a liveried footman waited to take the women's packages.

Closing the door behind them, Warwick turned back to Atlas. "If that is all—"

"It isn't." Atlas tossed the button back into the bin on the shelf, where it landed with a ping.

With a look from Warwick, the clerk vanished into the back area of the shop, leaving them to their privacy. "Pray state your business," the man said. "I do have an enterprise to run."

"So I have noticed. You seem to enjoy the custom of some of Mayfair's finest families."

"Indeed." Warwick drew himself up. "I owe a debt of gratitude to the late Duchess of Somerville—God rest her soul—for it was she who first drew society's attention to my haberdashery. She and her young daughters often frequented my establishment. Their end—her and his grace—was such a tragedy."

The late Duchess of Somerville, famed for her sartorial style, had been one of the beau monde's leading lights. Atlas's family never moved in such exalted circles, but gossip about the duchess's gowns and social activities had often graced the society pages during his youth, until both Somerville and his duchess had died in a carriage accident several years back. Warwick no doubt regretted the loss of a customer more than anything else. "And do her daughters also favor you?"

"Alas, both live in Scotland. One is a countess, and the sister lives with her and is said to be contentedly on the shelf." Warwick straightened some ribbons on an oak shelf. "But the duchess's influence endures, and many in the *ton* continue to frequent my humble establishment."

"Do you think they would so readily give you their custom if it became known that you sold your wife and are cruelly keeping her from her children?"

Warwick's busy fingers stilled, and he turned to face Atlas. "You think to threaten me with exposure?"

"I think the ladies of the *ton* will be aghast at your treatment of your wife. No one can cut a person as cruelly and catastrophically as the fearsome matrons of Mayfair."

Warwick moved to bolts of white muslin and began to organize them in exacting rows. "You've overplayed your hand, Catesby."

"Have I?" he asked mildly.

"Ask Lilliana. She fears exposure far more than I. Do you really want to subject her to public shame and degradation?"

"You have already done that." He spoke through clenched teeth. "Most thoroughly, I might add."

Warwick laughed. "You don't understand at all."

Uneasiness slithered through his gut. The man was too smug, too confident of his position in regards to his wife. "Perhaps you'd care to enlighten me."

Warwick met his gaze, but Atlas, who watched him carefully, detected uneasiness behind the confident manner. "She's hiding from someone or something. It's why she married me—me, an older man and likely of inferior social status, from the looks of her—and buried herself in the country during the entire course of our marriage."

"What do you know of her family?"

"Nothing at all, which is how she wanted it." He shrugged. "And what did I care? As a long-standing bachelor of six-and-thirty when we married, I was just happy to have a young girl of obvious quality in my bed."

Disgust trickled through Atlas's veins, even though it was not unusual for men of advanced age to wed much younger girls; at forty-two, Lord Berwick, one of Prince George's cronies, had married a girl of fifteen, although she was rumored to be a courtesan. But the image of Warwick, a man old enough to be his wife's father, grunting over the innocent sixteen-year-old girl as he bedded her, made Atlas want to call the bugger out then and there.

"You took advantage of an innocent young girl with no family, and now you have cast her aside," he said.

"You will soon learn Lilliana is not what she appears."

"Your behavior has been deplorable, sir. I should meet you at dawn and put an end to Mrs. Warwick's suffering."

Warwick laughed again, a grating, self-satisfied sound. "Fortunately for me, I am no gentleman and, as such, do not engage in duels."

"Mrs. Warwick has no family to lend her financial support. According to my barrister, you could be required to pay for her support."

Warwick's mouth curled with skepticism. "You purchased her. Lilliana's support is now your responsibility."

"The law might not see it that way. However, Mrs. Warwick is willing to forgo any financial assistance in exchange for being able to visit her children at regular intervals."

"As far as my children are concerned, their mother is dead, and I will do everything in my power to ensure that she never sets eyes on them again." Malice gleamed in his black eyes, and Atlas wondered what had passed between this man and his wife to put it there. "Nor do I expect to be held responsible for providing any type of support for Lilliana. I am not a fool, Mr. Catesby. If I were you, I would take care to remember that."

"Only a fool would act as you have acted." Atlas placed his beaver hat on his head as he turned to leave. "Rest assured, you will be made to pay for what you have done."

Warwick made a disparaging sound that Atlas heard just before he pulled the shop door shut behind him.

Chapter Five

Much later that day, Atlas arrived at his sister's house to find Thea engrossed in *The Times*.

"You were correct about Prudence Pratt," she informed him.

"Prudence Pratt?"

"Surely you recall the case of Miss Pratt and the murder of her half brother," she admonished. "The toddler who was the product of her father's marriage to the family's former governess after the death of his first wife."

"Of course I remember. The little boy vanished from the family home one evening only to be found in the garden the following morning with his throat cut." The case had fascinated him. As with puzzles, the intricacies of human behavior and motivation, life's conundrums in all forms, sparked his intellectual curiosity and drove his desire to decipher them. "Has there been a new development?"

"Miss Pratt, the sister, has been arrested in the death of her brother."

"It's little wonder. It's as clear as a bell that the girl did it." Once he'd read the details of the murder, Atlas had immediately deduced that the boy's jealous older sister was the culprit, a conclusion he'd reached even before the magistrates directed Prudence's arrest. "The missing nightdress is proof enough of that."

Thea regarded him over the top of the newspaper. "She maintains the cleaning lady stole it."

"Miss Pratt could hardly say otherwise. However, the cleaning lady has never before been accused of taking anything." He walked around to read the paper over her shoulder. "The sister obviously bloodied her nightdress when she cut her brother's throat and then burned it to destroy the evidence."

Thea shivered and folded the paper away. "I don't see how a sister could be quite so ruthless."

"A half-sister," he reminded her. "And the child was a male heir borne of a woman who was not Miss Pratt's mother."

"You do have a cold-blooded way of viewing the murder of an innocent child."

"Hardly. It's a terrible thing. However, once you sort through all the facts and view them with an objective eye, it's as clear—"

"—as a bell," she finished for him. "Yes, yes, so you often say. Except I own that many things only seem self-evident to you and not to the rest of us." She rose and went to her blackboard, which was covered with math equations scrawled in white chalk.

"Where is Mrs. Warwick?"

"She left for Buckinghamshire very early this morning."

"She went to Slough?" he asked incredulously. "Is she trying to see the children?"

Dressed in her usual black muslin, Thea stood with her back to him, one hand perched on her hip, the other cupping her chin as she stared at the blackboard scribblings. "She received a message late yesterday that her sister in marriage had succumbed to her malady. I believe Lilliana's gone to pay her respects to the husband."

John Warwick's wife was dead? Atlas recalled hearing mention of her illness, but he hadn't realized how dire the situation was. "How did Mrs. Warwick get there?" Alarm rustled through him. Godfrey Warwick might also have gone to Slough to be with his grieving brother. "Why didn't someone inform me?"

"And why, pray tell, should you be informed of Lilliana's whereabouts?" Thea pivoted to face him, and he saw that her dark gown was marked by smudged chalk. "Perhaps you're taking this idea of purchasing her to heart."

"Don't be absurd," he retorted. "If her husband is present when Mrs. Warwick arrives, he could reclaim her, and under the law, there's nothing any of us could do to help her."

"I hadn't thought of that." Concern caused two little wrinkles to appear between her eyebrows. "I sent her in my carriage with my coachman and a footman. She should be perfectly fine." She turned back to study her equations. "No doubt that jackanapes husband of hers is tied to his little shop on Wigmore Street here in Town. He doesn't seem the type to risk losing a shilling in order to comfort the grieving."

He walked over to stand beside the board, which gave him the opportunity to study his sister's face as well as the smudge of white chalk on her chin. He noted her stiff posture and the way she avoided looking him in the eye. "Why do I get the sense that you are not telling me everything?"

Keeping her focus on her equations, she scribbled something on the board, the chalk making quick tapping sounds. "I don't know what you mean."

"I think you know exactly what I mean. You said you *believe* Mrs. Warwick went to Slough to pay her respects to John Warwick. Does that mean she might have gone to see the children?"

She kept her eyes on the board. "Lilliana is a grown woman. She can do as she pleases."

He exhaled a long breath through his mouth. His sister could be frustratingly obstinate when she chose to be. He tried another approach. "Have you had an opportunity to learn more about Mrs. Warwick?"

She gave him a sideways glance. "What exactly do you wish to know?"

"I met with Warwick this morning. Fear of exposure to his aristocratic clientele did not seem to rile him in the slightest. He claims his wife has something to hide and that she would be far more distressed than he if her situation were made public."

"A deep, dark secret?" Charlton's voice sounded from the threshold of Thea's breakfast-room-turned-office. "How intriguing."

Thea glanced over her shoulder. "What are you doing here?" she asked, her words damp.

"I've come to learn why two plus two does not equal four." Clad in a fitted royal-blue jacket festooned with gold buttons and matching military-style braiding, Charlton headed straight for the most comfortable chair in the room. "And to bask, of course, in the dazzling brightness of your countenance."

"The only thing that is dazzlingly bright in here is your jacket," Thea said. "Goodness, I practically need a parasol to protect me from its brilliance."

Charlton frowned and looked down at his attire just as Mrs. Warwick entered the room.

"I do hope I'm not interrupting." She looked very well. Her manner was perhaps more subdued than usual, but her eyes sparkled, and for the first time in their short acquaintance, there was a healthy glow of color in her cheeks.

Thea set her chalk down. "Not at all. You're just in time for some tea out in the garden. We're taking advantage of a rare sunny day."

Atlas guessed at what had put that unexpected light in Mrs. Warwick's eye. "You went to see the children?" Wary of overstepping, he resisted the urge to warn her against placing herself in such a vulnerable situation. "I trust they are well."

She nodded. "Yes. Very. And they are well looked after by Mrs. Greene, the housekeeper, and Jamie, one of the houseboys."

Alarm stirred in his gut at the thought of Mrs. Warwick visiting her former home. "It could prove very dangerous were Warwick to catch you at the rectory with the boys."

"It is a risk I had to take. They are my children. I cannot be apart from them."

Thea dusted chalk from her hands. "Did you also call on your brother in marriage?"

A solemn expression came over Mrs. Warwick's face, and the reason for her muted demeanor became apparent. "Yes, John is in a terrible way. Verity's death was most unexpected."

"My deepest sympathies." This from Charlton, who'd come to his feet when Mrs. Warwick entered the room. "What ailed her, if I may ask?"

"She had a fever and severe stomach pains." Mrs. Warwick still seemed slightly dazed by the sudden, tragic turn of events. "The doctor said it was scarlet fever."

Thea said, "How very sad."

Mrs. Warwick nodded. "I find it difficult to believe that gentle Verity is gone so suddenly."

"You say her husband is not coping well?" Thea asked.

"No, he is not," Mrs. Warwick answered. "He is grieving, of course, but John is also very angry. It is so unlike his usual gentle and amiable countenance."

"What of their children?" Thea asked. "Can they not provide their father with some comfort?"

"John and Verity were not blessed with children," Mrs. Warwick said sadly. "Verity anguished over not being able to provide John with the heir he deserved, but he never recriminated her for it. And now he is truly alone."

Fletcher came in to announce that tea and refreshment had been laid out in the garden. The four of them filed out back and settled into the worn brick terrace's iron furniture. Three brick steps led up to a narrow, slightly overgrown garden, where shrubs and flowering plants crowded each other, seeming to compete for attention.

Thea's elderly butler shuffled behind them, overseeing the footmen who brought in the tea and frozen treats.

"Lemon ices?" Mrs. Warwick dipped a spoon into her frozen dessert. Ice treats were a luxury to have at one's home. "Where did they come from?"

Thea spoke around a small spoonful of the icy treat. "My icehouse."

Mrs. Warwick's delicate brows rose. "You have an icehouse here on the property?"

"Yes, my husband had it put in once he learned how much I adore lemon ice."

"Where is Mr. Palmer?" Charlton asked. "Why is he never in residence?"

"My husband spends most of his time at our property in Yorkshire. I prefer Town life, and he enjoys the country."

"Oh." The surprise on Mrs. Warwick's face was apparent. "I assumed . . . because you wear black—"

"That I'm in mourning?" Thea's eyes twinkled. "Not at all. I wear black to hide the ink stains from my work. You've no idea how many gowns have been sacrificed in the name of geometry."

Charlton sipped his tea, his pinky finger daintily extended. "Is your husband not afraid to leave his beautiful wife unattended for so long a period?" The earl had a flirtatious nature, and Thea's obvious lack of receptiveness did nothing to curb that inclination. "I certainly would be."

"Mr. Palmer and I understand each other perfectly," she said. "We don't see a need to be in each other's pockets."

"More fool he," Charlton replied under his breath.

"As I was saying," Thea continued, "we stock the icehouse with ice from the Thames when the river freezes so I can indulge myself all summer long, no matter how hot it gets. That icehouse is the only reason Atlas agreed to stay with me while he recuperated."

"Recuperated?" Mrs. Warwick looked at Atlas. "Have you been ill, Mr. Catesby?"

Atlas pressed his lips together. He loathed discussing his injury and the limitations it placed upon him. He was not accustomed to being a man of inaction.

But Charlton had no qualms about sharing his friend's private business. "Atlas was involved in a carriage accident several months ago. He jumped from the hackney as it tipped over and broke his foot in the process."

Mrs. Warwick's gaze darted to his injured foot and back again. She must have detected his limp, even though he went to great pains to hide it. "I am improved," he reassured her.

"Unfortunately, he still has pain." Thea sipped her tea. "Icing the injury helps alleviate his suffering. But as soon as he could walk again, he found his own apartments."

"I prefer to be on my own," he said tightly. He also preferred to end all conversation about his private affairs.

Mrs. Warwick set her spoon down, leaving most of her lemon ice untouched. "Did you not have a permanent residence in London?"

He shook his head. "I take temporary lodgings whenever I am in Town."

"Atlas is a restless soul," Charlton put in. "He travels extensively, spending months at a time abroad. He doesn't see the need to keep a household."

Thea scraped the last of her ice from the bowl. "His incapacitation has kept him in England far longer than he cares to be."

"Why are we speaking of me as though I am not present?" Atlas ground the words out.

"Don't be such a stick-in-the-mud, Atlas." Thea reached for her tea. "Mrs. Warwick is clearly interested to know more about us. She is staying here, after all."

He scowled. "Yes, but we seem to only be talking about me."

Mrs. Warwick gave him a considering look. "Will you be leaving again soon, Mr. Catesby?"

He dipped a spoon into his ice, which had begun to melt. "I expect so."

"I shall miss him when he goes." Thea sipped her tea. "But he sends wonderful letters. Atlas is a keen observer of the world around him and fills his correspondence with marvelous details of his travels. He gets his gift with words from our late father."

Mrs. Warwick stared at Thea. It seemed as though something clicked in her mind. "Silas Catesby was your father?"

Thea's pride was apparent. "Yes, indeed."

Atlas was surprised Mrs. Warwick hadn't made the connection before now. His father had been one of England's greatest modern writers and poets. Silas Catesby was so widely admired that he'd been awarded a baronage some twenty years earlier.

Mrs. Warwick looked from Thea to Atlas. "How was it growing up with Silas Catesby as your father?"

"Ever-changing." Thea smiled. "He'd lock himself away for days at a time when he was working. But then he'd emerge, and we'd go on family picnics and other outings until inspiration struck Papa again and he'd vanish back into his study." Mrs. Warwick asked several more questions about their father—inquiries both siblings had grown accustomed to answering over the years.

The conversation gradually moved on to other topics as they drank their tea in the gentle sunshine. When they were done, Atlas and Charlton rose and bade farewell to the ladies before taking their leave.

They'd walked a short distance and were crossing the damp street when Charlton glanced back in the direction of Thea's house. "I say, isn't that Mrs. Warwick's unpleasant husband?"

Atlas swung around in time to see the stocky man with a headful of gray hair lift the knocker on his sister's front door. "What the devil?" He began walking quickly back in the direction they'd just come.

"What are you about?" Charlton called after him. "Do you intend to pummel the man in the street?"

"Only if I have to," he said over his shoulder as he broke into a jog.

Chapter Six

Knowing it would take Thea's decrepit butler several minutes to answer the door, Atlas cut through the back alley that separated the mews from the houses, taking the direct route to the small iron gate that led to Thea's back garden.

As he approached, Godfrey Warwick's voice rang out. Atlas paused by the hedgerow, which gave him a view of the happenings on the patio without revealing himself. He was conscious of overstepping—Thea would never let him hear the end of it—but he was also discomfited by the thought of leaving Mrs. Warwick and Thea alone with the loathsome man.

"I do appreciate your looking after my wife, Mrs. Palmer," the scapegrace was saying.

"Someone has to," Thea retorted. She did not ask him to sit. Women of quality did not extend such invitations to tradesmen, but Atlas suspected his sister withheld the invitation to demonstrate her contempt for the man, not for his class.

"Yes, you are quite right." Warwick had the grace to appear chagrinned. "I have behaved most precipitously in regards to my wife, but I intend to rectify the situation."

"How so?" Mrs. Warwick asked.

"I've come to take you to the boys."

Mrs. Warwick sat up taller. "You'll allow me to be with them?"

"You are their mother. It is only right."

"I'm grateful." Relief washed over the refined lines of her face. "I'm certain we can work out an arrangement that allows me to be with the boys while you are at the haberdashery."

The man frowned. "I'm afraid you mistake my intentions. I've come to take you back as my wife, Lilliana, with all that entails."

Mrs. Warwick went very still. "You wish for things to be as they were."

"You are my wife, after all."

An indelicate snort sounded from Thea. "You seemed to forget that when you sold her. My brother holds a bill of sale that is proof of your dastardly conduct."

"Nonetheless, in the eyes of the law, Lilliana remains my wife," he said tightly. "As her husband, I have complete dominion over her."

"You took me to the center of town and sold me." Mrs. Warwick's voice shook with angry emotion. "I could have been terribly abused if I'd fallen into the care of someone other than Mr. Catesby. You have betrayed me in the worst way."

"I will admit my temper got the best of me. Come home, and all will be well."

"And what will you do when you become angry with me again?"

"I trust you've learned your lesson and will hold your tongue in the future when you think to oppose me."

"No." Mrs. Warwick's spine stiffened. "I will not put my fate in your hands again. You have debased me for the last time."

His eyes went wide, his surprise evident. "I beg your pardon?"

"And well you should." Her voice rang out loud and clear. "What you have done is unpardonable."

Flushed with anger, he placed his palms facedown on the table and leaned into her. "If you do not come with me now, you are choosing to abandon your children."

"I cannot . . . will not . . . go back to living with you as your wife," Mrs. Warwick said.

"You do comprehend that your access to the children will be at my good pleasure." He edged closer. She turned her head, avoiding his gaze. "A court could command that you restore my marital rights to me. A wife has her duties."

"I always endeavored to be a dutiful wife." She raised her gaze to meet his. "However, any sense of obligation I once felt as your wife was severed the moment you whored me out to the highest bidder."

Warwick appeared to be struck dumb, as though uncertain how to deal with this uncharacteristic show of defiance. "Under the law, you do not exist apart from me," he snarled.

Thea cut in. "You may leave us now, sirrah," she said bitingly. "And do not presume to return until, or unless, you are summoned."

Flushed, he glared at his wife. "Everything you do, every action you take, is at my sufferance. Do not push me, Lilliana."

He bowed stiffly before making his exit. When he'd gone, Thea reached over and patted Mrs. Warwick's hand. "Bravo," she said softly. "Are you well, my dear?"

"I am," Mrs. Warwick declared. "As a matter of fact, I tire of acting the victim. It is time my husband learned that I, too, won't be pushed."

Seeing that the women had the matter well in hand, Atlas quietly stepped away from the gate and went back toward the alley, setting off for home.

* * *

The following day, Atlas walked home to Bond Street after an invigorating hour-long swim in the Marquess of Granleigh's indoor plunge pool, his first swim in months.

During his travels to warmer climates, Atlas, a strong and enthusiastic swimmer, took a dip almost daily. Unfortunately, London weather was rarely as accommodating as the Mediterranean. Luckily, Charlton was well acquainted with Granleigh, an elderly marquess whose ill health kept him in the country, and had recently secured permission for Atlas to use the plunge pool during the old man's absence. The basin was somewhat small, but at least Atlas had been able to practice a few strokes. Swimming was the only truly vigorous exercise his foot allowed for these days.

The day was overcast, but that didn't stop people from crowding the fashionable shopping area, the pristine stone walkways keeping them above the muddy streets as they strolled past engravers, gentlemen's hairdressers, wine merchants, and confectioners. Stepping around a group of chattering young women, he wondered again why he hadn't taken a lease on a quieter street.

He went by a man repairing the signage above a clockmaker's shop where the letter *C* had fallen off the building. He smiled because it made him think of Phoebe. Reading imperfect signage had been a game between them when he'd been very young. He would have asked his sister to read the clockmaker's sign for him, and they both would have giggled when she pronounced it "lockmaker." It was strange how a silly childhood game between siblings was now a treasured remembrance. Would it have receded into the forgotten reaches of his brain, he wondered, had Phoebe lived long enough to create more memories?

Ignoring the twitch of emotion in his chest, he turned to walk down Piccadilly and was surprised to find Thea and Mrs. Warwick coming out of Hatchards bookshop, followed by Thea's footman, Miller, who was weighted down by several packages.

"Good day." He removed his beaver hat. "I hadn't thought to run into you ladies here."

Thea's eyes danced merrily. "Mrs. Warwick wanted to do some shopping."

"I see." He eyed the footman's many packages. "Have you seen fit to purchase every book at Hatchards?"

"Oh, no," Thea said. "We have visited a dizzying number of shops and purchased everything you might imagine—hats, slippers, reticules, shawls, gloves, the finest kid leather gloves you can imagine—in every color."

"In every color?" He wondered where Mrs. Warwick had obtained the funds for such extravagance.

"Oh, yes! Miller has already loaded many packages into my carriage," Thea said gleefully. "These are just the latest purchases."

He eyed his sister. Thea shopped when necessary, but she was not one to visit Bond Street for entertainment or to take such pleasure from it. "I've never known you to find shopping so . . . rewarding."

She grinned. "I don't think I've ever enjoyed a visit to Bond Street as much as I have today."

What sounded like a human roar of anger came from behind Atlas. He turned to find a red-faced Godfrey Warwick charging down the street, his furious gaze centered on his wife. "How dare you, you stupid wench," he growled. "Do you think to outsmart me with these antics of yours?"

Atlas stepped into Warwick's path, preventing him from coming too close to his wife.

"Hello, Godfrey. I've been enjoying a bit of shopping." His wife's voice was polite, but the devilish gleam in her eye sparked a strange sensation deep in Atlas's gut.

"Who do you think you are?" The angry words spewed from Warwick's mouth as he gestured to the bags in Miller's arms. "You have charged all this to me? You have spent dozens of pounds."

"Hundreds, I daresay," she said lightly. "Gowns can be most expensive, and I ordered an entire new wardrobe—morning dresses, afternoon dresses, even a couple of ball gowns."

His eyes bulged. "Ball gowns?"

"Once the merchants realized I was the goodly wife of their colleague merchant, the esteemed owner of the Warwick & Sons haberdashery, they kindly extended me a very generous line of credit."

Atlas eyed his sister, who was brimming with barely contained amusement. He suspected that Thea's reputation had also helped Mrs. Warwick obtain credit.

Warwick shook a fist at his wife, but Atlas's stalwart form kept him from getting close enough to the lady to do her any physical harm. "I will cancel all the orders at the modiste."

"Unfortunately, you cannot," she said, not seeming sorry in the least. "I had to pay a premium, you see, to buy the ready-made gowns, some of which had been made for other customers. But we convinced the modistes to sell them to us right away. At considerable expense, of course."

"If you think I will pay these bills, you are mistaken, madam." His voice trembled with anger, and the deep-red shade of his face suggested a man close to having an apoplexy. Shoppers on the sidewalk slowed, staring openly at the commotion Warwick was causing.

"Oh, but you must," Mrs. Warwick said. "Since I do not exist as a separate person from you, according to the laws of England, it is as if you yourself ordered these things, and as such, you are responsible for any and all debts I've incurred today."

Color leached from Warwick's face as her words sank in. "You will not get away with this," he said in a low, deadly tone.

"I do believe that I already have. According to the law, I cannot act on my own. It will be assumed that you ordered me to buy these things." She held herself erect and unflinching in the face of his anger, which prompted Atlas's deep admiration. She was quite a woman.

Disbelief stamped Warwick's face as he advanced on his wife. "You witch!"

Atlas stepped closer. "This is neither the time nor the place to discuss this matter," he murmured in the man's ear. "You are causing a spectacle that your patrons would not appreciate should word of this unfortunate encounter reach them."

Warwick's angry glare met Atlas's calm gaze. "This is all your doing. It must be."

"I assure you this is the first I have heard of Mrs. Warwick's shopping spree. Although I cannot say I disapprove of her methods."

Warwick craned his neck to peer around Atlas's burly frame until his wife came into sight. "You will pay dearly for this."

Atlas placed a warning hand on the man's shoulder. "I will call upon you soon to see if we can settle this matter." Miller also moved a little closer, positioning himself to intervene if needed.

For a moment, it seemed Warwick might come to physical blows with Atlas, but apparently realizing that he was badly outmatched, the man appeared to regain control of himself. "See that you do. You need to control your property, Catesby." He spun on his heel and marched stridently away.

"Well," said Thea with a huff of laughter. "I don't know when I've enjoyed myself so much."

Atlas looked at Mrs. Warwick, who exhibited no outward indication that the encounter with her husband had upset her, although the color on her cheeks was high. "Are you well?"

"Supremely well." Then she released a shuddering breath, and all the strength seemed to flow out of her, and he understood how difficult it had been for her to defy her husband. She gave him a measured look. "I gather you disapprove of my methods."

"Not at all," he responded honestly. "I am all admiration. That was a tactical move worthy of Wellington himself."

Thea clapped her hands together with delight. "I agree. Well done, Lilliana. How clever you are to have thought of this."

A small smile curved her lips. Her mouth intrigued Atlas. It was slightly lopsided, so that when she smiled, it was more of a haughty smirk. "Although the laws of marriage and divorce were written by men to be to their advantage, they neglected to take into account that women can be far more cunning."

Atlas laughed out loud. "Well said. I shall endeavor to remember never to cross you, Mrs. Warwick."

And yet, at the same time, it occurred to him that battling wits with such a woman might prove very amusing indeed.

Chapter Seven

Charlton took a draw on the water pipe, the sound of bubbles percolating through the air. Exhaling, he eyed the decoration in Atlas's bachelor apartments. "The person who chose these colors was either partially blind or had dreadful taste."

Atlas relaxed back into his overstuffed chair and lifted his troublesome foot onto the stool in front of him. The riot of color surrounding them was indeed startling. The carpets were crimson, the wallpaper a bright orange, the chairs and sofa covered in sky-blue paisley chintz. "These apartments were already furnished when I rented them. I don't really notice the decor anymore."

"How can you not?" Disdain tinged Charlton's languorous tone. "It's positively headache inducing."

Atlas took the shared hose from his friend and inhaled, enjoying the effects of the mellow tobacco taste. He'd long had an aversion to snuff and cheroots, but to his surprise, he rather enjoyed an occasional session with the nargileh, a habit he'd picked up in Constantinople. Charlton had also taken to the hookah pipe. "And yet you manage to visit often enough."

"One suffers as one must in the name of friendship."

Atlas smiled, still somewhat bemused by the unlikely bond that had formed between them after meeting at Cambridge. Not only did the Catesbys not move in the same rarified circles as earls, but after Phoebe's death, Atlas had developed an aversion to the peerage. Charlton, who'd always been surrounded by obsequious hangers-on desperate for a future earl's favor, had been intrigued by Atlas's ambivalence. For the first time in his privileged life, he'd had to earn someone's friendship and had vigorously applied himself to doing so. As such, before Atlas knew it, the two men had become fast friends.

Charlton surveyed the chamber. "Although the decoration leaves much to be desired, I do approve of the location. A Bond Street address is quite the thing for young bachelors about Town."

"Your approval relieves my mind." He hadn't taken the apartment because of its fashionable address. It was the first place he'd seen once his foot had healed enough for him to manage a flight of stairs. One could only take so much of Thea's hospitality. His sister tended to be overbearing at times.

He was comfortable enough here. His rooms consisted of a hall with a fireplace, a sitting room with twenty-foot ceilings, double doors that led into the bedchamber, and a dressing room with a hip bath. His servants, if he employed any, would have access to kitchens in the attic, but at the moment, he only had a cleaning lady who came weekly. "Not that it matters," he added. "I shan't be here for much longer."

Charlton held out his empty glass. "Determined to head off for foreign lands again?"

Atlas grabbed the decanter off the marble table beside him and learned forward to freshen the earl's drink. "As soon as I am able." He exhaled disgustedly while gesturing toward his hobbled foot. "That miserable appendage has kept me in London far longer than I'd anticipated."

"You really must get a valet to assist you while you are in Town," Charlton said. "Who will dress you for Thea's party this evening?"

"I shall endeavor to accomplish the task on my own."

"I don't know how you do it. I myself have never managed without making a hash of things."

Atlas drew on the hookah again, settling his head back against his chair to exhale high up toward the ceiling, enjoying the sweet, fragrant scent that filled the air. "You're in possession of an obscenely wealthy earldom. I am not. Circumstances required that I learn to do things for myself." The modest Berkshire property he'd inherited from his father provided an adequate income, if he lived simply. He would never possess anything near the earl's massive fortune.

"Oh, I almost forgot. I met someone the other day who knew you at Harrow," Charlton said. "His name is Robert Bentley. He's the third son of the Marquess of Langford."

"Bentley?" He thought back to his school days and searched his memory for the name. "I don't recall him."

"He remembers you very well. Says you were something of a legend there. A daredevil who would accept any challenge.

Bentley says all the boys there thought you had a death wish. Pity I was at Eton."

Atlas leaned forward, using tongs to tap ash from the glowing coals fueling the hookah. "You did not miss much." He preferred not to reflect back upon his days at the exclusive boarding school. It had been a dark period in his life, a time when he'd often flouted death, daring the reaper to come for him as he had for Phoebe.

Charlton sipped from his glass. "Should I regret that you had calmed somewhat by the time you reached Cambridge?"

"Definitely not," Atlas muttered, eager to change the subject. The near drowning of a fellow student he'd challenged to race across a wide stretch of the rain-swollen River Brent had thoroughly curtailed his most reckless tendencies. Atlas might have been perfectly willing to gamble with his own life, but he could not bear to have another person's death gnawing at his conscience. One was quite enough.

He did not care to continue this line of conversation. It recalled memories he preferred to forget. "I'm beginning to remember Robert Bentley." Irritation edged his words. "He always did talk too much."

"I found him most entertaining."

"I've no doubt." Atlas shifted, grimacing as pain pulsed in his foot. "You enjoy gossip more than any woman I've ever met."

"You're awfully ornery today. Perhaps you should take the tobacconist's wife up on her offer of extra hospitality." Charlton winked. "She makes no secret of her admiration, and she's uncommonly handsome."

"She's offered no such thing." Mrs. Disher, wife of the proprietor of the establishment below his apartments, was friendly enough whenever he stopped by to pick up his special-order tobacco for the nargileh, but he perceived her to be a virtuous woman. "She is my landlord's wife. Not some doxy to be used to slake my unrequited lust."

"Unrequited lust?" Interest sparked in Charlton's blue eyes. "And for whom exactly do you have unrequited lust?"

"No one in particular." Atlas handed the hose to Charlton. "I just haven't addressed that particular need of late."

"As you say." Skepticism hummed in Charlton's throat. "Speaking of your belowstairs neighbor, did you ever learn the reason for his vanishing tobacco stores?"

"As a matter of fact, I did." Charlton had been with Atlas several weeks prior when Mr. Disher had exited his shop and shared his concern that several pounds of prime tobacco seemed to have disappeared.

"And?" Charlton puffed on the end of the nargileh hose. "What was the outcome?"

"We set something of a trap and caught his clerk passing a few ounces of tobacco to his brother each evening when Disher left the shop to take his meal at home with his wife."

"Ah, mystery solved then." He replaced the hose on the hookah and rose, straightening his jacket. "I suppose I should make my way home to ready myself for Mrs. Palmer's affair this evening."

Thea was hosting a small supper party, mostly for her academic-minded friends, but she'd included Atlas, Charlton, and Mrs. Warwick on the guest list. Why she'd invited the earl, Atlas couldn't fathom, since his sister seemed to be in a constant state of annoyance whenever the man came around.

On his way out, Charlton paused by the pedestal game table near the sitting room window. "What are you working on this time?" He stared down at the half-finished frame of the puzzle Atlas had begun upon their return from Bath. Most of the pieces were still scattered atop the walnut surface, waiting to be put into some semblance of order. Charlton tilted his head. "I can't make it out."

"That one's a Gainsborough." Atlas stood and came over, wincing when he put too much weight on his injured foot. "It's called *Landscape in Suffolk*."

"I know that painting. It's all trees, landscape, and sky." Charlton picked up a green puzzle piece. "It'll be next to impossible to put together."

"If it were easy, there would be no challenge." He took the edge piece from Charlton and considered it for a moment, his attention moving to the part of the puzzle he'd already completed and then back to the piece in his hand. He leaned down to press the piece into place on the left side of the frame. "And where would be the fun in that?"

"Fun?" Charlton grimaced before continuing out to the front hall. "I'd rather have a tooth extracted."

An impatient knock sounded at the door before they reached it. Atlas was surprised to find his eldest brother on his doorstep.

"Jason," he said. "This is unexpected."

"Some most distressing news has reached my ears. I've come to make certain for myself that it isn't true." He glanced at Charlton, his eyes widening. "I didn't realize you had company."

Atlas introduced them. "Gabriel Young, Earl of Charlton, meet my brother, Jason, Baron Catesby."

"Well met, Catesby. I was just leaving." Charlton turned to Atlas. "I'll see you this evening."

Jason watched Charlton stroll down the steps and into the street before coming inside. "What on earth was the Earl of Charlton doing here?"

"Having whiskey." Atlas closed the door, and the two made their way back to the sitting room. "Can I offer you a glass?"

"No, thank you. I wasn't aware that you knew Charlton."

"We met at Cambridge." He settled back into his stuffed chair and picked up his glass.

"Cambridge?" Jason repeated, his brows shooting upward. "That was years ago. Why have you never mentioned your association with the earl? Must you always be so secretive?"

"I've rarely seen him since leaving Cambridge." They'd only recently renewed their acquaintance. Atlas's injury, and the long period of recuperation that followed, had allowed for that. He'd bumped into the earl while hobbling along Bond Street a couple of months prior, and they'd resumed their friendship as if the previous several years of separation had never occurred.

"He's excellent *ton*," Jason said approvingly.

"Yes, that is why I have befriended him." Sarcasm weighted Atlas's words.

"I'm relieved to see you are over the unreasonable acrimony you hold for the peerage."

"Rest assured, I still detest many of them, particularly those who think they are above the law." He settled the hand holding his glass on the arm of his stuffed chair. "Fortunately, Charlton is not one of them."

"Your irrational malevolence toward noblemen will not help Phoebe," Jason observed. "Our sister is dead. It is too late to save her."

"And well I know it." Grief knotted in his chest. Phoebe had been the eldest of the six Catesby children and Atlas the youngest. Given their twelve-year age difference, Phoebe had been something of a maternal presence in his life; the Catesby parents had loved their children, but their real adoration had always been reserved for each other. "I do not need your reminder that Phoebe is no longer with us. I should never have left her alone with Vessey. He killed her." And the Marquess of Vessey, a powerful peer, had known that his victim's powerless young brother could do nothing about it.

"You really must put it behind you." Jason's tone suggested the topic bored him. "Phoebe's death was a tragedy, but it is long over and done with."

It would never be over. Not as long as he or Vessey still lived and breathed the same air. Suddenly weary, he asked, "What brings you here, Jason? You rarely visit without a reason."

Jason made a face when he spotted the nargileh. "Really, Atlas, it's bad enough you mix with savages while abroad, but must you bring their heathen habits home with you?"

"Smoking the hookah relaxes me, which I find a particular need for when I am in our fair metropolis."

Jason stared at him. "How is that even remotely possible? You've always hated cheroot smoke, and you won't even sit in a room where cigars are being smoked."

He made a face. "Cigar smoke is particularly objectionable."

"Nonsense. English smoking implements are the finest in the world." Jason waved away the nargileh smoke in short, jerky movements. "I think the truth is that you enjoy being contrary."

"Perhaps. You were about to tell me why you are here," Atlas prompted.

"I may as well come straight to the point." His brother flicked out his coattails before perching at the edge of the chair Charlton had recently abandoned. "The rumor about Town is that you've purchased a doxy who was sold off by her husband."

Atlas remained silent.

"Is it true?"

"No."

Jason exhaled his relief. "Thank goodness."

"The lady in question is no doxy."

Jason started. "Are you saying you did purchase a female?"

"I will not say anything further that could damage the lady's reputation."

"Don't be ridiculous. She's already ruined. Being sold like that by her husband. How could you involve yourself in such a scheme?"

"I could not allow her to face any further degradation than her husband had already subjected her to."

Jason pressed his snowy kerchief against his pursed mouth. "We are newly come to the upper reaches of society, and this antic of yours will not help matters." Their late father had never cared for titles, even after he'd been awarded the barony, but the same could not be said of his heir. "Did you think nothing of the family name when you behaved so rashly?"

"I cannot say that I did."

"My stars! It's positively scandalous. What do you plan to do with her? Is she your mistress?"

"No, she is not. As I said, she is a respectable woman."

"What does your esteemed friend think of this?"

"My esteemed friend?"

"The earl."

"Charlton? He found it deplorable, of course."

"Naturally."

"Deplorable that the lady's husband would treat her in such a manner."

"Really, Atlas." Jason pursed his lips again, an affectation he seemed to have acquired since coming into the title. "Even for you, this behavior is beyond the pale."

"I cannot agree. Coming to the assistance of a lady in distress is completely within the bounds of proper behavior." Not that he gave two figs about such things.

"You have never seen fit to observe the proprieties."

"I think we just disagree on what the proprieties are." Atlas rose. Conversations with Jason were usually exasperating. "If you'll excuse me, I have an engagement this evening that I must ready myself for."

Knowing he'd been dismissed, Jason stood. "Have you gotten yourself a valet yet?"

Atlas led the way into the front hall. "No."

"Every gentleman should have one." Jason shook his head. "You really must learn to behave in accordance with your new station in life."

Atlas opened the door. "You are the baron. My situation is little changed, and I am content for it to be so. Besides, I don't anticipate being in London long enough to need a valet."

Once his brother had gone, Atlas dressed quickly. The mention of Phoebe had darkened his mood, but he still made his way to Thea's a little earlier than the appointed time. He hoped to discuss Mrs. Warwick's future with her before the other guests came. But he arrived to find she had gone out to Slough again.

"What is she doing in Slough?" he demanded to know. "She is trying to see the children, isn't she?"

"Oh, very well." A cutting slash of her hand belied Thea's annoyance. "If you must know, this is her third visit to see the boys. The housekeeper allows her to spend time with them without Warwick's knowledge."

He released an exasperated breath. "It's not safe."

"She'll do anything to see the boys, and it's secure enough, considering her loutish husband spends most of the week at his haberdashery."

Sounds of the front door opening reached them, followed by hurried footsteps coming up the stairs. Atlas, who'd been standing at the hearth in Thea's upstairs sitting room, strode out into the corridor in time to see a red-eyed, stark-faced Mrs. Warwick rushing toward her bedchamber. She was normally impeccably tidy, but today her hair and clothing were askew. Her sleeve was torn, and her dark hair had escaped its bonds, cascading in long ringlets about her shoulders and down her back.

"Mrs. Warwick?" he asked, alarmed by her disheveled appearance. "May I be of service?"

She avoided his gaze and waved him away, dashing down the corridor to her bedchamber and slamming the door behind her. He followed, coming to a halt before her closed door. He rapped softly.

"Mrs. Warwick," he said in gentle tones. "Are you well?"

"What kind of idiotic question is that?" Thea stood in the corridor outside the sitting room. "She's obviously overset."

"Obviously," he snapped. "Thanks to you encouraging her to enter that den of wolves all on her own."

"She wasn't alone," Thea retorted. "My coachman and Miller went with her."

Atlas stormed past her to the top of the stairs. "Miller!" he bellowed.

The footman rushed to the landing, his expression wary. "Yes, sir."

"Join us, if you please. Mrs. Palmer and I would like to hear what occurred in Slough today."

Before long, Miller was relaying the distressing tale. Mrs. Warwick had arranged to see the children on the day the butler, Warwick's man through and through, was off. She'd been visiting with them when Warwick arrived unexpectedly with the butler, who'd somehow learned of Mrs. Warwick's clandestine visits and immediately alerted his master. Warwick caused a great scene in front of the children, yelling at Mrs. Warwick for defying him and at the housekeeper for disobeying him and allowing his wife to see the children.

"A great commotion ensued," Miller said in grave tones. "John Coachman and I hurried into the house and up to the nursery, as Mrs. Palmer had charged us with ensuring Mrs. Warwick's safety and well-being."

"It's good that you did." A sickening feeling swirled in Atlas's gut at the memory of Mrs. Warwick's torn clothing and the ravaged look on her face. "What happened after that?"

"The youngest boy was on her lap, and Mr. Warwick grabbed the lady by her arm and shook her fiercely. John Coachman and I stepped forward and told him to unhand her. Both boys were crying and clinging to their mother, but Mr. Warwick and the butler tried to pull the children away. Mrs. Warwick was trying to calm them. She kept telling them everything would be well, but her husband, well, he just kept bellowing, putting the fear in those poor mites and making them even more upset."

Thea put a hand to her chest. "How terrible."

Miller nodded. "Finally, Mr. Warwick and the butler succeeded in pulling the boys away."

"Is that how Mrs. Warwick's clothing came to be torn?" Atlas asked.

"I suppose so. They carried the boys away and must have locked them in a chamber, because we could hear the boys screaming and pounding on the door, crying out for their mother."

Atlas swallowed down his fury. "What did Mrs. Warwick do?"

"She was begging Mr. Warwick to allow the housekeeper or the footman who looks after the children to go to the boys and comfort them."

"And what did Mr. Warwick say?" Thea asked.

"He threw the footman and the housekeeper out of the house, along with Mrs. Warwick. He said they had lost their positions, and he would give them no reference on account of their being so disloyal," Miller said.

Thea hugged her arms around herself. "Did you leave after that?"

"We did. We helped Mrs. Warwick into the carriage. She barely had the will to do it herself."

"I can only imagine." Thea slumped into the nearest chair. "The poor dear."

Atlas headed for the door.

Thea straightened. "You're leaving?"

"I'll be back soon."

"The party begins in an hour. I cannot cancel this late," she called after him as he trotted down the stairs. "Where are you off to in such a hurry?"

"I'm going to see Warwick, to settle this matter once and for all."

CHAPTER EIGHT

After talking to Warwick's clerk at the haberdashery, Atlas tracked his quarry down at a pub in Covent Garden called the Red Rooster. The man apparently hadn't wasted any time returning to London after throwing Mrs. Warwick out of the house in Slough.

Several framed paintings, mostly landscapes and portraits, adorned the pub's wooden walls, along with cheaper prints and woodcuts. The rich scent of coffee in a vat over the large fire filled the air. Some two dozen men sat around, drinking port or coffee and reading newspapers. A serving girl and a couple of young boys bustled about serving the coffee, while an older man, who appeared to be keeper of the coffeehouse, stood proprietarily behind the counter issuing orders.

One particularly well-dressed group of patrons spoke in Russian, interrupting a boisterous debate about Napoleon to raise their glasses, murmuring, "To your health, gentlemen," before resuming a lively conversation in their native tongue. Atlas had picked up enough of the language—from a Moscow scholar he'd once traveled with—to know they were denigrating the prowess of English troops. He doubted the Russians would have been so vigorous in their insults had they realized the Englishman walking past them understood their barbs.

Atlas spotted Warwick sitting alone at a corner table and made his way over. A shoeshine boy knelt before him, buffing his buckled, brown leather shoes. "May I join you?"

Warwick appeared unsurprised to find Atlas standing before him. He gestured toward a chair. "As you wish." He dropped a tip into the shine boy's open palm, and the boy touched a forelock before moving on in search of another patron.

Atlas pulled out a wooden chair, taking care not to disturb the squat, long-bodied German badger hound curled up in the corner, dozing near the table. A boy of around eleven came over to take his coffee order and then left them alone.

Atlas placed his folded hands on the scarred table. "I think we can both agree that this unpleasantness between you and Mrs. Warwick must cease."

"Indeed." Warwick took a long pull of his port, his face cast in shadows. The afternoon sun had begun to set, and a couple of young serving boys lit candles to counter the diminishing daylight coming through the windows. "That's why I've decided to take her back."

Atlas's gut tightened. He would return the woman over his dead body. "I'm afraid that's not possible. I have a bill of sale that proves she is mine, and I say Mrs. Warwick can choose her own future."

Malice gleamed in Warwick's eyes. "According to my solicitor, she remains my wife by law, meaning I retain all rights over her."

Atlas watched the serving boy pour a mug of coffee from a metal pot kept warm by the hearth. It was clear to him now that Warwick's pretense of indifference when threatened with exposure to his customers had been just that—pretense. The man clearly meant to have his wife back, and not for sentimental reasons. That he'd gone so far as to seek advice from an expert in the law was proof of that.

"Your sudden desire for your wife's return is heartwarming," he said, "but she has made clear to me that she has no interest in returning to you." The boy brought over Atlas's coffee and set it on the table before quietly moving away.

Dark amusement deepened the lines in Warwick's face. "Quite the gallant, aren't you? Have you not yet learned that the termagant isn't worth it?"

He forced himself not to react to Warwick's insult. "If that's how you feel, one can't help but wonder why you would want her back." The man sitting alone at the table next to them shifted in their direction. Their conversation seemed to interest him, although his overt attention remained focused on the plate of food before him.

"That is none of your concern." Warwick leaned forward, elbows on the table. "It seems to me that you would also face great censure if your role in purchasing my wife were to become public."

Atlas drank from his coffee. "I assure you that I have little interest in society gossip."

"But the same cannot be said of your brother the baron, can it? I understand he is very interested in observing the proprieties."

"My brother's opinion is his own and will have no bearing whatsoever on this negotiation."

"What you fail to understand is that there will be no agreement," Warwick said smugly. "I want her back, and I shall have her."

Atlas's fingers tightened around his mug. "If Mrs. Warwick does not wish to return to you, I will not force it upon her." The interloper at the next table stopped eating, and although he avoided looking in their direction, Atlas could almost see the man's ears twitching.

"Then I shall sue you for criminal conversation," Warwick said. "I will drag your good name through the mud."

"You bastard." Fury churned hot and sharp in Atlas's gut. The whoreson intended to sue him for adultery, shaming both him and Mrs. Warwick. If the damaging allegations were heard in open court, they would trigger the scandal of the season. As a gentleman, Atlas would survive the social disgrace, but Mrs. Warwick would be irretrievably ruined. "I never touched her."

"Surely you don't expect anyone to believe that? You've trespassed on my private property, my wife's body, and I intend to see you punished in a court of law."

Atlas stood abruptly, upending his chair, which clattered to the dark slate floor behind him. "You go too far."

"I would suggest you encourage Lilliana to return home before I pursue legal recourse."

"Do you think to threaten me?" Atlas clenched his fists by his side to keep from ramming one of them down Warwick's throat. "Don't push me."

"You're playing with an empty hand, Catesby. I hold all the cards." Satisfaction sparked in the man's malevolent gaze. "The only recourse left for you is to deliver my wife back to me posthaste."

"I'll see you dead before I allow Mrs. Warwick returned to you without her consent." He swung around and kicked the toppled chair out of his way, striding out of the coffeehouse before he lost what little remained of his temper and used his bare hands to tear the foul bastard apart, limb by limb.

* * *

By the time Atlas returned to Thea's house, the party was already under way. Sounds of conversation, soft laughter, and clinking glasses drifted out into the main hall.

"I'm going to take a moment to myself in the upstairs sitting room before I join the others," he told the butler when he handed off his hat.

Fletcher slowly bowed. "Very good, sir."

Atlas trotted upstairs, hoping to settle the outrage simmering in his blood before he joined Thea and her guests. He also did not care for Mrs. Warwick to see him in his current agitated state. When he reached the sitting room, he found it occupied.

Mrs. Warwick sat on the sofa in a white dressing gown with her legs tucked beneath her. Her hair was pulled loosely back, cascading spirals of midnight glinting in the candlelit room. She looked . . . beautiful.

"I gather I am not alone in wanting some time alone," he said.

Her smile was weary. "It's been a trying day."

His throat felt tight. "I'm sorry about what you went through this afternoon."

She looked into the fire. "It's hopeless."

He joined her on the sofa. Sitting at the opposite side, he rested his arm over the sofa back, taking care not to touch her. "What is?"

"He doesn't care about the children's well-being. He'll keep them from me just to spite me. And I dare not subject them to another scene like the one they endured today."

"Perhaps in time . . ."

"How much time?" she asked softly. "A year? Two?" Her eyes glistened with unshed tears. "The housekeeper and footman who looked after the children are gone because of me."

"No," he said ardently. "Not due to your actions. Warwick is the reason they are gone."

"Mrs. Greene and Jamie were kind to me and the boys. As a result, they find themselves without a situation, and my children are utterly abandoned."

"Do you know their direction? Your housekeeper and the footman? Perhaps Charlton and Thea could help them find a situation."

Some of the worry lines in her face softened. "It would relieve my mind greatly if that could happen."

"Then consider it done."

They were quiet for a moment. There was a strange sort of affinity between them, one that was not entirely comfortable, resulting from that terrible afternoon at the inn yard in Buckinghamshire. It was a bond her scoundrel of a husband had inadvertently sowed when he'd sold her to the highest bidder.

"I understand you went to see Godfrey," she said.

He avoided her gaze. "Who told you that?"

"Did it go so badly, then, that you cannot even look me in the eye?"

He cleared his throat, wanting to shield her from the full extent of her husband's ugliness. "He is a scoundrel of the lowest sort."

"What happened?" When he hesitated, she said, "Nothing could be worse than having my children taken from me. Whatever it is, I can survive it."

"It is nothing worth repeating."

"I deserve to know what is coming."

She did. But he hated to be the one to tell her that Warwick was out to destroy her. "He's threatened to sue me for criminal conversation."

She sucked in a breath, and all the color drained from her already-pale face. "But it's a lie."

"He is not interested in the truth. He knows the accusation alone will cause a terrible scandal."

She shook her head, her distress obvious. "He will ruin your good name when all you have done is behave in the most gentlemanly manner."

His eyes widened. "You worry for my good name? I can easily withstand anything he casts in my direction. But for you, as a female—"

She touched his hand where it rested on the back of the sofa. "Your concern is for me?" Her touch was light, like a butterfly. Or an angel. And it sent a pleasant ripple through him.

"You would not even be allowed to testify in your defense," he said heatedly. "You would be utterly ruined."

"You are a very decent man, Atlas Catesby." She met his gaze and held it; her eyes, rich and luminous, were the color of leaves in the fall. "I did not know there could be men like you in the world."

"I am sorry for what you have endured." He presumed to take her pale, fine-boned hand into his. When she allowed it, something sweet, yet also painful, stirred in his chest. He feathered his thumb over skin that was warm and as soft as a rose petal. "You do not deserve such base treatment."

They held each other's gaze. It was silent except for the rain that had begun to fall outside, a gentle patter sounding against the window. Her eyes glittered against the smooth porcelain of her complexion. A strange, fierce sensation kindled deep in his belly.

A throat cleared. "Excuse me, sir." Atlas tore his attention away from Mrs. Warwick to the young man standing on the threshold dressed in servant's clothing. Atlas didn't recognize him, but then Thea often hired extra help for her parties. "Mrs. Palmer asked if you will be joining the others for dinner, sir."

He pulled his hand away from Mrs. Warwick's, regretting the loss of her touch. "I gather you are not joining them," he said to her.

"No." She came to her feet, and he rose as well. "I'm not up to socializing this evening."

"If I were to go down to dinner, there would be an uneven number, since you are not there." He was greatly relieved to have a reason not to join the festivities. "Send my regrets to Mrs. Palmer," he instructed the young man.

After the servant left, he escorted Mrs. Warwick down the corridor to her bedchamber. "I hope you will be able to get some much-needed rest."

"I will try." She paused after opening her door. "Thank you for all you've done on my behalf. Most men would not have behaved in such a chivalrous manner."

"It has been my privilege," he said before bidding her good evening. A fierce desire to protect her swept through him. "On my honor, I will do whatever is in my power to help you be with your children again."

* * *

When he arrived at home, Atlas sat to work on the Gainsborough puzzle, an activity that usually helped to clear his head and settle his mind. That evening, though, the puzzle did not have the desired effect, for his thoughts remained unsettled. After about an hour, he gave up and retired to his bedchamber, where he spent a restless night, the rumble of thunderstorms adding to his sleeplessness.

He rose early the following morning and had just completed his toilette for the day when he noticed a message had been slipped under his door. It was from Godfrey Warwick.

For a certain sum, this situation can be rectified.
Please attend me at the shop at your earliest convenience.

GW

He threw the note down with a colorful curse, wondering what game Warwick was playing at now. The man obviously enjoyed keeping Mrs. Warwick dancing on a string; perhaps he fancied doing the same with Atlas.

It was late morning by the time he entered the haberdashery, fueled by curiosity and a desire to assist Mrs. Warwick. The shop was in the same tidy state—with gleaming surfaces and neat, well-stocked shelves—as when he'd last visited. He approached the curly headed clerk standing alone behind the mahogany counter, whom he recognized from his previous visits. "I'm here to see Mr. Warwick."

"I'm afraid that's not possible." The clerk pushed his spectacles up the bridge of his nose with his pointer finger. "Mr. Warwick has not come down yet this morning."

Irritation flickered. "Does he normally stay abed this late?"

"No, Mr. Warwick is usually down before I even arrive."

Atlas didn't know what Warwick was up to, but he was in no mood to be toyed with. He hadn't slept well, and a headache threatened. He peered behind the clerk to the door leading to the private back area of the store. "I have an appointment with Mr. Warwick." He stepped closer, knowing his size and high-handed manner would intimidate the boy. "Pray go and tell him I am here."

The boy blinked and stepped back. "Mr. Warwick does not like to be trespassed upon in his private quarters."

"And I don't care to be kept waiting. Go and summon your master at once."

The clerk wavered while Atlas stared hard at him, and then he gave a nervous cough. "Very well. I shall go and inquire as to whether Mr. Warwick is available."

While the clerk was gone, Atlas speculated about Warwick's motivation for summoning him. It was likely another game, although it was possible Warwick wasn't as well breeched as he appeared. Perhaps the shopkeeper was truly in need of chink.

His musings were punctured by an ear-piercing scream from somewhere above him that seemed to shudder through the stucco walls. The animalistic howl was pitched so high that, at first, Atlas thought it belonged to a woman. His blood turned cold, and he bolted toward the narrow steps leading to the upper floors. When he reached the bottom step, the clerk appeared on the landing and staggered down the stairs with horror etched on his face, his skin an ashy gray.

"What is it?" Atlas reached out to steady the fellow.

"Mr. . . . Warwick." The clerk gagged and covered his mouth. Wrenching violently away, he stumbled past Atlas and across the shop floor, throwing open the door just in time to cast his accounts all over the stone walkway.

Atlas ran up the stairs, taking them two at a time until he reached the top. The mahogany door to what he assumed were Warwick's apartments was wide open, leading to a well-ordered sitting room with comfortable stuffed brown furniture, a desk, a wooden table, and two spindle-backed chairs. The only item that looked amiss was a heavy pewter candleholder lying on the rug. He moved toward the double doors that led to the bedchamber.

A sickly sweet odor reached him. There, on the crumpled bed, lay Warwick, clad only in trousers. He was on his back with his arms flung out wide, his head hanging over the side of the bed. His face had turned a sickening shade of dark purple, while the skin on his exposed upper body, chest, and arms coated with silvery fur was bluish gray and waxy looking. His stomach appeared distended, unnaturally swollen. Eyes that had gleamed with malice only a few short hours before were now open and unseeing, staring blankly at a world he was no longer a part of.

Atlas spun away from the gruesome sight, his breakfast threatening to reappear when his own belly lurched. He put a fortifying hand on the wall and leaned into it, forcing himself to breathe evenly while his mind processed what he'd just seen. There was no doubt about it.

Godfrey Warwick was dead.

Chapter Nine

"How long have you known the deceased?"

Atlas rubbed the back of his neck. "A short time. Approximately three weeks." He sat atop the haberdashery counter, answering questions put to him by the corpulent Bow Street runner who'd arrived shortly after the clerk had discovered Warwick's corpse.

"How did you come to make his acquaintance?"

"We met by chance at an inn when I was passing through Slough in Buckinghamshire. He has a country box there."

The runner was a rumpled-looking man of about forty who'd introduced himself as Ambrose Endicott. "He *had* a country box, you mean to say. You are aware Mr. Warwick is deceased."

"I'm aware. It was hard to miss."

Endicott studied him with eyes that looked like black currants among the fleshy folds of his face. "So you only met three weeks ago."

"Yes, I didn't know him well."

"But you were well acquainted enough with the man to threaten him?"

The hair rose on the back of his neck. "Where did you hear that?"

"What difference does it make?" The runner consulted his notes. "Ah yes, here it is. You threatened to meet Mr. Warwick at dawn to put an end to Mrs. Warwick's 'suffering,' as you put it."

Atlas recalled saying as much to Warwick during his previous visit to the haberdashery. "The clerk obviously has keen hearing."

Endicott nodded agreeably. "Young Mr. Stillwell's information has been most helpful. Most helpful. Do you deny threatening to challenge the victim to a duel?"

"I do not deny it. However, I never issued the challenge, and I fail to see how that's relevant, since we are not currently standing on the lawn at Hyde Park."

"A most valid point. Most valid." The runner scratched his head and consulted his notes again. "You were also heard to say that Mr. Warwick would pay for what he had done."

Atlas exhaled through his nostrils. "Am I being accused of something?" All signs suggested to him that Warwick had been killed and that the pewter candlestick on the floor was the likely murder weapon. But he hadn't noted any overt signs of injury to the man's skull. "Was he hit in the head?"

"Possibly." Endicott chewed on the back of his pencil. "Could be a natural death. But it also could be poison. We'll have to wait and see. The medical examiner's report will help determine if we are dealing with murder."

"These questions about my relationship with the man could very well be pointless." But Atlas did not think they were. He would do just about anything to get his hands on the medical examiner's report once the postmortem had been completed.

"Perhaps, perhaps not, but it is best to be thorough." Endicott spoke in an amiable manner. "I am interested to know why you hated the man and what precisely any of this has to do with his wife."

"It has nothing at all to do with Mrs. Warwick." Atlas struggled to hold onto his temper. The last thing he wanted to do was to sully Mrs. Warwick's name any further by making her husband's outrageous behavior more publicly known than it already was.

"Let's come back to that, shall we?" Endicott pulled out a bolt of fabric. "Fine muslin. My missus would appreciate this, but it's rather too fine for a runner's modest wages."

Impatient, Atlas came down off the counter. "If that is all." He wanted to tell Mrs. Warwick about her husband before someone else did.

Endicott looked up from the fabric. "Just one more thing. What were you doing here today?"

"I had an appointment with Mr. Warwick." He straightened his jacket. "He sent a note requesting that I visit him here at the shop today."

"Is that so?" He came over. "May I see the note?"

Atlas pulled the missive from his pocket and dropped it into Endicott's open palm. The runner read the words quietly to himself and then again aloud. "For a certain sum, this situation can be rectified." He tilted a look at Atlas. "To what situation does he refer?"

"I have no idea," he lied. "Warwick enjoyed toying with people. Now if that's all—"

"One more question. Do you know where I can find Mrs. Warwick?"

There was no reason to obfuscate. "She is a houseguest of my sister, Mrs. Thea Palmer, who lives in Bloomsbury."

"A houseguest? Mr. and Mrs. Warwick were staying with your sister?"

"No, Mrs. Warwick is the sole houseguest."

"And where was Mr. Warwick staying?"

"I was not the man's keeper." Atlas ground out. "Although I understand he stayed most evenings in his rooms here above the shop."

"They were staying apart, were they?" Endicott rubbed his chin with thick fingers topped by clean, short nails. "Interesting, that. I suppose Mrs. Warwick will need to be made aware of her husband's sad demise."

"It will be quite a shock for her. I'd like to tell her myself, if you don't mind."

"Would you now?" Interest flickered in the man's black eyes. "No, I don't mind. Not at all. And after we finish up here, I'll call on the good widow myself to extend my condolences."

* * *

Atlas found Mrs. Warwick in the library, reading one of her newly acquired books on the particulars of English law.

"Your sister is out." Putting the book aside, she stood to greet him. "But you've come in time to save me from seeing for myself, in black and white, just how dire my legal situation is."

He bowed, his gaze sweeping over her. She wore one of her new gowns, a fashionable, dark bottle-green print that flattered her dark hair and eyes. This was the first time he'd seen her dressed in the first stare of fashion, and it suited her.

Dreading what he must tell her, Atlas went to stand before the unlit hearth with his hands clasped behind his back. "If it were in my power, I would spare you from any further unpleasantness. Lord knows you've been through enough."

Alarm replaced the relaxed expression on her face. "What has Godfrey done now? Stealing my children and threatening to publicly brand me an adulteress isn't enough?"

He cleared his throat. "I have grave news."

"What is amiss?" She crossed over to him. "Is it something to do with the boys?"

"No, nothing of that sort. The children are fine, as far as I am aware." He moved closer, and he could see her surprise when he took both of her hands into his. Her palms were smooth and warm. "But something of a very distressing nature has occurred."

She looked at their joined hands and then back into his face. "What is it?"

"Perhaps we should sit."

Her fingers tightened around his. "Just tell me. Please."

"Very well." He paused. "I've just come from the haberdashery."

"Yes?" She appeared to brace herself. "What has my husband done now?"

"It is more of what has been done, or may have been done, to Mr. Warwick."

"I don't take your meaning."

"I regret to inform you that Mr. Warwick appears to have taken ill and is now deceased."

She stiffened. "Deceased?"

"Yes, his clerk found him this morning in his apartments above the shop."

She withdrew her hands from his. "Godfrey is dead?"

"Yes, and you have my deepest sympathies."

She stared at him, her expression dazed. "Are you certain?"

"There can be no doubt. I saw . . . him . . . for myself, and the runners are there at the shop as we speak."

"The runners? What is Bow Street doing there? I thought you said Godfrey took ill."

"They are taking every precaution. The body will have to be examined."

"What about the boys?"

"As I said, I have no reason to believe they are not well."

"I must go and get them." She started for the door. "Their father is dead, and Mrs. Greene and young Jamie are no longer there to comfort Robin and Peter. Godfrey's butler doesn't possess a nurturing bone in his body. Once he learns about Godfrey, I wouldn't put it past him to abscond with the silver and abandon the children."

"Lilliana." Atlas closed a hand around her upper arm, gentle but firm. She halted, swinging around to look at him with large eyes. He'd never been so familiar as to call her by her given name. "Mrs. Warwick," he corrected, "it might not be wise of you to go immediately. We must see about the status of the children's guardianship."

Alarm shadowed her eyes. "From what I've just read, Godfrey had the right to assign a guardian to look after the children in the event of his death. Do you think he's done such a thing?"

"I suppose it's possible."

"I'm going to them." But before she reached the door, Fletcher appeared, effectively blocking her exit.

"A visitor to see you, Mrs. Warwick."

She tried to step around him. "I am not at home to anyone."

"It is a Mr. Ambrose Endicott." The old servant repeated the words slowly and distinctly, as if he'd taken pains to remember the name. "He says it is an urgent matter."

"Endicott?" Atlas said with some distaste. "That was rather quick."

She glanced back at him. "Who is he?"

"The Bow Street runner investigating your husband's death."

The heavyset man appeared behind Fletcher. "Mrs. Warwick, I presume?"

"Yes?"

Fletcher bristled. "Sir," he said loudly, "you were to wait until I showed you in."

"No need for that," the runner said cheerfully, maneuvering his unwieldy form around the butler. "I managed to find my own way in."

Fletcher drew himself up as if to protest, but Atlas headed him off with a staying hand. "It's all right, Fletcher. You may leave us."

Once the butler departed, shuffling away with a restrained huff, the runner turned to Mrs. Warwick. "My condolences, madam, on the death of your husband."

"Thank you." She still seemed stunned. "It hardly seems real."

"I assure you it is very real."

She nodded and took a seat, inviting him to do the same. He lowered himself into a lacquered ebony chair with graceful tapered legs that appeared too delicate to withstand his girth. She took a position across from him, while Atlas stood by the hearth with one elbow resting on the stone mantle.

"Was your husband in poor health, Mrs. Warwick?" Endicott observed her closely with canny dark eyes.

"No." Her voice had a distant quality. "He seemed to be quite robust the last time I saw him."

"And when was that?"

"Just yesterday."

Atlas could well imagine the nightmarish scene Thea's footman had described—Warwick barking at her while the boys cried and clutched at their mother, desperate to hold on as the butler and their father dragged them away.

"I see," the runner said. "And where exactly was that?"

"At . . . our home in Buckinghamshire . . . with our children."

"Buckinghamshire. Is that where you grew up?"

"No, I come from Bewerley, in Yorkshire."

"Bewerley? Lovely place." Curiosity glimmered in his eyes. "My mother's people hail from near there. What is your family name?"

Atlas found himself listening intently for her answer. Perhaps this would be his first real insight into the lady's true origins. "Hastings."

"Hastings. Hmmm." The runner appeared to strain his memory. "No, I can't say the name is familiar."

Atlas shifted his weight from one foot to the other. "Perhaps we should return to the matter at hand, since this is not a social call."

"Just so. Just so," the runner said easily. "On the matter of your husband, Mrs. Warwick, did you notice anything amiss with his health yesterday when you saw him?"

"No, he seemed his usual self."

He proceeded to ask more about Godfrey's health and his daily routine. Mrs. Warwick answered his questions in a calm, almost distracted manner. She was still clearly in shock from the news.

"Very well," the runner said at length, rising heavily from his seat. "I won't impose on you any longer for now. I perceive this is a difficult time for you."

Atlas stepped forward. "What happens next, Endicott?"

"Next?" Endicott gave Atlas a thoughtful look. "We wait to hear the results of the postmortem and proceed from there." He turned to go. "I'll see myself out."

Once he'd departed, Mrs. Warwick said, "I cannot believe Godfrey is gone." She spoke more to herself than to Atlas, as if saying the words aloud might make it seem more real. "That it's truly over."

Atlas had a sinking feeling in his stomach. "I pray that is so."

Chapter Ten

The sounds of an argument were the first thing to reach Atlas's ears when he visited his sister's house in Bloomsbury three days later.

"The shop is no place for children." Thea's indignant voice rang out from the morning room. "For the love of God, I am childless, and I know better."

"I cannot continue to impose," Mrs. Warwick's voice returned, the words quiet and determined.

He cleared his throat to alert them to his presence.

Thea's attention swung toward him. "Thank the Lord you are here." Hands on her hips, she stood by the round breakfast table, which was cluttered with notebooks and papers. "Perhaps you can talk some sense into her."

Mrs. Warwick stood before the window with her back toward the room, her arms crossed over her chest. It was the first he'd seen her since the day she'd learned of her husband's demise. Warwick had been buried in Buckinghamshire the previous day. Atlas had not attended.

"Good morning," he said.

She turned at the sound of his voice, her expression wary. "Good morning." She had not taken on her mourning. Instead, she wore a simply cut teal gown that highlighted her elegant figure and flattered her dark hair and fair coloring.

"Why does my sister think you've taken leave of your senses?"

One side of her sensuous mouth quirked upward. "Mrs. Palmer has been very generous, but—"

Thea interrupted in a burst of exasperation. "She wants to take the children to live above the shop."

"Shop?"

"The haberdashery."

"I cannot take advantage of Mrs. Palmer's generosity any further."

"Of course you can." They all turned toward the sound of Charlton's voice.

Thea frowned. "How did you get in?"

The earl flashed a charming smile, baring a row of bright-white teeth. As usual, he was impeccably dressed in a double-breasted aubergine tailcoat with shiny brass buttons. "I assured Fletcher that, as a close friend of the family, I do not need to be announced."

She harrumphed. "I shall have to have a word with him."

"If he can hear you," Charlton murmured as he moved to stand before Mrs. Warwick. "My dear lady, allow me to extend my deepest condolences on your loss."

"Thank you," Mrs. Warwick said. "It is kind of you to come."

His interested gaze swept over her teal gown. "I see you've adopted a new style of mourning."

She flushed, color arching high over her cheekbones. "I hadn't expected to receive callers today."

Thea shook her head. "Really, Charlton. You barrel your way past my butler, invading my inner sanctum, and then you dare to censure *Mrs. Warwick* for not observing the proprieties?" She sat at the table, practically disappearing behind the stacked notebooks and papers. "For an earl, your manners are atrocious."

Charlton flattened a hand against his chest. "On my honor, I meant no insult. The late Mr. Warwick was an odious fellow, and it pleases me no end that Mrs. Warwick hasn't turned sentimental or maudlin solely because the man had the courtesy to kick the bucket at a most opportune time."

"Charlton." Atlas's tone held a note of warning. He didn't want to risk upsetting Mrs. Warwick any more than she already was.

But she surprised him with a light laugh. "No, Mr. Catesby, it is quite all right. Truly. The earl provides a note of levity when we could all use it."

"I'm glad to be of service," Charlton said. "Now, do tell, why can you not take further advantage of Mrs. Palmer's hospitality?" He straightened his perfectly wrought cravat. "If she offered as much to me, I would surely take her up on it."

"You turn up all the time anyway," Thea retorted without looking up as she sorted through some papers. "I cannot begin to imagine how much more you'd be underfoot if you were actually invited."

Atlas turned to Mrs. Warwick. "What's this about moving over the shop, if I may be so bold as to inquire?"

A resolute expression came over her face, erasing any traces of mirth. "The boys and I cannot stay here forever."

"Are the children here?" he asked.

"They remain in Slough but will join me shortly. I visited with them all day yesterday while the men attended to the burial." So she had gone to Buckinghamshire. He'd wondered. Females, including wives, generally attended funerals but rarely went to the burial itself.

"Perhaps it is premature to make plans until you know of the status of the children's guardianship," he said gently.

She moved to take a seat at the table. "John and I met with Godfrey's solicitor yesterday after the burial," she said. It took him a moment to put together that the John she referred to was her late husband's brother. "Godfrey had a will. The boys have inherited everything."

Atlas exhaled through his nostrils. "You have been very busy." It pricked at him, even though it shouldn't, that she had attended to important business without him. He felt left out, which was silly of course, but since their first meeting at the inn, he'd taken on the role of her protector. Now it seemed she no longer needed him to act in that capacity.

Perhaps she meant for their acquaintanceship to draw to a natural close. He couldn't blame her, especially considering the way they'd met, which was an embarrassment to her. That could explain her desire to distance herself from Thea as well.

"The boys do have a guardian," Mrs. Warwick continued. "John is that guardian and is happy to relinquish them into my care, although, as their uncle, he naturally hopes to continue to have a role in their upbringing."

"Naturally." It appeared the head of her late husband's family had moved into the role of Mrs. Warwick's champion. A peevish part of Atlas wondered whether John Warwick, himself a recent widower, had designs on his late brother's wife. They could never marry, of course—the law prohibited a man from taking his brother's widow to wife—but even so, Mrs. Warwick and the boys offered John the family he had never managed to build with his late wife.

"And you choose to move your children to live over the shop?" Charlton made a moue of distaste as he settled himself into his favorite overstuffed chair. "How pedestrian of you. What of the quaint country box in Buckinghamshire?"

"I will never live there again," she said tightly. "Those are memories best left in the past."

Atlas could only imagine what had occurred in the old rectory to give her such a deep aversion to the place that she preferred to install her children in small apartments above a haberdashery.

"All the more reason for you to stay here with the boys." Thea threw down her wooden graphite pencil. "I live alone in this huge mausoleum and would welcome the company."

Mrs. Warwick's expression softened. "You've been very kind to me. But boys are noisy, rambunctious creatures. They will create a fuss when you are trying to work."

"It is a sound I had hoped to hear for many years." Wistfulness clouded Thea's usual no-nonsense gaze. "I would welcome the sounds of children running through the halls."

Surprise illuminated Mrs. Warwick's face. An awkward silence descended. Mrs. Warwick darted an uncomfortable glance Atlas's way while Charlton pretended to examine the cuffs of his jacket.

Atlas was stunned by his sister's show of emotion. He had always assumed Thea's childless state was of her own choosing, that she preferred to immerse herself in her equations. Lord knows she complained often enough about her husband being underfoot during his occasional visits from his country estate. Atlas had long suspected Charles Palmer would prefer to be at his wife's side even though he indulged her need for solitude and independence.

"I suppose I could bring the boys here to stay for an interim period," Mrs. Warwick said slowly. "If you are certain, Thea."

His sister had already picked up her pencil and was scribbling away. "I am," she said, recovering her usual brusque manner.

"You are very kind," Mrs. Warwick said.

"Nonsense." Thea reached for one of the notebooks stacked to her side and opened it up before her. "Now all of you go away—I have work to do."

As they exited, Thea called out to Atlas. "Don't forget. We dine at Jason's this evening."

He resisted the urge to groan. Since he was so often abroad, he mostly managed to miss the monthly gatherings, family dinners with all his siblings in attendance—all except for Phoebe. It was not an event he looked forward to, but Thea was not one to let him escape easily.

"I'll pick you up in my carriage," she said. "Be ready at seven."

* * *

"Could Warwick's death present a problem for you?" Charlton asked as they stepped onto the sidewalk after taking their leave.

"Yes, I believe it could." They turned down Great Russell Street, walking past a boarding house, which had once been a grand home. Bloomsbury was now solidly middle class, home to doctors, artists, writers, and politicians. Palmer had fancied a residence on George Street, off fashionable Cavendish Square in Mayfair, but Thea would have none of it, saying she preferred the intellectual vigor found in Bloomsbury. "I'd like to get ahold of the medical examiner's report."

"I've made certain inquiries. It appears Warwick died of a harsh blow to the stomach."

"Did he?" He'd assumed Warwick had died of a blow to the head, but apparently someone had taken the pewter candlestick to the man's gut rather than bashing his brains in. He looked at his friend. "Wait. Is this your way of asking me if Warwick and I came to blows?"

"Did you?" Charlton cut him a sidelong glance. "He certainly deserved a thrashing, especially after threatening to sue you for crim-con."

"I did not." Rather than take insult, Atlas found himself appreciating his friend's directness. "Although I dearly wanted to on more than one occasion. Why did you inquire into Warwick's death?"

"You mentioned wanting to see the report. The runner you spoke of seems to have set his sights on you, considering the questions he put to you after the body was discovered."

They crossed the street to avoid the construction of new terraced homes being built on land where the Dukes of Bedford had once lived in grand style. The current duke preferred the fashionable West End, so his old mansion had recently been demolished.

Atlas buttoned his tan overcoat against the chill of the overcast day. "Are you certain of how Warwick died?"

"Quite certain. The physician who performed the postmortem has an excellent reputation for being an exacting man of science."

"I'd like to learn more about what he discovered."

"I thought you might." Charlton's smile could only be described as smug. "I happen to know that he would welcome a visit from us."

"He would? And why is that?"

"I recently made a significant contribution to the good doctor's research endeavors." Charlton played at being the dandy, but Atlas had learned long ago that his friend wasn't as vapid as he purported. The earl stopped and extended a graceful arm to hail his carriage, which had been trailing behind them. "You'd be surprised at what one can access when one is in possession of the proper resources."

* * *

Dr. Archibald Rivers kept an office in Smithfield not far from St. Bartholomew's Hospital. Out front, the breeze carried the slight stench of animals and waste from the nearby meat market. But once within, the doctor's office resembled a gentleman's study, with its dark wood paneling and studious air. Rivers was a careful, cordial man with a slender build and an extraordinarily high forehead where his hairline had once been.

"You'd like to know how the victim died?" Rivers gestured for them to sit in the chairs opposite his desk. "It's quite simple, really. He bled to death."

"Bled to death?" Atlas asked incredulously. "Impossible. I viewed the body, and there was no blood."

"That is due to the fact that the bleeding was internal. May I offer you some tea?"

"No, thank you," Atlas spoke for both of them without pausing to consider whether Charlton might care to wet his throat.

"How could a blow to the stomach cause Warwick to bleed to death internally?"

"Whoever hit him ruptured his spleen."

"And where exactly is the spleen?" Charlton inquired politely.

"It is about the size of your fist"—Rivers pointed to an area below his chest—"and is located in the upper-left quadrant of the abdomen . . . just under the rib cage."

Atlas leaned forward. "How does rupturing a spleen kill you?"

"As I said, you bleed to death internally," Rivers explained. "The spleen bleeds into the stomach, which decreases oxygen to the heart and brain."

"How long would it have taken him to die?" Atlas asked.

"In such cases, death can occur anywhere from a few hours to a few days."

"How long before he would have felt some pain?"

"The deceased likely would have experienced some discomfort immediately after the injury occurred. The pain would have become more acute as the hours passed. Mr. Warwick probably grew light-headed and confused. It's possible he fainted first, before he eventually died. I found all his blood in his abdomen."

"Were there any other signs of disruption to the body?" Atlas asked. "Any sign he struggled with his attacker?"

"No, not that I could tell."

"Besides a blow to the abdomen, is there any other way this injury could have occurred?"

"Sometimes we see this type of trauma following a carriage or a riding accident. And, of course, we sometimes find the condition in pugilists."

After a few more questions, Atlas and Charlton thanked Rivers and took their leave. As they climbed into the earl's waiting carriage, Atlas mulled over what they'd just learned.

"You seem to be concentrating very hard," Charlton remarked. "What are you thinking?"

"Rivers said there were no signs of a struggle," Atlas said.

"Is that significant?"

"There was also no evidence that someone had forced themselves into Warwick's apartments." In fact, the space had been quite orderly. No overturned chairs, nothing out of place except for the pewter candlestick on the floor in the sitting room.

"What do you deduce from that?"

"That it is very likely Warwick knew his attacker, which narrows the field of suspects considerably."

Chapter Eleven

Charlton dropped Atlas off at his Bond Street bachelor quarters, where he found an earnest-looking young man with a wide face and large, heavily lashed brown eyes sitting on the top stair near his front door.

When he spotted Atlas coming up the stairs, the boy leapt to his feet and pulled off his cap. "Sir, Mr. Catesby, sir."

"Yes." Atlas reached the landing and inspected the youth more closely. His clothing—a murky threadbare coat and rough brown trousers—marked him as working class. "And who might you be?"

"James Sutton, sir." He licked his lips. "But everyone calls me Jamie."

Atlas withdrew his key from his pocket and unlocked his door. "And how may I help you, young Jamie?"

He twisted his cap between his hands. "Mrs. Palmer sent me, sir. She says you are in need of a valet."

Thea had sent him a valet? His sister was hardly in the habit of worrying about his staffing concerns. She could barely be bothered with her own. He motioned for the boy to follow him inside. "And how did my sister come to recommend you?"

"From Mrs. Warwick." The boy stood awkwardly in the front hall, shifting the weight of his tall, gangly form between his two feet. "Mrs. Warwick is helping me to find a situation, sir."

He realized who the young man was. "You're the footman who worked for the Warwicks in Slough?"

The boy's face brightened. He looked like an eager puppy. "Yes, sir. That's me."

"I see." He took in the boy's scruffy appearance. "How much do you know about serving as a valet to a gentleman?" The boy's face fell, which made Atlas feel like he'd kicked a harmless puppy. "Never mind. As I am just barely a gentleman and you are just barely a valet, I daresay we'll rub along well together for as long as I remain in Town."

Jamie's face glowed with unrestrained excitement. "You'll take me on, sir?"

"Yes, but it won't be for long—a few weeks at most. After that, we'll see about arranging another situation for you." Atlas blew out a hard breath. Having the boy underfoot might very well be more of a nuisance than anything else, but he'd promised to help Mrs. Warwick find employment for the servants who'd assisted her and her children. "You don't perchance know how to cook?"

Jamie shook his head. "No, sir," he said cheerily. "I can't say that I do."

"Very well." He withdrew a few shillings from his pocket. "Why don't you run down to Pressler's and get us something to eat?"

"Pressler's?"

Atlas forgot the boy had only recently come up from the country. Becoming accustomed to London would be challenge enough for him without the added strain of learning how to become a gentleman's valet. "Pressler's is a grocer just down the street."

"Very well, sir." The boy started for the door.

Atlas sighed at the thought of the challenge ahead. Training young Jamie was the least of his concerns. Considering the suspicious circumstances surrounding Warwick's murder, he was certain it was only a matter of time before Endicott came calling again. "Oh, and Jamie."

The boy spun around, an expectant expression on his face. "Yes, sir?"

"Stop by Sanford's as well. It's not far from Pressler's."

"Very well, sir. And what do they sell there?"

"Wine." The mild pain in his left foot that had dogged him all day was getting worse. The devil! A flare-up was the last thing he needed to cope with at the moment. "Tell Mr. Sanford it's for me. He knows what I like. Now go, and be quick about it."

* * *

Not even the finest wine from Sanford's could take the edge off of a family supper at Jason's house. The gatherings were a Catesby tradition that Jason had insisted upon continuing after the deaths of their parents. For Atlas, these dinners were a poignant reminder of who was no longer with them more than anything else.

"Did you kill the old man?" his brother Hermes asked Atlas as soon as the main course had been served. "The bastard certainly seemed to deserve it."

Herm, the third son, was tall like Atlas but far more slender, almost sylphlike. They also shared the same gray eyes, but the similarities between the two brothers ended there. While Atlas did not care for superfluous things, Herm was a dandy whose primary concern was maintaining a fashionable appearance, which at present included breeches in a bright-yellow nankeen—a more cost-conscious choice than buckskin, which had to be replaced frequently to retain a fashionable skintight fit.

"Really, Hermes," Jason said. "Must you be so crass?" They were seated in the baron's dining room, which seemed like it had been dipped in gold. Everything in the room that could possibly be gilded was. To say Jason enjoyed ostentatious displays of wealth and rank was an understatement.

"A man was murdered." Herm took a large gulp of wine. "Of course I'm curious."

"And what would you know about it?" Atlas asked coolly. Frustration rippled through him. Private matters never stayed private for long in the Catesby family.

"A bit." Herm ran a light hand over his wildly unruly hair, a look favored by the fashionable, which was painstakingly achieved by infrequent washing and the artful application of hair wax. "Thea said you purchased the chit at market."

Atlas scowled at his sister, who had the grace to appear chagrined before snapping at Herm. "You're quite the town crier, aren't you? Remind me never to share anything of interest with you ever again."

"Gad," Herm protested. "You didn't ask me to keep any confidences."

Atlas gritted his teeth. Herm was a fop who never meant any harm, but he also didn't know when to curb his tongue. "Why don't we leave off on this?"

"I agree," Jason interjected with an admonishing glare at Herm. "That is quite enough."

"Why?" Herm shot back, not cowed in the least. "We finally have something of interest to discuss."

Jason dismissed the two attending footmen with a pointed look. When they were gone, he spoke. "Murder is an unseemly discussion."

Herm leaned toward Atlas. "Did you do it? You saw the body. What did it look like?"

Thea grimaced. "Really, Herm, we are trying to eat."

"If I had killed him," Atlas said, "do you think I would confess my crime?"

Herm considered that for a moment. "Would you?"

Atlas shook his head and reached for his wine. "No, I did not kill Warwick, but I do wish I had thrashed him."

Herm grinned. "You've done worse."

Atlas couldn't deny it. After Phoebe died, he'd spiraled out of control, swamped with overwhelming emotions he didn't know what to do with. Uncertain of how to manage him, his parents, who were consumed with their own grief, had packed him off to boarding school.

It was there—at Harrow—that he had become fully acquainted with the extent of the privileged class's sense of entitlement. Harrow was full of people like Vessey, the man who'd killed his sister, who thought title and rank placed them above everyone and everything, including the law. As the lowly fourth son of a newly minted baron, Atlas was expected to know his place, which was well below that of the blue-blooded scions of viscounts, earls, marquesses, and dukes.

When the bullies among them had presumed to teach Atlas that lesson, they'd unwittingly unleashed the furies of hell. The spawn of men like Vessey were ideal targets for the cauldron of pent-up rage that churned within Atlas.

His fearsome reputation had solidified by the end of the first term, when the second son of a duke, older than Atlas by at least three years, had tried to assert the dominance he believed his high birth accorded him. Atlas had savagely rebuffed the attempt, teaching his transgressor that neither rank nor privilege shielded one from a sound beating. Atlas spent six years at Harrow, and while no one challenged him after that first year, he'd often used his fists on bullies who preyed upon the younger, weaker, poorer, or otherwise more vulnerable students.

"You should distance yourself from the widow," Jason was saying as he sipped his wine. "Both you and Thea. Not only is she a fallen woman, but our family name should in no way be associated with something as crass as murder."

Thea snorted. "Oh, do shut up, Jason. Lilliana is welcome to stay with me for as long as she likes."

Atlas dug into his food, determined to ignore his brother's provocation and get through supper as quickly as possible. His other brother, Apollo, was fortunate to be away in the country.

Jason's nostrils flared. "I'm a baron now, and everything you do reflects upon me."

Herm hiccupped a short laugh. "Thank God Father was only awarded a barony."

Jason turned to him. "Why do you say that?"

"I shudder to think what would have happened if it had been a dukedom. You'd be even more insufferable—if that's possible."

Jason pursed his lips. "You're a second son. You wouldn't understand."

Herm rolled his eyes, but Jason didn't notice because he'd turned his attention to Atlas. "I hope you at least plan to keep your distance."

As if he would abandon Mrs. Warwick now, in her hour of need. "If calling upon Mrs. Warwick tomorrow at my sister's home is what you consider keeping my distance, then yes, I intend to keep my distance."

Jason flushed while Herm laughed out loud and reached for more wine.

* * *

"You ride very well," Atlas observed, admiring the way Mrs. Warwick sat a horse. Her posture was excellent, elegant, and straight-backed, and she seemed perfectly comfortable riding the mare they'd borrowed from Charlton, who kept an excellent stable in Town. Her mount was a fine blood, a spirited and intelligent animal she handled with skillful ease.

Mrs. Warwick raised a brow. "Why do you seem surprised?" She presented a lovely picture in her black, military-inspired riding costume, with her skirts flowing down the left side of her mount. He presumed it was one of the items she'd acquired during her recent shopping spree.

"I suppose I assumed Warwick wasn't the sort to allow you to ride at your leisure."

"I learned as a girl, and it has been far too long since I've been able to ride regularly."

He mentally filed away this small clue to her past. It was further evidence—as he'd suspected from the first—that she came from a genteel family that could afford to purchase horseflesh. Otherwise, she wouldn't have such an excellent seat.

He'd invited her to go riding shortly after he'd called upon her that morning and found her restlessly pacing the conservatory. The boys were with their tutor, and when she'd mentioned, rather wistfully, that it was a beautiful day for a hack, he'd immediately offered to escort her.

It was two o'clock when they reached the gravel trail lined with mature trees and wooden fencing. At that time of day, there were few riders or carriages to impede their way. Mrs. Warwick had insisted upon avoiding the fashionable hour on Hyde Park's bridle path; Mayfair's finest didn't typically put themselves on exhibit along Rotten Row until well after four.

After a brisk run along the Serpentine, they slowed until their animals walked side by side. Atlas kept tight control over Charlton's beastly tempered stallion, lest he try to cause trouble with Mrs. Warwick's handsome mare. Once he felt satisfied the animal was in hand, Atlas shared what he'd learned about the postmortem on her late husband.

Her marble composure firmly in place, she showed no emotion. "Do you believe Godfrey was murdered?"

"The word 'murder' is too strong, perhaps." He chose his words with care. "Given the way Mr. Warwick died, it seems possible he provoked someone to anger, someone who reacted by hitting him without thinking about the action beforehand."

She considered this. "Someone who didn't necessarily mean to kill him?"

"It is possible. The physician says it's unlikely he died immediately."

"It's a terrible thing. I despised him, but I never wanted him dead. My children are now orphans."

"They have you now, and I daresay they are the better for it."

She kept her focus on the path ahead. "The boys believe Godfrey fell ill. I did not want to tell them the truth of why they are now fatherless."

Atlas studied her regal profile, the straight nose and defined chin, and wondered if, despite everything Warwick had put her through, she regretted becoming a widow. He couldn't fathom it. After all, she could now be with her children.

The boys had been delivered to her shortly after the funeral. He had yet to meet them but sensed an inner contentment in Mrs. Warwick that hadn't been there before their arrival.

They directed their mounts to the side to make way for a finely appointed, bright-yellow barouche approaching from the opposite direction. The black hood was down, revealing the two passengers within. One was a young man who appeared to be in his midtwenties, while the other gentleman was older, a head of gray hair apparent beneath his hat. There was a seal of some sort on the side of the carriage, but before Atlas got a clear look at it, Mrs. Warwick's mount burst into motion.

"Let us run," she called back as she picked up speed down the row. As Atlas made to follow, he caught sight of something that made his stomach twist. The young man in the carriage stared after Mrs. Warwick in obvious disbelief. Shock tinged with apparent joy, and an emotion that seemed almost intimate, stamped the man's aristocratic features.

Atlas barely had time to register the strange reaction before his stallion took off with a start, likely outraged at the idea of another animal besting him. The beast carried Atlas away, his hooves beating hard along the path, chasing after Mrs. Warwick's mare. Atlas felt the young man's stare burning into his back as they raced down the lane.

Chapter Twelve

The deep, rich scent of tobacco followed Atlas as he climbed the stairs to his quarters. Just as he reached the landing, the door opened, and an anxious-looking Jamie poked his head out.

"You have a visitor, sir."

"Who is it?"

"Says he's a runner, sir. He's waiting for you in the sitting room."

"How long has he been waiting?"

"Not long, sir, about twenty minutes."

Atlas handed his black top hat to his valet—although Jamie still required extensive training before he could seriously be considered worthy of the very top vocation for men in service. In larger households, as valet, Jamie would be above all other servants. Ironic, considering that the boy still had no idea how to tie a cravat. Atlas had even had to show him how to brush out his master's clothes.

He dropped some money into the youth's open palm. "Run and get some coffee and sweet buns. Purchase enough for yourself as well."

"Very good, sir!" The enthusiasm gleaming in the boy's eyes made Atlas recall the constant hunger that had dogged him at Jamie's age. He made a mental note to ensure the youth had enough to eat in the future. Once Jamie was off on his errand, Atlas joined the Bow Street runner in the sitting room, where he found him looking down at the puzzle pieces scattered atop the walnut game table.

"Mr. Endicott."

The runner looked up. "Mr. Catesby. I hope I am not intruding."

"Not at all." The orange-and-red colors of the room appeared even more garish in contrast to Endicott's somber gray coat. "If you had sent word of your impending visit, I'd have arranged to be here to receive you instead of keeping you waiting."

"No trouble at all. No trouble." His attention went back to the game table. "I was looking at your puzzle. I don't think I've ever seen one quite this complicated."

"Probably because they do not exist." Most puzzles were far too rudimentary for his tastes, with large pieces that provided no challenge at all. "I had that one made to my specifications."

Endicott pointed a beefy finger at the puzzle. "This was especially created for you?"

Atlas nodded. "I order them from an engraver and mapmaker off Oxford Street."

"Fascinating." Clasping his hands behind his back, the runner leaned forward for a closer view. "Is it a painting?"

"Yes. A Gainsborough reproduction."

Endicott's sparse brows lifted as he studied the pieces. "The only puzzles I've ever seen are of maps."

Atlas pressed his lips inward, a mix of nerves and impatience. If only the bloody runner would get on with it. "A map hardly tests one's abilities if one knows where all the countries are located."

"True, very true."

His patience snapped. "What can I do for you, Endicott?"

The runner straightened. "I'll come directly to the point."

Finally. "Excellent." He sat and gestured for the runner to do the same.

Endicott moved to a blue chintz chair and wedged his portly form into it. "The postmortem shows Mr. Warwick died from a severe blow to the stomach."

"I see." He crossed one knee over the other, outwardly at ease, even though his blood began to pound hard through his veins. "Do you believe he fought with someone shortly before his death?"

"I do not. I think he was likely caught unawares."

"And why do you deduce that?"

"There were no signs of a struggle in Warwick's apartments. There was no other bruising on the body and no scrapes or scratches on his fists to indicate that the victim engaged in any kind of struggle."

Atlas was beginning to realize it would be a mistake to underestimate the runner. The man was no one's fool. "And what, may I ask, has any of this to do with me?"

"I've been to Slough to interview the victim's brother, Mr. John Warwick, and learned something very interesting."

A knot hardened in Atlas's stomach. "And what is that?"

"He tells me you purchased Mrs. Warwick from her husband outside of an inn in Buckinghamshire."

Atlas remained silent.

"Do you dispute that?"

"I've no wish to impugn the lady's reputation. She's suffered enough."

Endicott watched him with an unwavering gaze. Behind the runner's facile manner, Atlas detected a well-disguised but unmistakable shrewdness. "Then you don't deny the truth of it?"

His neck heated. "The truth is that Warwick was a blackguard who treated his wife abominably."

"Clearly so, clearly so." Endicott nodded his head in grave agreement. "My own missus would serve me up my own ballocks on a platter if I tried such a thing, but murder is still frowned upon in our fair metropolis, no matter how deserving the victim."

"Is there a point to this conversation?"

Endicott studied him in silence for a moment. "What is the nature of your relationship with Mrs. Warwick?"

Tension contracted in his chest. "I don't know the lady particularly well, considering I only became acquainted with her a few weeks ago."

"True." Endicott scratched his forehead with sausage-like fingers. "Although you did meet under unusual circumstances."

"I would characterize them as unsavory circumstances."

"To be sure, to be sure. But when a man pays money for a woman, he usually does so with one very particular purpose in mind."

Atlas's grip on the chair's armrests tightened. "What are you insinuating?"

"Only that you are obviously a healthy young man who might have acted accordingly. Not that anyone would blame you. Mrs. Warwick is a very handsome woman."

"Nothing improper has occurred between us." He gritted his teeth. "The only indecency that has occurred is that Mr. Warwick saw fit to sell his wife, subjecting her to great degradation and humiliation."

Endicott's gaze seemed to take in every expression, each mannerism. Atlas felt like a specimen under a microscope. "And naturally, you being a decent gentleman and all, that angered you."

"Warwick's actions offended me, most certainly, but they did not make me angry enough to kill." He held Endicott's unflinching gaze. "That is what you are getting at, is it not?"

Sounds of the front door opening were followed by footsteps, and then Jamie appeared bearing the coffee and sweet buns. He placed them on the table between the two men, the fragrant scent of freshly brewed coffee filling the air. "They're still warm, sir. The lady at the bakeshop said they just came out of the oven."

"Thank you, Jamie." Atlas reached for his coffee. "That will be all." The youth retreated with his own coffee and sweet bun.

Endicott made no move to reach for the refreshments. "Sir, where were you the night Mr. Warwick was killed?"

"I visited any number of places that evening." Atlas drank from his coffee—hot and bitter, just as he preferred it—although he barely tasted it. "I'm afraid you'll have to be more specific."

The runner reached into his coat pocket. "Very well. Perhaps you could tell me when you last saw Mr. Warwick alive."

He kept a bland tone. "At around seven o'clock on the evening of his death."

"Is that so?" He pulled out a notebook. "And where was that?"

"At the Red Rooster—it's a coffeehouse in Covent Garden."

He extracted a cedarwood-encased pencil from his other pocket. "And what were you doing there?"

"I went looking for Warwick. I was hoping to reach an agreement that would allow Mrs. Warwick to see her children. He was keeping them from her."

Endicott scribbled something on his pad. The scratch of the pencil's graphite tip filled the silences between the volley of the runner's questions and Atlas's answers. "And what did he say?"

"He was not receptive to any sort of compromise."

Endicott pondered this. "Yet he sent you that note the following morning, suggesting he might welcome some sort of agreement, provided it involved the exchange of funds."

"Precisely." He fought the urge to shift in his seat. "Mrs. Warwick tells me her husband was very fond of money."

Endicott tapped the back end of his pencil against his lower lip. "And after you left the Red Rooster, where did you go?"

"I returned to my sister's house. She was hosting a gathering."

Putting his notebook aside, Endicott reached for his coffee, his girth making the movement a challenging one. "So any number of people saw you there."

"Actually, no. The footman and the butler did, of course, because they let me in. But I was feeling unsettled by my meeting with Warwick, so I went abovestairs to my sister's sitting room to calm my nerves."

Endicott took a sip of coffee. "And later you eventually joined the party?"

"No, I found Mrs. Warwick in the sitting room. She was also not inclined to socialize. We spoke for a few minutes, and then I left."

"Where did you go?"

"I returned here to my apartments. I worked on the puzzle and then retired for the evening."

"So your servant"—Endicott gestured toward the corridor where Jamie had disappeared to—"can vouch for your whereabouts."

"No." He felt the beads of perspiration coalescing on his upper lip and fought the urge to wipe them away with his kerchief. "Jamie has only recently come into my employ, and I have no other servants."

"I see, I see. So you were alone."

"Yes."

"That's unfortunate."

"Is it?" Atlas spoke with care, sensing that Endicott had carefully laid a trap and was now waiting for Atlas to step into it. "Why is that?"

"We found the street urchin who delivered Warwick's note to you the evening of Tuesday, September second, the night the victim was killed."

"You're mistaken," Atlas impatiently corrected him. If the runner meant to solve the crime, he really ought to remember the details. "I received the note Wednesday morning, September the third, the morning after Warwick died."

"So you said. However, the boy says he put it under your door Tuesday evening well before midnight. And he has no reason to dissemble."

Atlas had to agree. He couldn't see any reason for the urchin who left the note under his door to lie about when he'd placed it there. "If he did, I didn't see the note until the following morning. How does when I received the note signify?"

"If you got Warwick's message Tuesday evening, that presents a very compelling alternate scenario."

Atlas sucked in a breath as the runner's implications sank in. "You think I received the note and went to Warwick's the evening he died." It was a damning theory, one that put him squarely at the scene of the crime at the time of the murder.

"It's possible."

"And what happened next, according to your theory? I suppose we argued and one thing led to another."

"It's entirely possible. Probable even, some might say." Endicott gave him a considering look. "Perhaps you reacted precipitously in the heat of anger. You might not have intended to kill him."

"I didn't kill anyone." Although his palms were sweaty, Atlas resisted the urge to discreetly swipe them against his trouser legs. "Neither accidentally nor on purpose." He came to his feet. "If that is all, I have an appointment." He didn't, but he'd had quite enough of Endicott's theories for one afternoon.

"Of course, of course." Endicott leaned forward to set his coffee down before pushing heavily to his feet. He gave that perennially genial smile, which Atlas now saw for what it was—a facade that masked the man's true cleverness. "Do you mind if I take a roll with me?"

Atlas looked at the untouched sweet buns. He'd lost his appetite. "Help yourself," he said without enthusiasm.

"Why thank you. Don't mind if I do." He reached for the bun and took a bite. "Delicious. Excellent." He paused, looking down at the table. Next to the buns were precisely cut flat wooden fragments in various shapes that Atlas had arranged into a perfect square. "Another of your puzzles?" he asked.

"It's an Archimedes' Box that I picked up in Greece." The words were terse. "The challenge is to put the pieces together to form a box. If one is very clever, he can also shape the pieces into various animal figures."

Endicott studied him with dark, unfathomable eyes. "I suspect you are a very clever man, Mr. Catesby."

"A clever man would have an unassailable alibi if he intended to commit murder," he said acidly.

Appreciation flickered across Endicott's face. "Unless he didn't intend to commit a crime and was overwhelmed in the heat of the moment." When Atlas didn't respond, he continued. "Or, say, if he was trying to protect someone."

Atlas scoffed. "Who would I be protecting?" His voice rose in disbelief as the runner's insinuation sank in. "You cannot seriously believe a gentlewoman such as Mrs. Warwick is capable of killing another being."

"In my experience," he calmly returned, "almost all women are capable of murder when it comes to protecting their children. And you must agree Mrs. Warwick seems to be a most devoted mother."

"A surplus of maternal affection makes one a murderer, does it?"

"We shall see." Endicott shrugged his hefty shoulders. "The investigation is ongoing." He paused. "You mentioned visiting Greece. I understand you travel quite a bit."

"Yes, I am rarely in London. I've injured my foot, which has kept me in Town far longer than is my norm."

"Will you be leaving again soon?"

"My cousin's frigate should come into port in the next week or so. When it sails out again, I expect to be aboard."

"As we are in the midst of an investigation, I trust you won't depart without speaking to Bow Street first."

"You may depend on it."

After the runner had gone, Atlas went back into the sitting room and stared down at the Archimedes' Box. He scattered the pieces and used a few to make the shape of an elephant.

His thoughts drifted back to the murder of Godfrey Warwick. Surely others had a motive to kill the man. But who? How difficult would it be to track the killer? Endicott struck him as clever, but was he cunning enough to catch the true murderer? Atlas had no intention of waiting until the fat bastard threw him into Newgate to find out. Scattering the pieces on the table, he quickly formed them back into a box again and then went over to sit before the unfinished Gainsborough puzzle.

He'd completed the top third of the painting, the clouds and sky, and had turned his focus to the trees. It was here, while doing puzzle work, that he felt clearest and most focused, a state of mind needed to intelligently mull over his conversation with the runner.

Endicott wasn't a fool. It was only a matter time before he learned of the terrible scene that had occurred when Mrs. Warwick's children were forcibly taken from her. Warwick had been killed just a few hours after that regrettable incident, the same evening Atlas had publicly confronted the dead man about the encounter.

He pushed a murky piece of puzzle, part of some tree bark, into place and felt a surge of satisfaction. He found it immensely gratifying when everything fell into place; he was drawn to the order of it. His thoughts drifted back to the runner, who was closing in and making no secret of it. Atlas had both motive and opportunity to commit the murder as well as no alibi.

Unfortunately, Mrs. Warwick was in the same predicament. She'd retired early on the night of Warwick's death. He supposed it was possible for her to have slipped out during Thea's party to do away with her husband. The man had done vile things to her, and she could have acted out in a moment of passion. But he just couldn't see Mrs. Warwick as a killer. He sensed she was hiding something, but he doubted it was murderous tendencies.

What of other possible suspects? If neither of them had done it, who had? He exhaled and stared at the scattered puzzle pieces. He couldn't trust Endicott to find the true killer, and he wouldn't leave his fate—or Mrs. Warwick's, for that matter—in someone else's hands.

He'd have to do it himself. It was time to begin his own investigation into the murder of Godfrey Warwick. He'd start by riding out to Slough to gather information on the people Warwick associated with.

He needed to uncover who—besides Warwick's widow—had hated the dead man enough to kill him.

* * *

"Are there affairs you must put in order, Lilliana, my dear?" Thea asked. "Regarding Mr. Warwick's business concerns?"

They were parked in the shade under the maple trees in Berkley Square, across from Gunter's Tea Shop, one of Thea's favored destinations. Atlas stood by the barouche, leaning against the square's railing while he made quick work of his sorbet.

The ladies ate their ices as they sat in Charlton's shiny carriage, which Atlas had borrowed because it was a fine day for a ride in an open carriage. He thought the fresh air would do Mrs. Warwick good. She hadn't ventured out of Thea's house for several days and had refused all his invitations to go riding in Hyde Park again. She seemed preoccupied of late, which he assumed was due to her recent widowhood and what her abrupt change in circumstances portended for her future.

"There is the matter of the haberdashery, but John has said he will look into finding someone to manage the shop." Mrs. Warwick poked a spoon into her lemon ice. "He has also discussed the possibility of selling the enterprise."

Atlas straightened. "Can Warwick's brother be trusted to look after the children's best interests?"

"John has always been kind to me and the children," Mrs. Warwick said. "He has given me no cause to distrust him."

Thea scraped the last bit of dessert from her glass bowl. "That is something to be grateful for at least." She glanced over at the other woman's uneaten dessert. "You haven't had any of your ice, Lily. At least try it."

"I am not much for sweets." Mrs. Warwick scooped up a small amount and brought it to her lips. "But I must bring the boys here. They enjoy frozen treats."

"Young Peter rivals me in my love of icy desserts," Thea said. "We can barely keep him away from the icehouse."

Concern lit Mrs. Warwick's face. "I have told him to stay away from the icehouse because it is not safe, but he seems enthralled by the sight of all that ice when it is relatively warm outside."

Atlas remembered his and his brothers' fascination with the icehouse at Langston Park, their family home in Berkshire, where they'd all grown up. It had been forbidden to them too. But in the heat of the summer, they'd sometimes sneaked inside to cool off, running through the tunnel, which was curved to keep out the warm air.

"Did Warwick never bring the boys to Gunter's, given Peter's love of frozen ice?" Thea asked. "It's not far from the haberdashery."

"Oh, no." Mrs. Warwick tried another spoonful. "The boys and I stayed in the country and never came to Town. And even so, Godfrey wasn't one for family outings."

Atlas felt a fresh rush of anger toward Warwick for never treating his family to the simple pleasure of a visit to Gunter's nor to any other excursion for that matter. When his own father hadn't been holed up in his study working on his latest poem, the Catesby family had gone on numerous picnics and other jaunts—exploring ruins, attending theatrical performances, or visiting Town to take in the Tower of London and the crown jewels.

Atlas had often grumbled about those mandatory family trips. The journeys were usually cramped and noisy, and as the youngest, he'd often been relegated to the worst seat, at least until his legs grew too long. But now he looked back upon those excursions with extreme fondness.

He could still picture Phoebe on those occasions, her smile light and ethereal while she drew something in her sketchbook. Gentle Phoebe had been nothing like her indomitable younger sister. While Thea could easily take on the world, Phoebe had been far too naïve and trusting of people. And she'd paid the ultimate price for it.

"Lilliana, there's nothing to stop you from bringing the boys here now," Thea was saying. "They might also enjoy visiting the

British Museum. It's so close to the house that you could go at any time, don't you think so, Atlas?"

"Most assuredly." He inhaled deeply to ease the tightness in his chest and pushed thoughts of the sister he'd failed from his mind. "I shall be delighted to escort you and the boys to Gunter's or elsewhere whenever you care to bring them."

He had yet to meet the children; he'd been waiting for their mother to introduce them, which she had declined to do so thus far for reasons she hadn't articulated.

Mrs. Warwick leaned forward, peering across the square. "Is that Lord Charlton?"

Atlas and Thea both followed her gaze to the well-heeled horseman coming their way clad in buff breeches and a lemon tailcoat with shiny brass buttons glittering in the sunlight. "It certainly is," Thea said. "He would be hard to miss in those bright colors. He looks like a peacock."

Atlas straightened. "I wonder what he's doing here. When I borrowed the barouche this morning, he said he had an engagement."

Thea sighed. "That man is always underfoot."

"You are very hard on him," Atlas observed.

"I agree," Mrs. Warwick put in. "I quite like the earl. He's amusing, and it was kind of him to lend us his barouche."

"Yes, certainly it was." Thea eyed the pricey vehicle's sleek lines and plush seats. Unlike the earl, she was not a spendthrift and had little use for creature comforts. "But it's a bit ostentatious."

Atlas laughed. His friendship with Charlton had helped him see past his blind animosity for every member of the peerage. He'd been at Harrow and Cambridge long enough to know there were decent sorts scattered among the knaves. Charlton, for all his foppish ways, was one of those honorable men. "Everything about the earl is ostentatious. It's part of his unique charm."

Thea pressed her lips tightly together as she watched Charlton approach. "Charlton is possibly the least serious man I have ever met."

"Alas, we cannot all be mathematicians," Atlas said before turning to greet his friend. "Hello, Charlton. This is unexpected."

"Good day." The earl removed his hat as he drew nearer. Smiling, he inclined his head toward the carriage. "How fortunate to have come across each other."

"We could hardly overlook you in that jacket," Thea said.

"Why, Mrs. Palmer, my heart will be broken if you tell me that you do not care for my attire."

Atlas spooned the last bit of his icy confection into his mouth. "I thought you said you had an engagement this afternoon."

"I was able to conclude my affairs earlier than expected."

Thea snapped open her fan. "How fortuitous."

The earl's blue-eyed gaze gleamed as it met hers. "My thoughts exactly."

Thea looked away and effectively rebuffed the earl by shifting her body to focus her complete attention on her brother. "What are you going to do about the runner who keeps dogging you at every turn?"

Irritation tugged at him. He preferred not to bring up Endicott's murder investigation in front of Mrs. Warwick, who had enough to worry about with the children and the fate of the haberdashery. "This is neither the time nor the place for such a discussion."

"I disagree," Mrs. Warwick interjected, her bronze eyes flashing, revealing a suggestion of temper. It was another fissure in the icy armor in which she'd encased herself. "After all, you would not be in this situation if it were not for me."

Thea handed her empty dish to the waiter who'd dashed across the street to collect the bowls. "You are my brother, and I know you very well—well enough to surmise you are already halfway to figuring out who killed Mr. Warwick."

"You give me far too much credit." He did not care to go into detail about his decision to look into Warwick's murder on his own.

Unfortunately, Charlton had no such qualms about the ladies' sensibilities. "From what I understand, Endicott has set his sights on you as his primary suspect."

Atlas didn't bother to ask his friend how he knew that. He assumed a few palms had been greased. "One can hardly blame him," he said lightly. "I had both motive and opportunity. He will likely look no further for the real killer."

"Which is why you must search for the killer yourself," Thea pronounced. "Your latest investigation."

It really was aggravating to have a sibling who knew him so well. He and Thea were barely a year apart in age. She'd always possessed a bossy nature and had made it her business to know everything about her little brother. Even as adults, she resisted relinquishing the role of interfering elder sister.

"This is a serious matter, and the runners are already investigating," Atlas responded.

"They are idiots." She waved an impatient hand. "You've more brains than the lot of them put together. Besides, you've always liked to solve mysteries, and this one is the ultimate challenge."

"Has he?" Mrs. Warwick looked from Atlas to Thea. "What types of mysteries?"

"All sorts." Thea smiled at the memory. "There was the time Papa's hound became enceinte by an unknown canine when Atlas was twelve. He was determined to find out who the puppies' sire was." She looked from Mrs. Warwick to Charlton. "He investigated all the neighboring dogs and interviewed the village veterinarian until he was able to identify the culprit."

"One woman's culprit is another man's lucky dog," Charlton intoned.

Thea ignored him. "And remember just before my come-out when a secret admirer kept leaving notes for me by the servants' entrance?"

Charlton's ears practically twitched. "Secret admirer?"

"He was all of fourteen."

Atlas remembered how thrilled he'd been to trace the notes back to the son of the local vicar.

Charlton leaned against the railing. "Atlas also discovered who was stealing from Disher, the tobacconist on Bond Street."

"But that was all a lark," Atlas said. "This is murder. It's a bit more serious."

"But you are good at murder too," Thea said enthusiastically. "You were correct about Prudence Pratt, after all."

He scowled at her indelicate reference to a disagreeable subject in front of Mrs. Warwick. "I have heard as much."

Thea scooted forward on the barouche's leather seat. "The young lady was apparently so overwhelmed with guilt that she confessed to the killing, even after being cleared of her half brother's brutal murder."

"Yes, I saw it in today's *Times*," he said. "Miss Pratt went to Bow Street court and admitted carrying out the crime."

Thea's eyes glittered. "You had the right of it all along. The sister was the killer."

"She'll no doubt hang now," Charlton mused. "I say, Atlas, why were you so certain Miss Pratt was the guilty party?"

He shrugged. "Once one considered the evidence, it was as clear—"

"—as a bell." Both Thea and Charlton finished his sentence for him.

"Yes, we know," the earl added, flashing an amused smile at Thea in light of their shared retort.

When she pointedly ignored him, Charlton returned his attention to Atlas. "If you don't wish to investigate Mr. Warwick's death yourself, you could always hire your own runner."

"I could, but I have no intention of doing so. I plan to see to it myself."

"What does that mean?" Charlton asked.

"I knew it!" Thea exclaimed in triumph. "He is going to investigate the murder himself."

Mrs. Warwick looked at him with wide eyes. "Truly?"

"Yes, I may as well take matters into my own hands. Otherwise, I might find myself in the gaol." He did not mention Mrs. Warwick's precarious position as a suspect. "Now, would anyone care for more lemon ice?"

Chapter Thirteen

The following day, Atlas rode to Slough to meet with Godfrey Warwick's brother.

Heavy gray clouds drooped from the sky during the two-hour ride. He set the ornery stallion at a moderate pace as they made their way through the encroaching fog, which obscured the road ahead like a ghostly snowfall.

John Warwick lived in a white stucco manor house with black-framed sashed windows on the first two floors and dormers on the third. Mist enshrouded the property, which exuded a certain sense of calm, not unlike the man Atlas remembered. He had a brief recollection of John Warwick from the morning after he'd first encountered Mrs. Warwick.

Atlas had no idea whether the man would agree to talk to him. However, the fact that Atlas's brother was a baron might work in his favor. It would be difficult for a member of the gentry to refuse him.

The mourning wreath hanging over the front door appeared several weeks old; the flowers were shriveled, and the dried leaves had lost their color. Atlas realized the hatchment served a dual purpose; within the past month, John Warwick had lost both his wife and his brother. As a servant led him into the parlor, they passed a mirror draped in black, another sign of a house in mourning.

They came to a bright space decorated in creams and red velvets. A portrait of a woman hanging over the hearth was draped in black. She had a sweet half smile and a gentle expression. Perhaps this was Verity Warwick, John's late wife. According to Mrs. Warwick, John had cared deeply for the woman. He wondered if the brothers had been close as well and how keenly John Warwick now felt his younger brother's loss.

"Mr. Catesby."

Atlas turned from the painting to find John Warwick entering the parlor. He wore country clothes. A black band on his left arm was the only overt evidence of his grief, yet deep lines etched his face, and each leaden step seemed burdened by the weight of his sorrow.

"My late wife," he said of the portrait. "Although I do not think the likeness does her justice."

"I do beg your pardon for intruding during your time of grief."

A shadow crossed John's face. "The loss has been difficult." He bore a passing resemblance to his brother—the same coloring and similar features, although his were a bit more sharply cut.

"Mrs. Warwick . . . Mrs. Lilliana Warwick, that is . . . has spoken very warmly of your late wife."

"She was a fine woman." John contemplated the painting. "I would have forgiven her anything."

The choice of words struck Atlas as odd, and for a fleeting moment, he wondered whether Verity Warwick had done something that required a husband's forgiveness. Not that it would matter now.

John lowered himself into one of the red velvet chairs and gestured for Atlas to do the same. "What can I do for you, Mr. Catesby?"

"I am looking into the matter of your brother's death."

"Why would you do that?" Warwick placed his interlaced fingers on his chest. "A Bow Street runner—Endicott, I think his name is—came to see me about the case."

Atlas had decided beforehand to come straight to the point. "I do not have confidence in his ability to correctly identify the person who killed your brother."

"It's a herculean task, no matter who undertakes it. My brother was a . . . difficult man to like."

The man's directness took Atlas aback. "Did you like him?"

John did not seem surprised by the question. "He was my younger brother. I always looked after him. His actions often disappointed me, none more so than his abominable behavior toward Lilliana, but he was family, after all."

"Do you know of anyone who would wish your brother harm?"

"Besides you? And possibly Lilliana?" When Atlas stiffened, Warwick continued. "Be at ease, Mr. Catesby, I am not accusing you of nefarious behavior. And I know Lilliana well enough to comprehend she is not capable of that sort of violence."

"Then what are you saying?" Atlas allowed a distinct edge to creep into his voice.

John shrugged. "The truth of the matter is that is there are probably more people who hated my brother than those who thought well of him."

"These people who did not care for your brother, are they mostly in Slough and the surrounding county?"

"It is hard to say. Godfrey spent most of his time in Town. He only came to Slough on Saturday afternoons and would depart early Monday morning."

Atlas wondered if the man was deliberately trying to be unhelpful. "So you cannot direct me to anyone here in Slough who might have been involved in some sort of dispute with your brother."

"Nothing worth killing over." John sighed. "But to be frank, Godfrey did not confide in me overmuch."

Atlas was beginning to think the journey out to Slough had been for naught. "Was there anyone your brother did confide in?"

"Bole. He and Godfrey had been friends since boyhood."

"Bole." The name sounded slightly familiar.

"You will remember him as the magistrate who threatened to throw Lilliana in the gaol."

Distaste slithered through his gut. "I do remember."

"Bole has a house on Upton Street." John shifted in his seat. "Now, if there is nothing else."

Atlas rose, taking John's cue that the interview had come to an end. "One more thing." He paused. "Do you mind telling me where you were the evening your brother died?"

John did not appear to take offense to the question. "I was here at home. There was a terrible storm that evening. It wasn't the kind of weather that invited going out."

Atlas recalled the downpour. "No, it wasn't." He turned to go. "Thank you for your time."

Warwick remained seated as Atlas exited the room. "Mr. Catesby."

He halted and turned around. "Yes?"

"In case you are wondering, I agreed to see you today because of your chivalrous behavior toward Lilliana. She's not one to give easy praise, but she has spoken highly of you."

Warmth swirled in Atlas's chest at the unexpected accolade from the cool Artemis, and he went out with a little more bounce in his step.

* * *

When Atlas called at Bole's modest timber-framed dwelling on Upton Street, he found the magistrate rushing out the door with his black top hat in one hand. When he spotted Atlas by his front gate, he slowed and stiffened, his posture becoming rigid.

"What would you be wanting?" he asked, his light-blue eyes like narrow slits in a square, fleshy face. He was not a tall man, and his body was almost as square shaped as his face.

"Good day." Atlas kept his manner easy and cordial. "Mr. John Warwick told me where to find you."

Bole placed his hat on his head. "As you can see, I am in a hurry." He stepped around Atlas and continued on his way.

Atlas followed and fell in step with him. "My condolences on the death of your friend."

Bole shot him a skeptical look. "I'm certain you're pleased to have Godfrey out of the way."

It seemed to Atlas that Bole did not appear overset by his friend's violent demise. "Why would you say that?"

"Godfrey told me everything the last time he was in Slough. About how you were shagging his wife."

Atlas, who had clasped his hands behind his back in an amiable posture as they walked, now clenched his fists tightly but managed to reply in a calm and even voice. "Even if that were true, which it is not, I had purchased Mrs. Warwick from her husband, so I hardly needed to kill him to make her mine."

"She wanted the children, and he was keeping them from her."

They rounded a steep curve in the road. The tower of the parish church loomed ahead. "If a man kept a mistress," Atlas said, "I imagine the last thing he would want is to have her children underfoot while he attempts to have his way with her."

Bole peered hard at him. "What is it that you want from me, Catesby?"

"You were closer to Godfrey Warwick than just about anyone else. You are in a position to tell me if he had any enemies, anyone who hated him enough to kill."

Bole sidled a bit away from Atlas, widening the distance between them. "Godfrey told me you threatened him more than once, and I told that runner, Mr. Endicott, all about it."

Atlas made a concerted effort to unclench his jaw. "Warwick's treatment of his wife was an outrage, and it certainly offended me, but if I had wanted to kill the man, I would not have done the deed in secret—I would have called him out on a field of honor."

Bole seemed to roll the words over in his mind and ultimately appeared to accept the truth of them. "I never could understand why any man in his right mind would fight over that harridan."

"Watch your tongue, Bole."

"Godfrey regretted marrying her. Oh, she was biddable enough at first, but that changed over the years." He paused. "She also had a strong dislike of the marriage bed, unlike the lusty wenches we are accustomed to here in the country. Of course, that did not deter Godfrey from bedding her whenever he was down from London. He did want children, even if begetting them was a chore."

Atlas's neck heated. "Are you saying Warwick forced himself upon his wife when she was unwilling?"

"Forced himself?" Bole regarded him with surprise. "As if such a thing is possible. She was his wife, and he had certain rights. But the answer to your question is no. Godfrey said Lilliana knew her duty. She submitted as she should, but it was not a pleasant experience for either of them."

"It is abominable to think that any man, gentleman or not, would discuss what occurs in the privacy of his bedchamber." Atlas struggled to keep his rising temper in check. "She was a young maiden of just sixteen when she came to him. Warwick should have treated her with more care."

"A virgin?" Bole scoffed. "Perhaps," he added quickly when he registered Atlas's negative reaction. "But Godfrey found no proof of a maidenhead when he took her."

Atlas didn't believe it. He couldn't imagine crystalline Mrs. Warwick lying with any man before marriage. "Did Warwick confront her about that? Did he question his wife about whether there'd been a man before him?"

"She denied everything, of course. She could hardly admit to it." He leaned closer to Atlas, his tone more secretive. "But

Godfrey went through her things once and found an old letter from the cove, whoever he was. It was dated from the year before they married."

Mrs. Warwick would have been just fifteen when the letter was written. "What precisely was in the missive?"

"Godfrey never said, but he was convinced it was from the man who'd taken her innocence."

"What was the man's name?"

Bole adjusted his top hat. "I don't believe Godfrey ever said."

"Is that why he sold her?" If Bole's account were true, it would explain why Warwick had been so furious with his wife.

"No, she'd done something more recently that angered Godfrey."

"What was that?"

"He wouldn't say precisely, but I gathered she'd threatened to disclose something he preferred to keep private." Bole came to a stop before a neat stone structure. "Now if you will excuse me, I am due in magistrates' court."

Atlas had more questions, but it was clear he wouldn't learn anything more from Bole today. "Of course. Good day."

Bole halted abruptly just short of the door and turned back to Atlas, his expression pensive. "Something occurs to me."

"Oh? And what is that?"

"What if Lilliana's lover has admired her from afar? He had no hope of coming anywhere near her while Godfrey was still alive."

"You make many assumptions."

"Perhaps. But in locating Lilliana's lover, you might also find the man who killed her husband."

* * *

Once he returned to Town, Atlas decided to stop in at the haberdashery to question Godfrey Warwick's clerk. His conversation with Bole had left a foul taste in his mouth, and he welcomed the diversion.

It was late afternoon by the time he got to Wigmore Street. The shop showed no outward sign of its owner's demise: the handsome bowed windows, shiny black door, and gilded *Warwick & Sons* sign all looked as they had when Warwick had been in charge.

The bell over the door rang when he entered the shop. The spotless floors, shiny mahogany counter, and shelves stocked with notions were orderly and well presented, as if the proprietor had just stepped into the back for a moment rather than having been murdered upstairs a short sennight ago.

"Good afternoon, I shall be with you presently," someone called from the back. The bespectacled clerk with the mop of curly hair appeared. His coloring had improved since the last time they'd met, when he'd stumbled out the door and retched after discovering Warwick's corpse.

The solicitous smile evaporated when he saw who'd entered the shop. "Mr. Catesby."

"Good afternoon, Stillwell. It is good to see you still have a situation here."

The clerk licked dry lips. "I am grateful to still have a position, especially after Mr. Warwick . . ." The color drained from his face as if he were remembering the sight of Warwick's corpse. He cleared his throat. "What can I do for you, sir?"

"I have a few questions that I hope you can help me with."

"About what, sir?"

Atlas removed his top hat and placed it on the counter. "I am attempting to discover who killed your employer."

"I'm not sure how I can be of any service—" He paled again. "Unless you are accusing me of something."

"Not at all," Atlas reassured him. "I thought you might be able to tell me whether your employer had any enemies that you knew of."

"I'm sure I cannot say."

"Perhaps he argued with someone? Or had a payment dispute?"

A crisp feminine voice sounded from the stairwell. "Mr. Catesby?" Mrs. Warwick glided down carrying a bulky black ledger in her arms.

"Mrs. Warwick," he said with some surprise. "What are you doing here?"

"I could ask the same of you." She wore a becoming black gown with white cuffs and a high-standing white collar, a sign she'd taken on mourning despite everything that bastard Warwick had done to her.

"I hoped to ask Stillwell a few questions."

"And I am attempting to gain an understanding of my late husband's assets." She handed the ledger to Stillwell. "Thank you, Henry. I'll take the next one, please."

"Yes, Mrs. Warwick." He vanished into the back with the book of accounts in hand.

Atlas returned his gaze to her. "You are wearing black."

"Yes." She looked down at her gown. "Despite everything, Godfrey was still my legal husband at the time of his death, and I do have the boys to consider. It would hardly be appropriate for them to take up mourning while their mother does not."

"You look very well."

"It's quite a nuisance, really. All my new gowns have been dyed black." She caught his eye. "I know it's terribly heartless of me to speak so when my husband is dead."

"Not at all. I was acquainted with the man, after all."

"I regret the manner in which Godfrey died, truly, but I am not sorry he is out of my life."

Stillwell reappeared with two hefty account books. "Here you go, ma'am."

"Allow me." Atlas stepped forward to take them.

He followed her up the stairs and into Warwick's apartments, taking care to leave the door ajar to protect her reputation. The only other time he'd been here was when he'd found her husband's body. He glanced in the direction of the bedchamber. The door was closed. He wondered if she knew Warwick's body had been found on the bed.

"How goes the investigation?" she asked. "Thea tells me you went to Slough to see John. How did you find him?"

He placed the ledgers on the table. "His grief appears to have taken a heavy toll on him. Was he close to Godfrey?"

"He often took his brother to task for his objectionable behavior, which Godfrey detested, but John cared for Godfrey, even though my husband did not deserve his brother's love."

"John said he didn't see much of his brother and could think of no one who would want to do him harm. I thought perhaps

Stillwell would know of someone who might have had a dispute with Warwick."

He was hesitant to mention his visit with Bole, especially given the man's scurrilous allegations regarding her honor and virtue, but it couldn't be helped. "There is something I must ask you."

When he paused, she said, "Well, get on with it. It can't be all that bad."

"Bole says you threatened to disclose some matter Warwick preferred to keep private. A threat that made him very angry."

Surprise, then wariness, lit her eyes. "You saw Felix Bole today?"

"I did. It is true?"

She dipped her chin. "It is. I overhead Godfrey threatening a gentleman."

"When did this occur?"

"A few weeks ago." One delicate pale hand absently smoothed her skirts. "The man arrived in Slough early on a Saturday afternoon, not long after Godfrey had arrived from Town. He was extremely agitated."

"Did you recognize him?"

"No, he was a stranger." She carried the ledgers over to the escritoire by the window. "I was in the garden with the children. There are double doors in Godfrey's study that lead outside. It was a beautiful day, and one of the doors was ajar. I heard the arguing and ventured closer to see what the fuss was about."

"In what way did Warwick threaten him?"

Setting the books down, she turned back to Atlas. "Godfrey demanded money from the man. Otherwise, he said, he would tell all of Mayfair the truth about him."

"What truth was that?"

She lifted her shoulders. "I have no idea. But after the man left, I confronted Godfrey and told him extorting money from the man was dishonorable."

He admired her fearlessness; she'd been unafraid to take her husband to task, despite his brutish behavior toward her. "Which he no doubt appreciated."

"Godfrey told me I would pay for my meddling." She gave him a wry smile. "And he was certainly true to his word."

"You say you did not know the man Warwick was extorting?"

"No, but I would most certainly recognize him if I saw him again."

"Why is that?"

"He had very dark hair except for a streak of gray running from one temple all the way to the base of his neck." She smiled. "The children giggled when they saw him and said he looked like a skunk."

"Did he appear to be a gentleman? Warwick threatened to disclose his secret to Mayfair, which suggests he might be a member of the peerage."

"I cannot say for certain, although his clothes were well tailored and of high quality."

Atlas looked toward the window and saw the day was growing short. He had taken up enough of her time. He offered to escort her home, but she declined.

"Thea's coachman will be along for me in an hour's time." She gestured toward the ledgers she'd moved to the small desk. "Until then, I have much with which to occupy myself."

He wondered if her presence at the shop meant she intended to take over its management. "Have you decided to take up trade?"

She seemed amused by the question. "You think it is beneath me? I do need to look after the boys as well as myself." She sat at the desk and began to write. "You cannot be my champion forever. I have imposed enough as it is."

Yet he still felt a strong urge to keep her safe. "It was no imposition. Common decency dictates that I assist in any way I can."

She ripped something carefully out of the notebook she'd been writing in and stood, holding it out to him. "This in no way absolves my debt to you, but it is a place to start."

He realized it was a bank draft written out in the amount of thirty pounds. The sum he'd paid Warwick for her that shameful afternoon at the inn. He stepped back, insulted. "I will not take your money."

"Technically, it is Godfrey's." She continued to hold the draft out to him. "Please accept it."

"No." The words were sharper than he'd intended. "You insult us both by offering."

"Why? Because I refuse to pretend my husband did not sell me to a stranger? As if I could ever forget it." She held herself erect, her bearing proud but her voice trembling. "I cannot bear to have this between us. Please accept the money."

Determination blazed in her autumn-hued eyes as she stood, pale-faced, with her arm extended, the bank draft fluttering from her tapered fingers. He suddenly understood that returning the money was the closest she could ever come to undoing the degradation her husband had subjected her to. It also became clear to him that the terrible way they'd met would always be a chasm between them. One that might prove unbreachable.

"Very well." With a heavy heart, he took the draft and stuffed it into his pocket. Then he bade her good evening and left her alone.

Chapter Fourteen

"Excuse me, Mr. Catesby," the clerk said when Atlas reentered the shop.

He was no longer in the mood to talk. It had been a long day, and his conversation with Mrs. Warwick had left him somewhat dispirited. "Yes, what is it?"

"You asked if I might know of anyone who had a dispute with Mr. Warwick."

He paused, regarding the clerk across the counter. "Have you remembered something?"

"Yes, a few days before Mr. Warwick was . . . left us . . . a gentleman came into the shop, and the two had words."

Could this be the same man Warwick had extorted money from? "Did you recognize this gentleman?"

"No, sir, I'd never seen him before. He wasn't a regular customer."

"What did they argue about?"

"I can't say." The clerk adjusted his spectacles on the bridge of his nose. "Mr. Warwick sent me out of the shop. He said it was to bring him coffee, but I think he wanted to speak with his visitor in complete privacy."

"Then how do you know they exchanged words?"

"I saw them arguing through the window when I returned with the coffee. At one point, the gentleman pushed Mr. Warwick against one of the shelves and pointed his finger in his face."

"You say this man was a gentleman?"

"Oh, yes. He was very finely dressed and carried himself like a prince. He could have been a royal duke, for all I know. I never got a good look at his face. He kept his hat on and his chin down. It was almost as though he didn't want to be recognized."

"Could you tell if he had dark hair with a streak of gray growing through it, like a skunk?"

Stillwell frowned. "No, sir. Like I said, I didn't get a good look at him, but he did wear the largest signet ring I've ever seen."

A signet ring. Which meant Warwick's caller was indeed a peer of some sort. The clue wasn't much to go on, but at least it narrowed the field down from London's one million denizens to a more manageable few hundred members of the *ton*. "What did this ring look like?"

"It was gold, with the largest red ruby at the center. That ring must be worth a fortune."

"Thank you, Stillwell." It wasn't much, but at least it was a start. He reached for his hat. "You've been most helpful. Please don't hesitate to send word if you think of anything else of interest."

The bell above the door jangled as Atlas pulled it open. A rush of damp air reached him. It had started raining again.

"Mr. Catesby."

He paused, looking over his shoulder. "Yes?"

"You mentioned someone with dark hair and a streak of white running through it?"

"Yes." He faced the clerk, his posture alert. "Do you know someone who matches that description?"

"Yes, sir. But he's no peer. He's a tradesman. His name's Kirby Nash."

His heart sped up. Here was his first genuine lead. "Did this Mr. Nash visit Mr. Warwick here at the shop?"

"No, not that I ever saw."

"How do you know him?"

"I've worked here a long time, and one comes to know other merchants in the area."

"What is Mr. Nash's trade?"

"He's a tailor, sir. He has an establishment on Pall Mall in St. James."

"Thank you, Stillwell." He placed his hat on his head. "You've been most helpful."

* * *

Like the cold rain beating down on him, the thoughts that accompanied Atlas on his way home were not pleasant. He couldn't help wondering whether Mrs. Warwick had truly had a secret lover.

His mind kept returning to the well-heeled man in the park who'd stared after her as if he'd seen a ghost. There was something about the man that had nagged at his mind for days. Perhaps it was the obvious joy that had illuminated the man's face when he'd beheld Mrs. Warwick, his attention riveted on her as she'd ridden away. It was a preposterous assumption, not supported by any evidence, but he couldn't help wondering if the man could be Mrs. Warwick's secret lover. And the lady was now free. Ice flowed in his veins at the thought of the two of them taking up with each other again.

His jealousy was ridiculous. It wasn't as though she was his or ever would be. But the thought of her giving herself to another man clawed at his insides. Not caring to examine what his feelings of possessiveness might mean, Atlas tugged his collar up around his neck to ward off the chilling downpour and hurried home.

* * *

Late the following morning, Atlas walked over to Pall Mall to visit Kirby Nash, the tailor with a dark secret Warwick had threatened to expose. The streets were damp and muddy from the previous evening's storm, and the air remained thick with humidity, though the rain itself had ceased.

He entered Nash's establishment to find a tasteful shop furnished in deep greens and dark-paneled wood. A patron standing before a mirror was being measured by a clerk while, by the counter, another customer examined a top hat. There were three clerks on the floor attending to clients, but Nash, with the startling gray streak shooting through his black hair, was immediately recognizable to Atlas.

"What can I do for you, Mr. Catesby?" Mr. Nash asked after the introductions had been made. He ran an appraising eye over Atlas's clothing. "May I suggest a new greatcoat? Perhaps I can interest you in an exquisite aubergine wool facecloth I've just acquired for my most discriminating patrons."

"Thank you, but I don't think so."

"Are you certain? Double breasted would look very well on you. You have the figure for it." Nash was younger than he'd expected, less than thirty, with a lean, elegant form and an upright bearing.

"I would like a have a few words with you regarding Mr. Godfrey Warwick."

Nash's friendly demeanor melted away. "What about him?"

Atlas glanced around at the customers and clerks within hearing distance. "Is there a more private place where we might talk?"

Nash regarded him warily. "Are you a friend of Warwick's?"

"No."

"Then what is your interest?"

"I am keen to find out who killed him."

An odd expression came over Nash's face. It almost looked like relief. Perhaps Nash thought Atlas had come to continue the extortion Warwick had begun. "I'm afraid you've wasted your time in coming here. I barely knew the man." Nash turned away. "Now if you will excuse me, I have patrons to attend to."

"You knew Warwick well enough to visit him in Buckinghamshire," Atlas said to the man's back.

Nash froze and slowly pivoted to face him. "What do you know about that?"

"Enough to surmise that it might be prudent to have this discussion in a more private location."

Nash pressed his lips firmly together. "Very well. If you will follow me."

He led Atlas through to the back, into a well-lit workspace dominated by a large workbench. Apprentices and journeymen sat cross-legged on the wooden platform, cutting patterns, threading needles, and sewing. A wide sashed window provided ample light for their work. Nash had certainly done well for such a young man.

The tailor led him past this scene and into a small, dimly lit storage room stocked with fabrics.

Crossing his arms over this chest, he faced Atlas. "What is it you want to know?"

"I'll come straight to the point. I'd like to know why you and Warwick argued in Slough."

The guarded expression on the man's face didn't change. "It was regarding a private matter."

"Let me assure you that I have no interest in revealing any secrets you wish to keep hidden. However, I happen to know Warwick was extorting money from you, and I'd like to know why."

"What business is that of yours?"

"It might have a bearing on the case."

"Ah, I see." Understanding sparked in Nash's eyes. "You want to know whether my secret is terrible enough to kill for."

"Is it?"

"Decide for yourself." Nash actually seemed amused. "Follow me." They went down a narrow corridor and came to chamber filled with comfortable masculine-looking furniture and shelves overflowing with books. Paintings and maps adorned the walls, and books were stacked on one tabletop next to a sizeable globe nestled in a bronze stand.

"Well, here it is."

"Here what is?" Atlas asked.

"My secret."

Confused, he surveyed the space but saw nothing beyond the books and maps. "I don't follow."

"I'm a merchant who is impudent enough to indulge my literary and intellectual interests."

Atlas began to understand. The upper orders had nothing but contempt for tradesmen with cultivated tastes. They were viewed as upstarts who dared to place themselves on the same level as their betters. "Warwick discovered this room and threatened to disclose its existence to your customers? In particular, those who reside in Mayfair?"

"He threatened to ruin me. After all, a proper merchant who knows his place spends his free time in alehouses and taverns. I have the audacity to read and study a variety of subjects, which, in the eyes of the *ton*, is a crass attempt to get above myself."

Atlas surveyed the room, scanning the titles of the books, which covered many subjects—history, geography, metaphysics. On the table before him, next to the globe, an interlocking wooden puzzle caught his interest.

"You have a Chinese Cross," he noted. "May I?"

Nash waved a hand. "As you like. It was a gift, but I've never been able to figure the thing out."

Atlas picked up the three-dimensional structure, which easily fit in one hand, and fiddled with the cubic-shaped pieces. "I've seen these puzzles, but I've never worked with one." He looked up. "How did Warwick come to find this room?"

"I was out at a client's when Warwick paid a visit. A foreman who was new to my employ very indiscreetly directed Warwick back to my private rooms to await my return."

"And when you did, you found Warwick here among your books."

"Precisely."

"He wanted money from you in exchange for keeping quiet. How much did you pay?" As he spoke, Atlas quickly disassembled the six-piece puzzle.

"I was to deliver a set amount at the beginning of each month."

He began to reassemble the squared-off pieces, fitting two *C*-shaped pieces into a closed circular piece. "How many payments had you made before Warwick died?"

"Not a one." Nash's attention dipped down to where Atlas's hands worked on the puzzle. "I was to make the initial payment on the first of next month."

"But you had agreed to pay what he'd asked?"

Nash exhaled heavily. The decision had obviously weighed on him. "I felt I had no choice. The revelation could put my business at risk. There are many who depend on this enterprise for their livelihood, to support their families."

"Why have you agreed to show me this room?" Nash seemed almost too willing to share his secret. "You run a great risk in doing so. You do not know me or my character."

"I have heard you are a man of honor. I also know you are Silas Catesby's son."

He paused and looked up from the half-finished Chinese Cross. "Were you acquainted with my father?"

Nash shook his head. "Not personally, no. But I had the privilege of hearing him speak in public on two occasions. I know he did not set much store by the separation of the classes."

"No, he did not." That egalitarian outlook, along with a healthy disdain of the peerage, was why his father had been hesitant about consenting to Phoebe's calamitous marriage to the marquess. The unbidden image of his sister's broken body flashed in his mind. A painful sense of loss throbbed in his lungs. The sensation never really left him; he merely felt it more intensely on some occasions.

"I trust you will be discreet in regards to what you have seen here today," Nash was saying.

Atlas locked the sixth and final piece into place and set the puzzle back on the table. "You may depend upon it."

Nash picked up the Chinese Cross to examine it. "You've finished it." He blinked in surprise as he turned the symmetrical square-shaped structure over in his hands. "It took you less than five minutes. That's quite impressive."

Atlas dipped his chin, quietly acknowledging the compliment. "Who else knows about this chamber?"

Nash set the piece down. "No one. If that will be all"—he motioned toward the doorway as if to usher Atlas out—"I do have patrons to attend to."

Atlas paused. "One more question."

Lines of irritation puckered around Nash's mouth. "Yes?"

"Where were you on the evening of September second?"

His forehead wrinkled. "The second of September? I'm not certain. Why?"

"That's the evening Warwick was killed."

Nash huffed an incredulous breath. "You cannot seriously believe I would murder a man over a few books."

"I am merely attempting to be thorough in my inquiry."

Nash's countenance became decidedly unfriendly. "On whose authority are you conducting this little investigation of yours?"

"It is a favor to Mr. Warwick's widow, the mother of his two sons." Not exactly the truth, but not precisely a lie either.

"On the evening Warwick died, I was doing a fitting at the home of a client," he said curtly.

"How late did you stay?"

"Very late."

"May I trouble you for the name of your client?"

"No, you may not. I never discuss my patrons with anyone." He answered with a finality that signaled the conversation was over. "I'll see you out. I'm very busy at the moment." Nash personally escorted him to the door. Atlas sensed the man's solicitousness had less to do with courtesy and everything to do with making certain his unwelcome guest departed the premises. As they walked across the shop floor toward the exit, a familiar voice rang out.

"Atlas? Whatever are you doing here?"

He turned to find Charlton standing before a shop mirror, being fitted in a navy tailcoat. "I could ask the same of you."

The earl shrugged out of the jacket with help from the clerk. "I have ordered some new things." The clerk held up the next coat for the earl to try, this one in black.

"Black and navy jackets?" Atlas asked. "A little somber for your tastes, aren't they?"

"One always appreciates variety." Standing with his arms extended while the clerk pinned the sleeves, Charlton regarded Atlas through the mirror's reflection. "Do you suppose Mrs. Palmer will approve?"

"Thea?" Atlas was taken aback by the mention of his sister. "Why would it matter?"

Charlton concentrated on the actions of the clerk pinning his sleeves. "Are you here for clothing as well?"

"No, I had some unrelated matters to discuss with Nash here," he said of the tailor who watched their exchange with tense interest. "I was just leaving."

"I am done here as well." The earl shrugged out of the black jacket and allowed the clerk to help him back into his own coat. "I'll walk out with you." He finished giving the clerk detailed instructions about the fit of his jackets before they left together and strolled along Pall Mall.

"I wasn't aware that Nash was your tailor," Atlas said.

"He and Weston are the two I frequent most often."

"What is your opinion of him?"

"Of Nash? He's a fine tailor and has always dealt with me in an honest and forthright manner." He tilted his head. "Why do you ask? And what were you doing there?"

"I have reason to believe Warwick was planning to extort quite a bit of money from Nash."

"Truly?" Charlton's eyes rounded. "That haberdasher was one slimy bastard. It is no wonder at all that someone did away with him."

"You'll get no argument from me on that score."

Interest gleamed in Charlton's eyes. "But what dark secret could a tailor like Nash have?"

Atlas revealed what he'd seen in Nash's back room and the reason for Warwick's plan to extort money from the man. "The question is," he said after sharing what he'd learned, "whether a roomful of books is motivation enough for murder."

"Saving one's reputation and livelihood might be motivation enough for many men," Charlton said after thinking on it for a few moments.

"Would such a revelation be enough to ruin Nash?"

"I have heard of something similar happening to a milliner a few years ago. A peer discovered the man was studying with a tutor in the evenings and contrived to destroy the milliner's business."

"Solely for the crime of trying to better himself?"

"His clients began to accuse him of spending his time reading rather than attending to their orders. He lost almost half of his business."

Atlas thought of the clerks on the shop floor as well as the journeymen and apprentices he'd seen laboring in the back. Nash seemed to have a prosperous business and, therefore, quite a bit to lose had Warwick lived long enough to reveal his secret.

He and Charlton reached Bond Street and parted company—the earl heading for his club while Atlas made for home. As he trotted up the steps, he resolved to verify the tailor's alibi for the evening of the murder, which meant finding the mystery client Nash had supposedly been with the night Warwick was killed.

Chapter Fifteen

The following afternoon, Atlas sifted through the facts of the case as he cut through Red Lion Square on the boundary between Bloomsbury and Holborn. His footfalls drummed a steady beat along the path. He had nowhere in particular to go, but walking seemed to clear his mind, and except for a mild ache, his foot wasn't bothering him.

He was contemplating how to get a hold of a list of Kirby Nash's patrons—in hopes of tracking down the tailor's alibi—when a wooden hoop rolled across the grass and rammed into his leg. He caught hold of the hoop, wondering who it could belong to, when a dark-haired child raced across the grass and came to a screeching halt before him.

"Excuse me, sir, but that's my brother's hoop." The boy was out of breath, his dark eyes round and solemn. Atlas guessed him to be around seven or eight years of age.

"Is it? He seems to have lost control of his toy."

The boy shuffled his feet. "Yes, sir, we're only just learning how to use them."

A much younger boy dashed up to them and pointed to the hoop. "Mine!" he said indignantly.

"This is my brother, Robin," the older boy said. "And I am Peter."

"I am pleased to meet you both." He made a bow. "My name is Atlas."

"That's mine!" the younger boy repeated, refusing to be distracted by the introductions. He had a headful of soft brown curls and a sturdy little body that didn't seem to be completely within his control. Atlas judged him to be two or three years younger than his brother. "I was trying to roll it."

Both boys were smartly dressed in matching pale-blue skeleton suits with white ruffled cambric shirts underneath, outfits commonly worn by children of the upper classes. Their high-waisted trousers buttoned into the hem of a matching jacket, creating one long jumpsuit.

"It got away," the younger boy, Robin, said.

"I can see that." Atlas hoisted the hoop, twirling it on his arm. "The trick of controlling a hoop, while making it go as fast as possible, is all in the elbow."

The older boy, Peter, watched with rapt interest. "What do you mean?"

"There was a time when I was very young that I was quite the expert at bowling hoops." He winked at the younger boy. "I even beat all my older brothers in a race." He smiled at the memory of besting Jason and Apollo, even though they were older than him. Herm, a talented and agile athlete, had been harder to beat.

"How did you do that?" Peter asked.

"I could also jump back and forth through the hoop as it rolled." He'd been able to perfect a number of tricks with his hoop.

The younger boy, Robin, frowned as he ran his eyes over the length of Atlas's tall form. "But you are too big to fit through a hoop."

"Now, yes, I certainly am." Atlas returned the hoop to its young owner. "But once, a very long time ago, I was the size of you and your brother."

Holding his hoop with one hand, little Robin sucked three fingers in his mouth and continued to regard Atlas's statements with obvious skepticism.

"Have you ever played catch with a hoop?" he asked the older brother.

Peter shook his head, although interest gleamed in his dark eyes.

"Would you like me to show you?" Atlas asked.

Peter nodded vigorously. "I'll be right back." He scampered off to a bench where a woman who seemed to be his nurse had watched their entire exchange. Atlas thought it rather careless of the young nurse to allow her charges to speak at length with a strange man. He watched Peter snatch up a hoop lying in the grass near the woman.

Atlas followed, and as he drew closer, the young woman stood up, and he recognized her as one of his sister's maids. She curtseyed as he approached. "Mr. Catesby, sir."

He realized Thea's servant had allowed the boys to speak with him because she'd recognized him as her employer's brother. He struggled to remember her name. "Clara, isn't it?"

She beamed. "Yes, sir. The boys are trying to learn how to bowl hoops, and I'm afraid I am not very good at it."

It dawned on him then who her young charges were. Peter and Robin. He should have recognized the names. He recalled Mrs. Warwick mentioning them once or twice. He studied the boys with renewed interest. Peter, the older boy, had narrow shoulders and a slim build and was dark and serious like his mother. Robin's coloring was lighter, and he was sturdier and thick bodied, more like his father.

The younger boy tugged on his tailcoat. "Teach us," he demanded. "I want to play catch."

Clara reddened. "Now, Robin," she admonished, "that is not a polite way to speak to Mr. Catesby."

Atlas waved her off. "Please don't concern yourself." Children didn't normally interest him, but he found himself to be exceedingly curious about Mrs. Warwick's children. "I'll just show the boys a trick or two that they can do with their hoops."

The nurse seemed relieved. "I myself have no idea how to bowl hoops, sir, so the young masters will no doubt welcome the instruction."

He spent the next hour showing the children how to roll their hoops and perform assorted tricks. Before long, the boys were marveling at themselves for having learned how to play catch with their hoops.

"I want to race you," Peter said. He'd lost much of his polite wariness and was brimming with a little boy's energy and enthusiasm.

"Oh?" Atlas asked, amused. "Do you think you can best me now?" He was perspiring from his exertions, his cravat was askew, and his hair was surely a mess. Surprisingly, he was enjoying himself. Spending time with Mrs. Warwick's boys rekindled the fond memories he had of playing with his numerous siblings as a boy. "You think you've learned enough to beat me?"

Peter raced off, rolling his hoop with speed and precision. "There's one way to find out!" he called back over his shoulder as he dashed away.

"Cheater!" he shouted after the boy. He turned to young Robin. "Come on then. We must catch your brother and really show him how it's done."

They went running off, with Atlas rolling the hoop and Robin chasing after him, laughing and calling out to his brother. "We're going to catch you, Peter!"

Atlas was so focused on rolling the hoop that he didn't see Mrs. Warwick cross his path until it was almost too late. He barely avoided colliding with her before coming to an abrupt halt as the hoop rolled off without him.

"Am I interrupting?" she asked, obvious amusement twinkling in her eyes.

"Mrs. Warwick." Embarrassed at being caught behaving like a child, Atlas ran a hand over his unruly hair in a hapless attempt to tidy it.

"Yes, Mama," Robin cried out in frustration. "You are interrupting our race, and now Peter is the winner because we didn't have a chance to finish . . ." His voice trailed off as his eyes watered and his chin wobbled.

"Don't cry, my love." She knelt to take the boy into her arms. "You can have another race."

But the boy wasn't interested in being comforted. He wriggled out of his mother's embrace and grabbed the stick from

Atlas before rolling his hoop wobblingly off in the direction of his brother, who'd reached the end of the grassy square and turned back in their direction. "That wasn't fair," Robin called out to him. "Mama says we have to start over and do it again."

Mrs. Warwick stood and turned her attention back to Atlas. "You roll that hoop quite expertly. You're a man of many talents."

He tried to tug his cravat back into some semblance of order. He was sweating like a stevedore and no doubt reeked more than a Seven Dials cutpurse, while she personified the epitome of cool, serene loveliness. Her flawless pale skin was luminous against the black of her mourning gown, its square décolletage emphasizing the long, graceful column of her neck.

Masking the chagrin brought on by his disheveled appearance, he said lightly, "I confess bowling hoops is one of the activities at which I excel. I am also quite the expert at bilbocatch," he added, referring to a ball-and-cup game at which he was unbeatable.

She favored him with that crooked—yet somehow still imperious—smile of hers. "What a braggart you are. I wouldn't have guessed it."

He laughed at the setdown. "Touché."

"It is good of you to play with the children," she said on a more serious note. "Their father never did, so they are quite unused to masculine attention."

He abandoned his futile attempts to put his hair and clothing to rights. "It was my pleasure," he said with all sincerity. "I cannot remember the last time I enjoyed myself quite so much." Though his left foot was beginning to protest, and he suspected he'd suffer the aftereffects of the day's exertions.

Peter came running up, trailed closely by his younger brother. "Mama," he cried. "Don't say we have to go home."

An expression of profound maternal love and admiration settled on her face as she looked at her child. "Yes, darling. I'm afraid we must return to Mrs. Palmer's. Your new tutor has come to meet you."

Peter crossed his arms over his narrow chest. "It's not fair," he pouted. "Mr. Catesby was going to show me how to jump back and forth through a rolling hoop."

"I'm sure Mr. Catesby is a very busy man and has matters of importance to attend to today." She spoke in a firm voice while exchanging a look with Atlas. It took him a moment to realize he was supposed to reply in the affirmative.

"You'll need a much bigger hoop for that trick," he told the boy. "We shall have to get you one. In the meantime, I'll escort you all back to Mrs. Palmer's."

They walked down High Holborn and turned right onto Bury Street, which led to Great Russell. Along the way, the boys chattered excitedly, regaling their mother with stories about the tricks Atlas had taught them so far. It was the first time he'd seen Mrs. Warwick in the company of her children. Their presence softened her precise edges, and she was as relaxed as he'd ever seen her when she interacted with them.

At first, he was embarrassed to have his folly with the hoops recounted for the boys' elegant mother, until he registered the way her eyes shone when she looked at him, gratitude glimmering in those dark depths.

"I must admit young Peter gave me quite a run." Atlas handed his hat to Miller when they arrived at Thea's house.

"Mama got in the way," Robin said for at least the fifth time. Atlas was beginning to learn children certainly could be repetitive.

That put Peter's back up. "I can beat you any day. You're just a baby."

"Sir—" Miller said to Atlas.

"Peter, apologize to your brother for being rude." Mrs. Warwick's sharp words cut the footman off.

Peter stared at the ground. "I beg your pardon," he said with sullen reluctance to his younger sibling.

"Sir," Miller tried again.

"Mama is good at bowling hoops," Peter said, brightening. "She could even race Mr. Catesby."

Atlas looked at her. "Is that so?"

"I am quite accomplished," she said haughtily, good humor sparkling in her bronze-colored eyes. "I do believe I could best you."

He regarded her appreciatively. "Ahoy! That sounds like a challenge."

She laughed. "Perhaps it is. But I must choose the hoops to make certain they are the same." It was the first time he'd seen her completely stripped of her usual reserve. He'd never seen her as unencumbered as she seemed at the moment, as though a great weight had been lifted from her.

"I will not go easy on you just because you are a lady," he warned.

"La." She gave a careless wave of her hand, and he glimpsed for a moment the carefree young girl she must have been before her marriage. He stared at her in open admiration. It was as though she'd been wrapped in a tight cocoon when he'd first met her, and now the layers were slowly being peeled away to reveal her true self. Discovering the woman beneath could prove intriguing. "You've no idea what I'm capable of."

"Just what are you capable of, Mrs. Warwick?" said a familiar male voice from behind them.

The smile drained from Atlas's face when he caught sight of the portly man just off the front hallway.

"Mr. Endicott." All mirth left the lady's face as well. "This is a surprise."

"As I was saying, sir," Miller put in. "You have a visitor. Mrs. Palmer is out, but Mr. Endicott here said he would like to wait for you."

"So I see." Atlas shed his jacket and handed the garment to the footman. "What brings you here, Endicott? You seem to be making a habit of lying in wait for me." He wanted to plant the man a facer for destroying the convivial atmosphere.

Endicott glanced at the footman. "Perhaps we could talk somewhere a bit more private?"

Mrs. Warwick excused herself to take the boys to meet their tutor, saying she would join the men shortly, while Atlas led the runner to Thea's little-used blue parlor.

Endicott wandered over to examine a landscape painting above the hearth. "I'm pleased we have a moment alone before Mrs. Warwick joins us, because what I have to say is of a delicate nature."

Atlas kept his expression neutral. "Can I offer you a whiskey?"

"No, thank you." Endicott turned from the painting. "I'll come straight to the point. I visited the Red Rooster, the pub in Covent Garden where you met Warwick on the night he was killed. The people there remembered Warwick. And you."

Atlas poured himself a whiskey. "I see."

"One of the regulars even managed to overhear your conversation."

Atlas's scalp tingled as he turned to face the runner. "Did you learn anything of interest?"

"Only that Warwick was going to publicly charge you with adultery." His keen gaze was trained on Atlas. "Criminal conversation, I believe he said."

Atlas sipped from his whiskey and struggled to maintain a placid demeanor. "The accusation is untrue as well as unfounded."

"Still, being publicly charged with adultery in a court of law could have severely damaged your reputation."

A mirthless huff of laughter escaped him. "Do you truly believe concern over my own standing in society is why I've neglected to mention this sordid business to you before now?"

"It seems as good a reason as any."

"I am a gentleman, the brother of a baron and son of the beloved national poet Silas Catesby—"

"You don't say?" Avid interest shone in Endicott's eyes. "I didn't realize you were connected to *that* Catesby. Your father's work is a favorite of the missus . . . particularly, what is it called? 'Golden Time' or 'Golden Day,' or something to that effect?"

"'One Golden Hour.'" It was one of his father's most popular poems.

"That's it!" Endicott slapped his fleshy thigh and pointed at Atlas. "That's it. That's the one."

"As I was saying, given my connections, I could survive a scandal. However, crim-con allegations would be far more damaging to Mrs. Warwick."

Endicott stared at him for a moment. "And you are fond of Mrs. Warwick."

"As I've told you before, I do not know her very well, but I have felt a sense of responsibility to her since she came into my care."

"Would you say the two are you are . . . close?"

"Not particularly, no."

Endicott withdrew his notebook from his coat pocket and thumbed through it. "Let's see." He studied the page. "You deny that you and Mrs. Warwick are close."

He registered the underlying note of skepticism in the runner's voice. "As I have already made clear."

"I wonder if you can explain why a witness spotted the two of you together holding hands in an abovestairs sitting room in this very house on the evening of the murder."

Atlas froze and then quickly recovered himself. "I was merely consoling her." Atlas remembered trying to comfort Mrs. Warwick after his foul conversation with Warwick at the Red Rooster. He could still recall the smooth warmth of her hand from that too-brief touch. "She was upset about a matter regarding her children."

"Ah yes, the children." Endicott thumbed through his notes again.

Mrs. Warwick chose that moment to join them. "Have there been any developments in your investigation?" she asked, crossing over to take a seat.

"Not quite yet, I'm afraid," The runner regarded her thoughtfully with piscine eyes. "However, I am making progress."

"Oh?" Mrs. Warwick regarded him expectantly. "I'm pleased to hear it. Won't you sit?"

"Don't mind if I do." Endicott lumbered over and wedged his corpulent form into the largest available seat. "I learned something very interesting from Mr. Jobbins while I was in Slough."

Atlas was not familiar with the name. "Mr. Jobbins?"

"Mr. Warwick's butler." He regarded Mrs. Warwick. "Surely you are acquainted with him."

"Not really," she said carefully. "He came into my husband's employ just a few weeks before I ceased living there."

"But you had contact with Jobbins the day before your husband was found deceased, if I am not mistaken."

Atlas's grip tightened on his glass as Mrs. Warwick grew noticeably paler.

"Yes," she said.

"As Jobbins tells it, there was quite an ugly scene because you defied your husband's edict that you have nothing to do with the children."

"They are the flesh of my flesh," she said flatly. "I would never agree to stop seeing my children."

"Very understandable. Very." He spoke in agreeable tones. "But your late husband was determined that you should never see the children, isn't that right? Jobbins said the boys were instructed never to talk of you and to think of their mother as dead to them."

"I'm afraid I was not privy to what Godfrey told the children after I left our home in Slough." She spoke calmly, her posture impeccable as she sat with her hands clasped in her lap.

"And you left the home, as you put it, against your wishes?"

"Yes, I preferred to remain with my children."

"But Mr. Warwick—forgive my mention of a most unpleasant topic—sold you against your will to Mr. Catesby."

"Yes."

"So he sold you to a stranger and kept you from his children."

"Yes."

"And now that he is dead, the children are in your care."

"Yes. Their uncle, Godfrey's brother, is their guardian, and he has consented to my keeping the children with me."

"That's very convenient. You've had a happy ending then."

She gave him an icy look. "The father of my sons is dead. They are now orphans. Society does not look kindly upon fatherless children. No one could be pleased with such a terrible tragedy."

"That's very gracious of you, very gracious, considering how your late husband treated you." He scratched his scalp. "I imagine most women in your situation would be relieved."

Atlas's neck heated. "Now see here, Endicott, just what are you accusing Mrs. Warwick of?"

"Nothing at all. It's far too early in the investigation for that." He turned to Mrs. Warwick. "I should like to hear of your movements on the evening of your husband's death. Just to be thorough, you understand."

"Of course." She absentmindedly smoothed the skirts of her gown. "I was here all evening."

"But you did not attend Mrs. Palmer's gathering."

"No, I had a headache and retired early to my bedchamber until the following morning."

"Can someone attest to your remaining at home that evening? Did you see a maid? Perhaps you sent for some tea or a light supper."

"No, I was overwrought and exhausted. I fell asleep almost immediately."

"I see. I can imagine how upsetting it must have been to have that terrible scene with your children." Endicott scribbled in his notebook as he talked. "And then to learn that Mr. Warwick planned to sue Mr. Catesby for criminal conversation."

"Yes," she said. "Naturally, it was upsetting. It was also a lie."

"And you shared your concerns with Mr. Catesby."

"Yes, he is the person who told me Godfrey had threatened to sue him."

"I imagine Mr. Catesby was very angry on your behalf."

Atlas's chest burned. The fat little bastard seemed determined to establish that Atlas had been angry enough to kill Godfrey Warwick. He swallowed the last of his whiskey, determined to turn Endicott's suspicions in another direction. "If you were not so focused on the more salacious aspects of this case, you'd see there were many people who would have liked to see Warwick dead."

The runner stopped scribbling and focused his attention on Atlas. "Like who, for instance?"

"I understand there is a certain tradesman on Pall Mall who had reason to fear Warwick."

Awareness flickered across the runner's face. The man was no fool. He comprehended full well the true reason behind Atlas's sudden desire to be helpful. "And who might that be?"

"I do not have a name," Atlas lied. "There was also a well-dressed man, possibly a peer, who argued with Warwick a few days before the killing. They had a physical altercation at the haberdashery."

"Is that so? I don't suppose you know the peer's name either."

"I do not." This time there was no need to lie. He wished he knew the well-dressed gentleman's identity, but that detail still eluded him. "The clerk, Stillwell, saw the confrontation. Perhaps if you learn that gentleman's identity, you will come closer to finding the killer."

They both knew it would be next to impossible for a mere runner to make inquiries in the rarified world of the *ton*. The very idea of someone of Endicott's station interrogating a duke or an earl was laughable. But it was not so for Atlas.

There was some currency in being the scion of the great Silas Catesby as well as the brother of a baron. And he intended to harness all the leverage at his disposal to keep himself and Mrs. Warwick out of harm's way.

CHAPTER SIXTEEN

"Good Lord." Atlas stared at the hole in his cravat. "Not again."

Jamie's boyish face, already reddened by the heat of the iron, flushed even more. "I can't make sense of it, sir. I made certain the iron wasn't as hot this time."

It was the fourth neck scarf his hapless valet had scorched beyond repair, rendering them all impossible to wear. At this pace, trying to maintain even the most basic gentleman's wardrobe could soon bankrupt him. "How much beeswax did you use?"

Jamie blinked, his face blank. "Beeswax?"

Atlas exhaled loudly through his nostrils. "Yes, beeswax. Surely you are aware beeswax is needed to keep the hot iron from scorching the starched cloth."

The manner in which Jamie's mouth gaped open suggested beeswax was as alien to him as Russian caviar. "Perhaps you should wait until you purchase some beeswax before continuing on."

"Very good, sir," Jamie said with a smile, recovering his usual youthful cheeriness. Ah, to be young again. At two-and-thirty,

Atlas was hardly ancient, but at times his damnable left foot made him feel one hundred years old.

He watched the boy move to his bed, carrying a basket of laundered clothing. "Jamie, how long were you with the Warwicks in Slough?"

"About six years, sir, since I was thirteen. My mam is Mr. Warwick's—the elder's—housekeeper. My brother works there too."

"Your mother works for Mr. John Warwick?"

"Yes, sir. Since before my brother and I were born. My brother is older than me, so he got to work with Mr. John while I was stuck with that blighter . . ." He flushed. "Begging your pardon, sir. It ain't proper to speak ill of the dead."

"It appears many shared your opinion of Godfrey Warwick. Did he have any enemies that you knew of?" Having lived in the household for many years, Jamie might be able to provide some insight.

Jamie paused, his expression grim. "There weren't many who got on with him. He was friendly with the local magistrate until they fell out."

"Are you speaking of Mr. Bole?"

Jamie pulled a pair of Atlas's drawers from the basket. "Yes, Mr. Bole."

Interesting. The magistrate had given no hint of any conflict between himself and the murder victim. "What did they argue about?"

"I can't say." He folded the drawers before adding them to a neat stack of clothing on Atlas's bed. "But maybe the housekeeper, Mrs. Greene, could tell you. She always seemed to know everything about what went on in that old rectory."

He recalled that the housekeeper had also been let go without reference after Godfrey had learned she'd allowed Mrs. Warwick to see the children. "Do you know what became of her after she was dismissed?"

"Mrs. Greene?" When Atlas nodded, the boy said, "She's working at the haberdashery now, didn't you know?"

He hadn't known. Atlas left the boy with the pile of laundry to walk down to the haberdashery. Wigmore Street was about a ten-minute walk from New Bond Street, and he welcomed the opportunity to stretch his legs.

He entered the shop to find a middle-aged woman standing behind the counter, sorting through a kaleidoscopic assortment of buttons.

She looked up when the bell above the door rang. "Good day, may I be of service?" Mrs. Greene was a trim, no-nonsense woman with a tight, turned-down mouth that betrayed no evidence that she smiled or laughed easily.

When he introduced himself, approval glittered in her flinty eyes. "You've done right by Mrs. Warwick, by all accounts. She deserved no less after what Mr. Warwick put her through."

"I have only done what any gentleman would do."

"As you say." She returned her attention to a grouping of pearl buttons and tossed them into one of two wicker baskets lined up on the counter.

"I am trying to determine who killed Mr. Warwick."

She paused and then, without looking up, continued her sorting. "It wasn't Mrs. Warwick, if that's what you're getting at."

"I do not accuse her."

"Although no one could have blamed her, given what he put her through."

"You refer to the way he sold her."

"Even before that." She isolated a group of cut-steel buttons with tiny steel studs that glittered when the light caught them. "He always tried to bring her low. Said she put on airs like she was a duchess."

He wondered how much Mrs. Greene knew about Mrs. Warwick's mysterious past. "Do you know if she is indeed highborn?"

"I don't know anything about her family, if that's what you're asking." She scooped the steel buttons into a second basket. "I know she had a king's ransom in jewels that served as her dowry when they wed."

"Mrs. Warwick had fine jewels prior to wedding?"

She nodded. "Diamonds, rubies, and pearls. I saw them once before Mr. Warwick sold them."

"How did she come by them?"

"I'm sure I cannot say." Her mouth twisted with distaste. "But it is obvious Mrs. Warwick was gently raised and had no notion how to deal with a husband who treated her harshly."

A storm brewed in his gut to think of the mistreatment Mrs. Warwick had received at Warwick's hands. The jewels momentarily forgotten, he asked, "Did Warwick raise a hand to her?"

"Not that I saw, but he humiliated her. I think because he knew she was too fine a lady for him. Miss Verity had a narrow escape, if you ask me."

"Miss Verity?" He repeated with some confusion. "Do you refer to the late Mrs. John Warwick?"

"The very same. She and Mr. Godfrey wanted to marry, but he was a second son with no prospects or expectations. Her parents forced a marriage to Mr. John, the elder son, because he would inherit the family property."

Atlas blinked. "Verity married John against her will?"

Mrs. Greene nodded. "It was a fortunate thing for her that her parents forced the matter, if you ask my opinion. Master John is all that is good and kind. A more honorable and decent man you would not find."

He remained silent for a moment, mulling over the unexpected new information. "Did Verity and Godfrey continue to carry a torch for each other even after she became John's wife?"

She shook her head. "That fire seemed to extinguish as quickly as it had caught fire."

"How so?"

"They were young, and the heart is fickle at such an age." She came around the counter, carrying both baskets. "Mr. Godfrey came here to Town to make his fortune and stayed away for many years while he built this business."

"I have heard that Mr. John Warwick and his late wife were most devoted to each other."

"And so they were." She arranged the baskets of buttons on the shelves. "I do believe Miss Verity came to realize she'd wed the better brother."

"How did the two couples get along?"

She turned to face him. "Miss Lilliana and the boys spent quite a bit of time with Miss Verity and Master John while Mr. Godfrey was away tending to the haberdashery."

"And how did he and Miss Verity interact with each other on the occasions when they were all together?"

"From what I could see, with the usual courtesy and nothing more. Miss Verity loved Master John and was completely devoted to him. She anguished at not being able to give him children."

"Godfrey must have resented his brother a great deal. John not only inherited the family assets but also took the wife Godfrey had wanted for himself."

She crossed over to the opposite side of the shop to straighten rows of ribbons in every color. "I would say he was always bitter and envious of his brother, especially after Miss Verity became so devoted to Master John."

He wasn't certain the onetime romantic triangle between the brothers had any bearing on Godfrey's death, but he tucked the information away to mull it over at a later time. For now, he wanted to learn more about the more current conflicts the murdered man had been embroiled in.

"Turning to another matter, I understand that Godfrey Warwick feuded with his friend, the magistrate, Mr. Bole, in the weeks before his death."

"'Tis so."

"I don't suppose you have any idea what caused the rift."

"Not specifically. However, Mr. Bole did come to the house, and he was ranting about how Mr. Warwick was trying to ruin him."

His interest piqued. "Ruin him, you say?"

"Yes, but I heard nothing more of it."

"Thank you for your time." He replaced his hat on his head as he turned to go. "I suppose I should ask Mr. Bole about it for myself. It is not too late to ride out to Slough."

"You won't find him at home."

He paused. "Why not?"

She stepped back behind the counter. "Mr. Bole always takes his family away this time of year. He won't be back for at least a fortnight."

Atlas suppressed a groan at the inconvenient delay in the investigation created by Bole's absence. He thanked Mrs. Greene and saw himself out.

He returned home from the haberdashery to find a smartly dressed footman standing on the landing outside his door. From the bottom of the stairs, he saw a fine-looking young man, tall and broad shouldered, with powdered hair, wearing gold-and-black livery. The fancy coat alone probably cost more than Atlas's own frock coat. The footman was likely employed at one of the metropolis's best houses. Handsome footmen were showpieces wealthy nobles enjoyed putting on display for visitors, not unlike the fine pieces of art that adorned their mansions.

"Are you Mr. Catesby, sir?" he inquired.

"I am." He came up the stairs. "Who would like to know?"

The footman didn't immediately respond. When Atlas reached the landing, he handed him a sealed note. "I am to await a reply."

Atlas did not recognize the seal, but he noted the paper was of the highest quality. He tore it open and scanned the fluid, confident writing. Cost was of no apparent concern to the sender, since he had used an entire sheet of paper for the short note.

He was shocked to discover it was a summons from the Duke of Somerville, asking him to call at his earliest convenience, preferably this very afternoon. Confused, Atlas turned the paper over and studied his name before flipping it back over and rereading the message.

What could Somerville possibly want with him? He knew the man was a particular friend of Charlton's, but he himself had never met him. And except for his unlikely friendship with the earl, Atlas did not move in the same circles as someone like Somerville. His curiosity got the better of him. Of course he would go and see what the duke wanted.

He looked up at the footman. "Please tell His Grace that I will attend him this afternoon as he requests."

* * *

Atlas had never been to Versailles, but he thought it might be something like Somerville House, a neoclassical monster of a mansion that took up an entire Mayfair block bordering Hyde Park. He'd visited some great houses in the past but nothing as grand as the opulent ducal residence.

Everything seemed oversized here, including a mammoth marble statue that dominated the sizeable entry hall. The porcelains, silver, and paintings cluttering the walls and surfaces had to be worth a small fortune in and of themselves.

The butler who led him to the duke's drawing room identified himself as Hastings. The name struck Atlas as vaguely familiar, and by the time they reached their destination, which involved traversing down several corridors and making a few assorted turns, he realized why: Hastings was the same family name Mrs. Warwick had given the runner when he'd asked about her family origins.

It seemed farfetched, but he ventured to see if there was any connection. “I have some acquaintances named Hastings who hail from Bewerley in Yorkshire,” he said.

“Indeed, sir?” Some of that butler-like reserve slipped. “My family does hail from Bewerley.” It was on the cusp of Atlas’s tongue to inquire as to whether he might have a niece or cousin named Lilliana, when the duke entered, and shock rippled through him.

Chapter Seventeen

He stared at the slender nobleman, who was not a complete stranger.

Atlas had laid eyes on the elegantly sculpted face weeks ago in the park, when the young man had stared at Mrs. Warwick as if he'd seen a ghost. The realization roused his protective instincts. Why had Somerville summoned him here, and what did he want with Mrs. Warwick?

"Mr. Catesby, I presume?"

He bowed. "Your Grace."

The duke waved an imperious hand in Hastings's general direction. "That will be all." Young as he was, the duke had an easy air of command and the confident bearing of one used to being obeyed.

As the butler quietly glided out of the room, His Grace faced Atlas. He was young, perhaps in his midtwenties, with coffee eyes, strong cheekbones, and a soft jaw.

Atlas vaguely recalled that Somerville had been just a boy when his parents had died in a carriage accident and he'd come into the title. His father had been a leading force in parliament and the duchess widely admired for her wit and sartorial flair. Together they'd ruled the *ton* until their sudden, unexpected deaths had shaken society. Tales of the tragic couple and their three orphaned children had filled the rags for months.

"Can I offer you something to drink?" There was a twist of insolence to the natural set of the duke's mouth. "I have a fine French brandy."

With England and France at war, the spirits were most likely smuggled, but Atlas had always enjoyed a good brandy. "Yes, thank you."

The duke splashed the amber liquid into two crystal glasses and handed one to Atlas. He gestured for Atlas to take a chair opposite his. As Somerville drank, he kept his gaze on Atlas.

Atlas gently swirled the brandy in his glass before raising the crystal to his lips. He drank, savoring the liquid in his mouth as well as the rich, supersmooth finish when he swallowed. It was by far the best brandy he'd ever tasted. Young as he was, Somerville clearly had an appreciation of life's finer things.

"Good, isn't it?" Somerville said, as if he'd read Atlas's thoughts.

"Excellent." He placed his glass on the table beside him. "However, I doubt you summoned me here solely to sample your world-class brandy."

"You are very direct."

"We hardly travel in the same circles, Your Grace. I can only assume you've asked me here for a reason."

"Very well." He took a leisurely sip of brandy, his gold signet ring catching the light as he did so. "Let me come directly to the point by telling you Mr. Nash was here the evening the haberdasher was killed."

This was not the direction Atlas had expected the conversation to take. "Are you saying that you are the client Nash was with on September the second of this year?"

"Yes. I do not care to go to the shop, so Nash comes to me."

It made perfect sense that Nash would pay house calls to a personage as esteemed as the duke and that he himself would attend to Somerville rather than sending one of his assistants. A duke's custom would be of high value to any tailor. "What time did Mr. Nash leave here that evening?"

"He did not."

"I'm afraid I do not follow."

"It was storming, and Nash is apparently given to megrims, which are worsened by the weather." Somerville crossed one knee over the other. "He was most incapacitated. I had Hastings put him in one of the guest chambers."

Atlas drank from his brandy. "At what time did he retire for the evening, if I might ask?"

"It was very late. Perhaps midnight. I had parliamentary business to attend to first that evening. Nash was required to wait before I could see him to be fitted."

"And when did you see Mr. Nash next? The following morning?"

"I did not see him again for many days. The following morning, I had important matters to see to." Matters that were no doubt more important than concerning himself with a tradesman, but in truth, Atlas was surprised Somerville had given Nash a chamber at all. "The staff attended to him in the morning, and my carriage returned him to Pall Mall, as it always does when he comes for fittings."

"I see."

"You may ask Hastings about it, if you wish. I have already instructed him to answer any questions you might have."

"Thank you. That is very helpful."

The duke studied him. "I trust this puts the matter to rest."

Atlas placed his empty glass on the table beside him. "Once Nash retired for the night, he was alone and has no alibi."

"Ridiculous." Temper flashed in the young duke's eyes. "This is a large home with many servants, including footmen who stand at attention throughout the night."

"Are you saying it would have been impossible for Nash to leave in the night without being seen?"

"It would be highly unlikely." He reached for a small porcelain bell at his side and rang it. The butler appeared instantly. His Grace came to his feet, ending their meeting. "As a gentleman, I ask you to leave this matter alone and cause Mr. Nash no further distress."

"With all due respect, Your Grace, I must follow the truth wherever it leads me."

"I see." The duke's face darkened. He was, no doubt, unused to having his commands challenged. "Hastings will see you out."

Atlas stood and bowed. "Good day, Your Grace."

As Atlas followed Hastings from the room, he couldn't help wondering if he'd just incurred the wrath of one of the most powerful young men in the country. Walking down a long corridor lined with paintings that were undoubtedly priceless, they passed a well-dressed man of middle age with a shock of gray hair. Atlas recognized him as the person who'd ridden in the carriage with Somerville that day in Hyde Park.

The man paused, regarding Atlas with an imperious stare. "And who is this, Hastings?"

"A guest of His Grace's, Mr. Eggleston. He was just leaving." The butler's answer was polite and deferential, yet Atlas noted the reply did not provide the man with much information. The displeasure that crossed Eggleston's face suggested he'd noted the elusive nature of the answer as well, but he merely turned to continue on his way.

"Hastings," Atlas asked when they reached the entry hall and a footman stepped forward with his hat, "are footmen stationed at Somerville House throughout the night?"

"Yes, sir. Except for in the family wing. His Grace prefers his privacy."

"I see." A tradesman such as Nash would have never been given a chamber in the family quarters. "So if someone elsewhere in the house left in the middle of the night, he would be observed by one of these night watchmen?"

"Indeed, sir. Once the household is abed, it would be difficult to leave Somerville House without being detected."

"And you saw the tailor, Mr. Nash, leave the following morning after he'd fitted the duke the previous evening."

"Yes, sir. Mr. Nash took a light breakfast before His Grace's coach returned him to his shop on Pall Mall."

Atlas thanked him and, placing his hat on his head, left Somerville House just as a light rain began to fall on Mayfair.

* * *

"You are acquainted with Somerville," Atlas said later to Charlton, when the earl dropped by his apartments before going to dinner at his club. "What do you know of his character?"

"He's a good sort, especially considering he hasn't had the easiest time of it. He came into the title when he was twelve and has been advised by his guardian, the late duke's cousin, since then. Cyril Eggleston is his name. He's a rather boorish and overbearing man."

That explained the identity of the man who'd inquired into the duke's business after encountering Atlas in the corridor. "And what sort of man is the duke?"

"I begin to see why you asked me to stop by." Charlton stepped past Jamie, who was dusting, and settled into his favorite stuffed seat in Atlas's sitting room. "Do not tell me the duke is somehow related to your investigation."

"He is." Atlas went on to share what he'd learned during his visit to Somerville House, that the duke provided his tailor with an alibi and about how Mrs. Warwick shared the same family name and hailed from the same village as Hastings, the duke's butler.

"And you'll recall Godfrey Warwick insisted his wife was running from something," he said in conclusion after laying out the particulars, "and Warwick's housekeeper says Mrs. Warwick came into the marriage bearing jewels fit for a princess."

"From that, you deduce what exactly? That before she became Mrs. Warwick, the lady was the butler's daughter who made off with the family jewels?" As he spoke, Charlton's gaze slid to Jamie and then back again.

"I must consider every viable possibility," Atlas said, "although I have difficultly envisioning Mrs. Warwick in the role of a servant."

"I agree. She possesses a bit too much hauteur to have come from such modest circumstances." Charlton stared at the rag in Jamie's hands as the boy walked from the sitting room, leaving them alone. "I say, is that a cravat the boy was cleaning with?"

"Sadly, yes." Atlas sighed. "A number of my cravats have recently had an unhappy meeting with the iron."

Charlton shook his head. "You really must acquire some competent servants."

Atlas couldn't disagree. "What about Somerville?" he asked, returning to the matter at hand. "Is he an honorable man?"

"He has always acted in a manner that is above reproach. I have become better acquainted with him in the last few years since he's come up from university." Charlton smoothed a wrinkle out of his waistcoat. "All in all, he appears to be an earnest young man intent on fulfilling his duties and being a credit to his late father."

"Not an easy role to fill," Atlas observed.

"Indeed not. His father was much admired, both as a statesman and for the competent manner in which he ran the duchy."

Atlas saw the door slamming shut on the possibility of Nash as a suspect. "I do not suppose Somerville would be inclined to provide his tailor with a false alibi."

Charlton dipped his chin. "If the duke says Nash was at Somerville House when your haberdasher was killed, I can see no reason to doubt him."

"I'm inclined to agree. Still, I would like to learn more about Nash."

"What do you intend to do? He did not seem amenable to answering more of your questions."

"I suppose I shall have to become a patron. He will hardly turn my custom away."

"At the very least, your endeavor will result in an exquisitely tailored coat." Charlton rose. "Are you engaged this evening?"

"No." Atlas pushed to his feet to see his friend out. "I shall be here at home, ruminating about the dearth of suspects in Warwick's death."

"Why don't you join me for dinner at the club? We can ruminate together and see if we cannot unearth a few more potential murderers."

Atlas readily accepted. Dinner and conversation about the case sounded very appealing. On their way out, Charlton paused by the game table to ponder the half-completed puzzle. "I see the Gainsborough is coming along nicely."

"I've still a bit of work to do on it."

Charlton studied the piles of loose pieces Atlas had grouped together by color—shades of green, blue, brown, and gray. "Why are you sorting these out?"

"Grouping like colors makes it easier to put the entire puzzle together."

Charlton shook his head. "I don't know where you find the patience."

"I find it relaxing to work on before I retire in the evening."

"Relaxing?" He drew out the word. "Good Lord, if I had to put this thing together, I'd go to bed with a megrim and proceed to have nightmares." They crossed over to the entryway where Jamie tended to the fire.

Charlton paused. "Can you spare your man for a few days?"

"Jamie, you mean?" Atlas asked, surprised.

"Yes."

"Me, your lordship?" The boy did not even bother to pretend he wasn't listening, as a well-trained servant should. He straightened from his crouched position before the hearth, his eyes owllike in his boyish face.

"Certainly," Atlas said. At least his cravats would be safe during Jamie's absence. "But whatever for?" He happened to know Charlton retained some of the best-trained servants in Mayfair.

Charlton addressed Jamie. "Present yourself tomorrow morning at the servants' entrance of my house on Curzon Street."

Atlas didn't think it was possible, but Jamie's eyes rounded even more. "Yes, my lord."

"You will be trained in all the arts of a valet de chambre."

Alarm flickered in Jamie's eyes. "A what?"

Atlas took pity on the boy. "He's going to see that you are trained in all the duties of a proper manservant."

Jamie brightened. "Yes, your lordship. Thank you." The boy was astute enough to realize receiving training in an earl's household could only enhance his marketability.

"And the first place your training will begin," said Charlton as he walked out the door, "is in the scullery."

The boy's face blanked.

"The laundry," Atlas explained as he followed his friend out.

* * *

It did not escape Atlas's notice that Charlton chose Boodle's, a purely social gentlemen's club on St. James Street, rather than Brooks's or White's, whose members had well-defined political affiliations. He suspected this was not because Charlton had no interest in matters of state but rather because he preferred subtlety when it came to politics.

The exclusive gentlemen's club was dressed in dark colors with plush Axminster carpets, fine upholsteries, and gleaming marble fireplaces. To Atlas's surprise, they encountered the Duke of Somerville in the eating room, sipping wine and dressed to perfection in unfussy designs exquisitely cut to his slender form. It was not difficult to see why the duke favored Nash's tailoring. It suited him.

The duke was not alone. He was joined by Cyril Eggleston, his former guardian.

Charlton paused as they passed the duke's table. "Well met, Somerville, Eggleston."

Some of Somerville's hauteur eased as he greeted the earl in a friendly manner. "Hello, Charlton." His attention moved to Atlas. "Catesby. This is a surprise. I have not seen you at Boodle's before."

He made a bow. "The earl was kind enough to invite me. I am not a member."

"I presume the dukedom is keeping you busy," Charlton said.

"It is a great responsibility for one so young," Eggleston interjected.

At the duke's cool look, Eggleston blushed and reached for his wine, keeping his gaze averted from the duke's.

The duke turned his attention to Charlton. "As I'm sure the earldom likewise keeps you engaged."

"Actually, we have had a spot of trouble recently," Charlton said easily. "The countess fears a servant has absconded with some of her jewels."

Atlas stared at his friend. This was the first he'd heard of Charlton's mother being burgled.

Eggleston frowned. "It is an outrage. Servants should be grateful to have a position. Those who resort to thievery deserve to be hanged in the public square."

Somerville reached for his wineglass. "I do hope you've caught the culprit."

"We believe we know who is responsible, but the thief seems to have taken the jewels and vanished."

"That is most unfortunate." The duke sipped his wine. "Please give the countess my sympathies."

"I suppose such unfortunate incidences occur more than we'd like to think," Charlton said. "What about you, Somerville? I trust the family jewels are intact?"

"Most assuredly. Thank you. We are fortunate to have never suffered that kind of loss."

The waiter arrived with the duke's food, prompting Atlas and Charlton to excuse themselves and leave the duke and his guardian to enjoy their meal.

"Eggleston is always inserting himself where he shouldn't," Charlton remarked as they walked to their table.

"How do you mean?"

"He seems loath to relinquish the role of guardian, even though Somerville is now grown and has taken control of the dukedom."

"I imagine running a dukedom is a heady thing for a distant cousin." They reached their table. "And that it would be difficult to relinquish the influence that comes with it."

"True." Charlton pulled out his chair. "Eggleston is keen to retain the role of Somerville's intimate advisor."

"And does the duke wish for him to continue in that role?"

"Eggleston was Somerville's guardian for many years, since the duke was twelve, and he appears to have overseen the dukedom with an able hand. Somerville feels he owes the man his gratitude."

"But in truth wishes he could toss his former guardian out on his pompous, overbearing arse?"

Charlton grinned as they took their seats. "So it would seem."

"By the way," Atlas said, changing the subject, "when was your mother relieved of her jewels? You never mentioned the loss."

Charlton's eyes sparkled. "Because it didn't happen."

"Just as I suspected." He grimaced. "You have very adequately disproved my theory."

"Quite." He paused as the waiter appeared and poured their drinks. The servers at Boodle's clearly knew what vintage the earl preferred, since he had not ordered the wine. Once the waiter moved away, Charlton continued. "If Mrs. Warwick is the Somerville butler's daughter, we now know she did not make off with the family jewels."

Atlas released a long breath. "The discovery presents more questions than it answers."

"How so?"

"Who is Lilliana Warwick really? And does her background have anything to do with her husband's murder? Can it really be just a coincidence that she shares a surname with the Duke of Somerville's butler?"

Charlton shrugged. "There could be a distant connection, I suppose. Perhaps Mrs. Warwick's father is a distant relation to the butler, from a branch of the family that has some means. It could explain why she appears to have been gently born and was in possession of fine jewels when she married Warwick."

"Perhaps." He glanced over to where Somerville and his guardian were eating. The memory of the duke staring after Mrs. Warwick that day in the park came back to him. "Tell me about the duke and his reputation with women."

Charlton gave him a quizzical look. "Are we no longer speaking of the murder investigation?"

He ignored the question because he did not care to answer it honestly. "I cannot help but wonder what it must be like for one so young to be in possession of an ancient title and one of the greatest fortunes in all of England. He must be surrounded by willing women."

"I have heard he keeps a mistress in Kensington. She is said to be a beautiful artist, but he is discreet and does not flaunt her. He maintains only that he is her patron and supports her artistic ambitions."

"He has not talked of wedding and begetting an heir?"

"Just recently, he has spoken of taking a wife in a year or so."

The waiter appeared, and while Charlton quizzed their server about the evening's food choices, new possibilities began to form in Atlas's mind. Possibilities he wasn't prepared to share with anyone, not even his friend.

It was obvious to him that Somerville had recognized Mrs. Warwick that day in the park and that there was some connection between the two of them. There was no mistaking the happiness that had shone on the duke's face when he'd laid eyes on her.

What if Somerville had once been smitten with the butler's daughter? What if he'd given her jewels as a token of his esteem for her? Or perhaps the gems were in recompense when he'd eventually cast her aside. There is no question that he would have had to break with her; a duke could never wed a butler's daughter, even if he truly cared for her.

Their parting would not have necessarily been a bitter one. If Godfrey was to be believed, his wife had kept a letter from her lover among her prized personal possessions. Perhaps the warm feelings lingered. Somerville thought to take a wife in a year or so. Around the same time Mrs. Warwick would be out of mourning.

A strange sensation clenched in his gut. His thoughts concerning Mrs. Warwick were becoming more muddled. He did not know if his suspicions regarding Somerville were rooted in rational thought or outlandish near impossibilities brought on by burgeoning jealousy and protectiveness. What he did know was that he could no longer trust himself to be objective where Lilliana Warwick was concerned.

And that could prove dangerous for them both.

Chapter Eighteen

"Damn and blast!" Atlas slammed the paper down on his sister's breakfast table. "This is the last thing Mrs. Warwick needs. Has she seen it?"

"No." Thea sipped her coffee. "Lilliana has not come down yet. She prefers to take the morning meal with the children in the nursery."

"The story does not mention her by name," Charlton said mildly. "There is that at least."

"That is very little consolation," Atlas said coldly.

The blind item in the morning paper referred to a murdered tradesman who might have gotten what he deserved after selling his wife to a gallant gentleman of quality. It was Thea who'd first taken note of the story and immediately summoned Atlas. He'd received her message after returning home from a morning hack through Hyde Park with Charlton, who'd promptly invited himself along.

"At least it doesn't come out and outright accuse her of doing away with her husband," Charlton added. "And you come off well. Gallant and a gentleman. High praise, indeed. The maidens of Mayfair will soon be swooning over you."

Atlas paced the room. "It will not be long before she is identified and a terrible scandal is attached to her name. I hardly know how to help her in that event. I had hoped to keep Warwick's degradation of her quiet. Once it becomes known, there will be quite a stain attached to her name."

"You could marry her." Thea scooped up a spoonful of kidney pie. "That would help mitigate the scandal."

Atlas halted in his tracks. "I beg your pardon?"

"I should think it would be no hardship," Thea said matter-of-factly, "considering the way you ogle her when you think no one is looking."

Atlas bristled. "I most certainly do not ogle Mrs. Warwick, or anyone else for that matter."

"But she is a tradesman's wife—" Charlton began.

"Was," Atlas corrected before he could stop himself.

"And as such," Charlton continued, "is far beneath you."

Thea glared at the earl. "What a boorishly high-handed thing to say." She dropped her spoon onto her plate with a clatter. "Unlike you, my brother does not care for the judgment of society."

Charlton shrugged, obviously unapologetic. "I am merely stating the facts."

"Thea is right." Atlas slipped into a seat at the breakfast table. "I'm hardly one to follow society's dictates. I do not put such store in the family bloodlines. We were decidedly middle class up until twenty years ago when our father was awarded the barony."

"What nonsense." Charlton precisely sliced a neat piece of his beefsteak. "Your bloodlines are more rarified than mine.

I cannot claim to be a descendant of King Edward III, as the Catesbys can." He looked straight at Thea. "So you see, my dear lady, you have a noble and royal ancestry that surpasses mine and is equal to any of the *ton*."

"I do not set store in such things," Atlas said.

Thea leaned forward, eagerness stamping her face. "Then you will consider it?"

Charlton shot her an amused look. "Is this your way of keeping your brother on terra firma? It would be difficult for a man to sail away with a ball and chain attached to his ankle."

Thea scowled at the earl, who simply raised his brows and held her gaze.

Atlas absentmindedly straightened the silverware at the place that had been hastily set for him by Thea's staff. "Marriage would be an extreme solution to Mrs. Warwick's dilemma."

"It might ground you," she said. "You have been adrift for far too long."

"Adrift?" He didn't hide his surprise. "I enjoy traveling and experiencing new cultures. That hardly means I am somehow unmoored."

"Doesn't it?" Sadness touched her eyes. "It seems to me that you've been unable to find your bearings since Phoebe died."

"What rot." An uncomfortable pressure bore down on his chest. "Just because I don't choose to live my life as you would like, that doesn't mean I require fixing."

"Good morning." Mrs. Warwick glided into the room. Atlas felt his face heat as he and the others returned her salutations and then fell silent.

"Pray do not let me interrupt your conversation." Mrs. Warwick poured herself a cup of coffee.

After a beat, Charlton spoke. "We are discussing the small supper party I am hosting on Tuesday next. I hope you will come too, Mrs. Warwick."

"I don't think so." She seemed unsure of how to respond. "I am in mourning."

"It will be a very small private affair," Charlton said.

"Do say you'll come," Thea urged. "Do not leave me alone with Atlas and Charlton. It will be good for you to get out. You've been cooping yourself up at home for too long."

The earl's face brightened. "There you have it. Even Mrs. Palmer will be in attendance, which means we're likely to discuss mathematics in great depth. How can you resist?"

Thea harrumphed. "I doubt you could discuss the subject at all, much less in great depth."

Mrs. Warwick smiled as her gaze bounced between Thea and Charlton. "If it is an intimate party, I suppose I could attend." She turned to Atlas. "What brings you here so early in the day? Is all well?"

Still disturbed by Thea's absurd assessment of his life, it took Atlas a moment to realize Mrs. Warwick referred to the investigation. "Quite well, actually. I stopped by to inquire as to whether you will permit me to accompany the children to the park later this afternoon after they are done with their lessons. I have purchased larger rolling hoops for them."

Something in her aloof gaze softened. "That is good of you but unnecessary. I'm sure you are very busy."

"Not that busy, apparently," Charlton piped in.

"I should like for Peter and Robin to know I am a man of my word," Atlas said, ignoring his friend's impertinence. "I have promised to show them how to jump back and forth through a rolling hoop and should like to do so today, since the weather is fine."

* * *

A couple of hours later, Atlas caught sight of Mrs. Warwick standing at the edge of the park, watching from afar as he showed Peter how to jump back and forth through the rolling hoop. He wondered how long she'd been observing them. He and the boys had arrived more than an hour ago, accompanied by Clara, who was acting as the boys' full-time nurse while they stayed with Thea. Atlas had presumed their mother wasn't coming.

The skies rumbled, and Atlas looked up see the gray clouds rolling in ominous splendor, threatening to unleash a torrent of rain. Mrs. Warwick left her observation post and came toward them.

"We should head for home," she said as she drew near. "It looks like a storm is coming." When Peter and Robin protested and insisted on demonstrating their newfound skills for her, she applauded and exclaimed when they did. Peter caught a frog and brought it to her just as they were ready to leave.

"May I take it with me?" he asked her, gingerly cradling his prize in one cupped hand and covering it with the other to prevent the creature from making a leaping escape.

"You most certainly may not," she admonished. "What would Mrs. Palmer think if you started bringing nasty little animals into her home?"

Atlas smiled. "Such a circumstance would not be completely alien to her. I was known to keep a frog or two when I was not much older than Peter."

The boy's eyes lit up as he shifted his admiring gaze to Atlas. "You were permitted to keep frogs in the house?"

"Not exactly. But since I very much wanted to watch my tadpoles transform into frogs, my sister Phoebe helped me hide them in my room." He smiled wistfully at the memory. For as long as he could remember, Phoebe had been his ally. "When they grew into frogs, however, she made me release them back into the pond near our home in the country."

Peter cast a hopeful look at his mother. "May I do the same, please? I will keep Froggie for a little while and then release it when we return to the country."

"Given that your frog is quite grown, and since we shan't return to the country for some time," she said to her son, "you may free the creature now so we can be on our way."

His shoulders slumped with disappointment, Peter knelt to release his catch and watched mournfully as it hopped away and disappeared into the nearest bush. He pushed heavily to his feet. "Mr. Catesby was very lucky to have had such a sister," he said, his expression sullen.

Atlas's throat felt sore. "I certainly was."

"It sounds as if you had quite an ally in her," Mrs. Warwick said gently.

"You could say so." He looked away momentarily. "Shall we go?"

They began the walk back to Great Russell Street, the boys rolling their hoops up ahead with their watchful nurse nearby while Atlas and Mrs. Warwick lingered farther behind to discuss the investigation.

"Did you know that Warwick and Bole argued before your husband died?" he asked.

"Did they?" The notion seemed to surprise her. "Bole usually followed Godfrey without question. I cannot imagine what they would have fought about. Do you know?"

"I do not. Bole is away, so I have not had a chance to speak with him as of yet." He clasped his hands behind his back as they walked. "I have also learned something else," he said reluctantly. "About Mrs. John Warwick and your husband."

"Verity and Godfrey? What of them?"

"Are you aware that once, long before Warwick met you, he wanted to marry Verity?"

She halted, obviously stunned. "Where did you hear that?"

He also stopped and faced her. "From Mrs. Greene."

"I would never have guessed. I never saw any sign."

"Her parents forced the marriage to John because he was the older son and stood to inherit."

She shook her head, still in apparent disbelief. "Verity seemed utterly devoted to John. I truly believe she loved him deeply."

"Mrs. Greene says the infatuation between Godfrey and Verity was youthful folly on both of their parts. That Godfrey came to Town to make his fortune while Verity truly came to love her husband."

"Yes." She nodded slowly. "That would make sense. Verity could not help but realize that John treated her with greater kindness than Godfrey ever would have." She searched his face. "Do you think this has something to do with Godfrey's death?"

"If it does, I cannot yet see how."

The boys shouted back to Atlas, insisting he watch them run through the hoops. This time Robin would dash through the hoop first and then Peter would follow. He applauded. "That is very good," he called out to them. "Soon you will be ready to learn more tricks."

She paused. "It is kind of you to offer, but I do not think it would be wise for you to take the boys out again."

He frowned. "Why, may I ask, do you object to my seeing the boys?"

"I do not want them to be hurt."

He took offense. "You think I would do injury to them?"

"Not purposely, no. But once Godfrey's killer is found, I plan to take them away and start anew someplace where no one knows us. I don't want them to become attached to anyone here."

He felt a stab of disappointment. "You will go off alone, just you and the children?"

"The newspapers have already begun to make reference to how Godfrey sold me. They have not identified me by name, but they will. I do not want the boys to face that scandal."

"Will their guardian allow it?"

"My husband's brother? I have not discussed the matter with John as of yet. But he is coming to Town in a week or two to visit with the children and to deal with matters related to the haberdashery, and I will do so then."

"Running away is not your only option." His words were measured. "There is another way to erase the taint."

She regarded him expectantly. "How so?"

Thea's solution to Mrs. Warwick's problem no longer seemed quite so extreme. "We could marry."

Her eyes widened. "Marry?"

"You and the boys would have the protection of my name."

"And you would share the taint of mine." She was incredulous. "I could never reward your gallantry and kindness by bringing notoriety to your family name. You deserve a virtuous wife of unquestionable character."

"Perhaps I should decide for myself the type of wife I deserve."

"A gentleman does not wed the widow of a tradesman, especially one of low reputation brought on by a public sale of her person," she said.

"This one would."

"Why do you have a habit of rescuing women?"

He frowned. "What has that got to do—?" Comprehension set in. "You think that is what I am doing by offering you marriage."

"We have hardly been courting. I have brought you nothing but trouble."

"That is not true." Atlas took a breath. He rarely spoke of the sister he'd lost, and yet he'd mentioned her twice already that afternoon. "I am sensitive to the plight of females because my own sister, Phoebe, suffered greatly at the hands of her husband."

"Your offer is a noble one but—"

"Gallantry has nothing to do with my offer." He interrupted before she could reject his offer outright. "Surely you have realized I am far from indifferent to your charms."

Her cheeks colored in a most becoming manner. "But what of your travels?"

"What about them?"

"You have said you are often abroad and that you intend to leave England again as soon as you are able."

He could not imagine giving up his travels, and yet . . . "Perhaps you and the boys would care to come. Their tutor could accompany us."

She stared at him. "You would take us with you?"

"If you would care to go." He spoke carefully. "Or we could take a house, and you could remain here. You would have the protection of my name without being overly burdened with a husband."

"You are not a burden," she said softly.

"Do not give me an answer now," he said. "But promise me you will at least carefully consider my offer."

"I will think on it. Under one condition."

At least she had not immediately rejected him. Something akin to hope stirred in Atlas's chest. "You have only to name it."

"If we are contemplating marriage, perhaps you should call me Lilliana."

"If it pleases you." He could not contain his smile. "And I am Atlas."

She mirrored his smile. "Very well, Atlas. I give you my word that I will seriously consider your offer."

* * *

They arrived back at Thea's to find Ambrose Endicott waiting for them.

"We meet again," Atlas said by way of greeting.

The runner's assessing gaze moved over their little group—from the boys and their nurse, to Lilliana and Atlas, all coming in together from an excursion. "Been out enjoying the day, have you?"

The boys went up with Clara while Atlas and Lilliana joined Endicott in Thea's formal parlor.

"To what do we owe this visit?" Atlas asked, too grated by the runner's constant intrusions to bother with the niceties.

"In truth, I did not expect to find you here, Mr. Catesby," Endicott said in his usual congenial manner. "It is, after all, Mrs. Warwick who lives here."

"As does my sister," Atlas said sharply, resenting the runner's unsubtle implication. "And I visit her regularly."

Lilliana clasped her hands in front of her. "What can I help you with, Mr. Endicott?"

"It has come to my attention that you and your late husband had words in front of Hatchards bookshop shortly before his untimely demise."

"That is true."

Endicott withdrew his notebook and pencil from his coat pocket. "May I ask what the altercation was about?"

"Certainly. My husband felt I was overspending. He confronted me about it that day."

"But the two of you had already, ah . . . parted company, had you not?"

"I was still his wife, and a husband is responsible for all a wife's debts."

"I see." The twinkle in the runner's eye suggested that he in fact did comprehend exactly what Lilliana had been up to. "And he would have raised a hand to you, but luckily, Mr. Catesby was on hand to prevent it."

"Yes."

"I see." The runner scribbled something down. "Well, that clears that matter up."

"If that will be all," Atlas said, ready to boot the man.

"I have one more matter to clear up with Mrs. Warwick." Endicott's manner was almost apologetic now, which made Atlas's muscles stiffen with alarm. "Did you believe you could kill your husband and not be held to account for the crime because the law regards the husband and wife as one entity?"

She scoffed. "Of course not. That's beyond absurd."

He referred to his notebook. "Did you not tell Barrister Ramsey Barrow that if you killed your husband, the law would consider it suicide?"

"Did Barrow tell you that?" Atlas demanded, remembering their visit to the barrister to discuss Lilliana's rights just after he and Charlton had brought her to London.

Lilliana laughed. Although how she could find humor in anything at the moment was beyond him. "Mr. Endicott, surely you cannot believe I honestly thought that to be the case."

He shrugged one hefty shoulder. "One of Barrow's clerks overhead you saying as much."

Atlas had a vague recollection of a pale, bespectacled young man poking his head through the door during Lilliana's meeting with the barrister.

Lilliana looked heavenward. "It was something said in frustration, in dark humor, nothing else. I assure you I recognize that murdering one's husband is a crime, and I would never even contemplate such a thing."

Endicott closed his notebook. "Even the best of people have been known to respond in a criminal manner when pushed beyond all endurance."

"That's it." Atlas struggled to keep ahold of his temper. "I think you should leave. Mrs. Warwick has answered your questions more than adequately."

"Yes, yes." Endicott slipped his notebook and pencil back into his pocket. "Oh, and one more thing, Mrs. Warwick? It's really a most curious matter."

"Oh?" she inquired politely. "And what is that?"

"No one in the village of Bewerley in Yorkshire seems to remember you. Isn't that strange? The Hastings are known there, but no one recalls a Lilliana Hastings."

Atlas doubted the runner detected the slight slip in Lilliana's composure before she recovered herself. "My parents and I left there when I was a very young girl. And they would remember me as Elizabeth. Lilliana is my middle name."

"I see," the runner said brightly. "Yes, of course, that explains everything most thoroughly." Atlas didn't think so, and he doubted Endicott did either. He accompanied the man to the front door, mostly to ensure the runner quit the premises without lurking around. He would not put it past Endicott to eavesdrop for valuable information if the opportunity presented itself.

"Quite a cozy picture of domesticity you present," the runner said in that infuriatingly amiable manner of his. "You and Mrs. Warwick and the children."

"What are you getting at, Endicott? Speak plainly." Atlas didn't bother to dissemble. "Are you wondering whether Mrs. Warwick and I did away with her husband so that our cozy little tableau could continue unimpeded?"

"*Did* you kill Mr. Warwick?" he asked. "You had motive, certainly, and opportunity. By all appearances, he was a hateful sort."

"If I had," Atlas said with some exasperation, "why would I return to the scene of the crime the following morning?"

They reached the entry hall, and Miller rushed to open the door. "As I said, I must consider all possibilities." Endicott went out. "Good day."

Atlas resisted the urge to slam the door on the runner's back. He was not so smitten with Lilliana that he would kill for her, but could the same be said for her supposed lover? His mind kept returning not only to the Duke of Somerville but also to the well-dressed older gentleman with the ruby ring who'd accosted Warwick at the haberdashery shortly before the man was killed. Who was he? What was his quarrel with Warwick? Did he have anything to do with Lilliana?

He returned to Lilliana, who watched him with worry in her eyes. "He can't possibly believe I admitted my intention to kill my husband and then carried out the crime, can he?"

"He must consider all possibilities. And he seems to favor the theory that Godfrey's killing was a crime of passion."

"That passion being hate, I presume?"

"Is there a man who cares so strongly for you that he would kill for you?"

She huffed a mirthless laugh. "If there is, I have not met him."

"Endicott clearly suspects me, but I fear he is also speculating about your possible involvement in your husband's death. If there is another viable suspect, you must tell him."

She stared at him. "What is it that you are asking me?"

He found it difficult to form the words. "Bole told me Godfrey suspected there had been a man before him."

Her face went white. She shook her head. "It isn't true."

"I do not sit in judgment of you. But if you are protecting this man at the possible cost of your own freedom—"

"Is that what you think? That I am motivated by some sort of noble love? It isn't true, although Godfrey believed it was."

"Why would he believe that?"

"I was a maiden when I wed Godfrey." She turned away. "But a man has certain expectations about . . . what he will find once he beds his wife . . . and Godfrey did not find it."

It took him a moment to understand what she was trying to tell him.

"I don't know why he did not find it. I had never submitted to a man in that way before, and I haven't since."

Comprehension settled over him. She hadn't bled when Godfrey had taken her, which led her husband to deduce there'd been another before him. It was just as Bole, the Slough magistrate, had said. "I will take you at your word."

"Will you?" she asked, her demeanor cool. "That is more than my husband ever did. And he never let me forget it."

Chapter Nineteen

After taking his leave of Lilliana, Atlas went directly to Smithfield, not far from St. Bartholomew's Hospital, where Archibald Rivers kept an office. He kept watch from across the way until he spotted the medical examiner leaving the building.

He crossed the street, dodging a fast-moving curricle and trying to avoid the muddiest patches. Pain flared in his left foot, which felt swollen and tender, suggesting that his decision to undertake the forty-five-minute walk from Mayfair, rather than hail a hackney, had been ill-advised. He managed to get to the other side of the road in time to cross paths with Rivers.

"Mr. Catesby, isn't it?" Rivers said, clearly remembering their meeting to discuss the cause of Warwick's death.

"Yes," Atlas replied. "Good afternoon." They exchanged the usual niceties, and then Atlas fell silent, uncertain of how to broach the sensitive subject that had brought him to Smithfield. At his core, he took Lilliana at her word, but he was no longer objective where she was concerned and didn't want his lack of impartiality to hinder the investigation.

Rivers seemed to sense his discomfort. "I'm heading toward the hospital if you care to walk with me."

Atlas fell in beside him, trying not to limp even though his injured foot protested with every step. "I have a medical question of a very delicate nature," he began.

"I assure you that anything we discuss will be held in the strictest confidence."

"It is about . . . the female anatomy."

"Go on."

His cheeks warmed. "Is it possible for a maiden not to . . . erm . . . bleed on her wedding night?"

If the question shocked Rivers, he showed no sign of it. "Indeed it is. Some females are born without the membrane that ruptures when a woman's body is breached on her wedding night. The bleeding from the torn membrane is what is seen as proof of a female's maidenhead."

"And in other cases?"

"I suspect many maidens break this membrane or partially tear it long before their husbands bed them."

"How does that happen?"

"In a variety of ways. Physical activity, such as riding a horse, is often thought to be the cause of such ruptures."

Lilliana was an able and enthusiastic equestrian, as were most gently raised young ladies. Atlas wondered how many innocent young women of quality had come pure to the marriage bed only to be censured when their husbands found no tangible evidence of their chastity.

Rivers came to a stop, and Atlas realized they'd reached the King Henry VIII gate at St. Bart's. Above the arched entrance, the dour face of the king who'd done away with several of his wives stared down at them. He thanked Rivers and prepared to bid him farewell.

"One more thing, Doctor, if I may," he began hesitantly. "It's about my foot."

Rivers nodded. "I couldn't help but notice it seems to be troubling you."

"Yes." He'd begun to fear the affliction was permanent. "I broke it several months ago, but it still pains me."

"That is understandable. There are more than two dozen bones in the foot and even more joints."

"I gather you are telling me that all adds up to a plethora of opportunity for pain," Atlas said grimly. "I worry the broken bones in my foot did not heal properly."

"Did you see a bonesetter?"

"I was treated by a qualified surgeon, Dr. Armitrage."

"I am acquainted with him. Armitrage is an able surgeon." Rivers nodded his approval. "Did he fashion a splint along the anterior surface?"

"Yes, and I kept it elevated for weeks." His damned recuperation had seemed interminable, and his foot still wasn't properly healed. "Can I expect it to return to normal?"

"Allow it time to heal, and ice the injury when you can, especially after you exert yourself. That will help alleviate the discomfort."

After the two men parted ways, Atlas hailed a hackney on Giltspur Street to take him back to Mayfair. He intended to stop by Thea's on the way home to get some ice for his foot. Settling back into the cramped cab, he thought of Lilliana's assertion that there had been no other man. He'd just learned that medical science could explain why she hadn't bled on her wedding night. The possibility of Lilliana having a lover who had killed Warwick now seemed more remote than ever.

The new developments meant he could eliminate Somerville as a suspect; the duke had no apparent motive for wanting Warwick dead. The identity of the man with the ruby ring remained a mystery, but for the moment, there was nothing connecting him to Lilliana.

There was still the matter of the supposed love letter Godfrey had found among Lilliana's things, but at least no other man had been in her bed. That piece of knowledge heartened him, although the painful throbbing in his foot was the very devil.

* * *

When Atlas arrived at Thea's, he found the place practically deserted. Fletcher, who remained on duty, informed him that Thea was out and that most of the servants had the afternoon off to attend the wedding celebration of a former housemaid.

Presuming Lilliana was with the children and not wishing to intrude, Atlas headed out to the icehouse, intending to be on his way once he'd gotten some ice for his foot. However, as soon as he stepped onto the brick patio, something smacked him in the head.

"So sorry, sir." Miller, Thea's footman, bounded over and caught the ball in midair as it bounced off Atlas.

Peter, followed by his younger brother, scampered down the narrow brick stairs leading from the cramped garden and came to a screeching halt when he spotted their visitor. "Mr. Catesby, come play catch with us," Peter pleaded, his face damp and red from exertion.

Atlas didn't think his aching foot was up to the task. "I'm afraid I cannot, boys. My old injury is bothering me, and I've come for some ice to put on it."

"You're going to the icehouse?" Peter's eyes lit up. "May I come with you?"

Recalling Lilliana's concerns, he decided it best not to abet the boy's infatuation with the icehouse. "Perhaps another time."

"Please, please, please," Peter implored, the words like rapid-fire bullets.

Robin wrinkled his nose. "It's cold and dark in there."

Atlas looked around for help but saw no sign of either Lilliana or Clara. "Are you on duty with the children?" he asked Miller.

"Just until Mrs. Warwick returns, sir." Miller bopped the ball between his two hands. "Clara went to the wedding, so I told her I'd look after the boys."

"Where is Mrs. Warwick?"

"Cannot say, sir. She was supposed to go up to the nursery to relieve Clara, but when she was delayed, I offered to step in."

"Do you know what kept Mrs. Warwick?"

"No, sir. She must have stepped out. It's only been about twenty minutes or so. I expect she'll be back shortly."

Seeing no way to put Peter off, Atlas consented to the boy accompanying him to the icehouse while Robin went inside with Miller to see if Cook could offer them a cool drink.

The icehouse was a small, rudimentary, but solid-looking structure. Made of stone, it had a short, wide-bolted door at its front. Greenery grew on its roof and around its sides. Atlas unbolted the door and pushed it open. A rush of cool air greeted him. Peering into the darkness, Atlas wished he'd remembered to bring a candle, but Peter wasn't put off by the uninviting conditions. He eagerly stepped inside.

"Careful," Atlas warned. "Stay with me." It wasn't as if the boy could get lost inside the place. Thea's icehouse was very small, but Atlas wasn't taking any chances with the boy's safety.

They took a few steps farther inside, Atlas squinting as his eyes adjusted to the darkness. He rubbed his arms. It was freezing. He wanted to obtain his ice and get back outside to the relative warmth as soon as possible.

Dim light from the open door barely illuminated the large chunks of ice stacked up against the walls. His foot touched something. He peered down at the shadowy, indistinguishable shape on the floor before them.

"What is that?" He addressed the question more to himself than to the boy.

Peter knelt down for a closer look and reached out to touch the still form. "I think it's Mama."

* * *

"Fetch a doctor." Atlas spoke sharply to Miller as he placed Lilliana's limp form on her bed. "And be quick about it."

"Very good, sir." The footman paused at the door. "Shall I send word alerting Mrs. Palmer as to what has occurred?"

"No. There's no use interrupting her afternoon. Perhaps after the doctor arrives and we know what we are dealing with. But do stay with the children. Peter is still in the garden. Make certain both boys are safe."

Fletcher appeared in the doorway, concern lining his forehead. Despite his advanced age, Thea's butler always seemed aware of everything that occurred under her roof. "How may I be of service?"

Atlas stared at Lilliana. His gut clenched at the blue tint of her fair skin. He needed to get the wet clothes off her; they encased her like a sheet of ice. "She needs her lady's maid. Send for her at once."

"I believe Mrs. Warwick uses Cleo, Mrs. Palmer's maid, but Cleo has the afternoon off. She left after dressing Mrs. Palmer."

"The devil!" His head spun. He somehow needed to get Lilliana warmed up. "Send any one of the female servants up immediately."

Fletcher cleared his throat. "There is no one, sir. Aside from myself and Miller, most of the servants have the afternoon off."

He cursed. "Then we shall have to wait for the doctor."

Fletcher withdrew, closing the door behind him.

Atlas swallowed down his rising panic at the sight of Lilliana on the bed—lifeless, her face deathly white, her lips a frightening shade of blue. When they'd found her motionless in a fetal position, her body icy to the touch, he felt as though someone had twisted a knife in his gut. Although, not wishing to alarm Peter, he'd reassured the boy that she was merely resting before whisking her back to the house. God help him if he had come too late. A tap on the door was followed by the reappearance of Fletcher. "The doctor is delayed. He is attending to the Duchess of Trentham and will come as soon as he can."

"What the devil are we to do in the meantime?"

"The doctor says to warm Mrs. Warwick up as much as possible."

"Have you checked on the boys?" If someone had tried to hurt Lilliana, they could very well have gone after the children too. He'd tasked Peter with bolting the icehouse door closed. He'd wanted to distract the boy from his mother's condition.

"Yes, they are well. And Miller has instructions to stay with them in the nursery." Fletcher bowed out, leaving Atlas feeling helpless.

If no one else was here to warm Lilliana, the task fell to him. Determined to do so as quickly as possible, he turned her gently over so he could access the tiny buttons running down the length of her gown. He made quick work of them and shifted her chilled body so that he could remove the thin gown, shuddering at the thought of Lilliana alone in the dark in the frosty icehouse with nothing to shield her from the cold but this flimsy muslin gown.

He unlaced her stays and pulled them off, leaving her in her shift and stockings. He reached under her shift and ran his hands up her stockings until he felt cold, velvety skin and untied her garters. He relieved her of her stockings, one after the other, averting his gaze to afford her what little privacy he could, leaving her only in her shift. He pulled the cover-pane over her inert form and found two more blankets in the wardrobe to place on top of that. Still, every part of her body remained icy cold.

Desperation riled through him. There was nothing to be done for it. Shrugging out of his own jacket, he stripped down until he wore only his smallclothes and the hand-shaped amulet on a chain around his neck that he rarely took off. He slipped into bed beside her, determined to use his own body warmth to bring her circulation back.

Ignoring his own discomfort as her glacial skin touched his, he wrapped his arms around her and encased her in his body heat. He was on his side and turned her to face him so that they had full body contact, their legs interlocked. Gritting his teeth against the frigid iciness of her body, he ran his hands over her skin to help warm her and pressed his cheek against hers, saying a silent prayer as he did so.

He did not know how long it was—it seemed an eternity—before her body finally seemed to absorb some of his warmth. He rubbed his hands over her arms and shoulders, desperate for some sign of wakefulness. Seeing Lilliana this way, still and expressionless, wrenched his insides.

Hope thudded in his chest when she began to stir. She nestled against him, and her eyes finally fluttered open.

"Lilliana? Can you hear me?"

Eyes the color of autumn leaves blinked a few times before focusing on his face just inches from hers.

"Darling, can you speak?" The endearment seemed to slip out of his mouth of its own volition. "It's Atlas."

"What . . . happened?" she asked in a gravelly voice.

"You were locked in the icehouse." He feathered a hand across the cool porcelain skin of her cheek, relieved to find it merely cold instead of frigid. "Do you remember?"

"Yes, I think so." Her face clouded. "It was so cold."

"Can you recall how you ended up there?"

"The servant said Peter was playing in the icehouse again, and I went to get him."

He stiffened. "Which servant?"

"William, I think his name is." She licked her dry lips. "I was surprised to see him. He does not usually venture abovestairs."

Dread crawled up his spine. "Did he accompany you to the icehouse?"

She nodded. "And then he locked me in." When she shivered at the memory, he drew her closer to the warmth of his body. "It was awful. There was no escape. I anguished about what would happen to the boys if I were to—"

"Shhh." He pressed a light kiss to her forehead. "You are safe now." Inside him, fury churned. William had deliberately tried to hurt Lilliana. She'd been left to freeze to death inside the icehouse.

Her eyes fluttered as she looked past him, as if she'd just become aware of their surroundings. "Where are we?"

"In your bedchamber."

Her gaze dropped to his bare chest. Confusion clouded her eyes when she looked down at her own body and realized she wore nothing but her shift. Some color tinged the pallor of her face. Relief flooded him at the sign her circulation was returning to normal.

"What . . . ?" She stammered. "I don't understand why . . ." Her questions trailed off.

"We are awaiting the doctor," he explained. "You were so cold, your lips were blue. I feared for your life, so I used my body heat to encourage your body temperature to return to safe levels." As he spoke, now that his fear for her had eased, he suddenly became physically aware of her as a woman. One who appealed to him. Very much.

The most masculine part of him became sensitive to the subtle curves of her willowy body snuggled against his, soft breasts pressed against his bare chest, their limbs still intertwined in an intimate fashion.

His body reacted, hardening in a quick swell. Cursing inwardly at his own baseness, he broke away from her softness and bounded up from the bed with the alacrity of a man escaping a raging fire.

She watched him with growing alertness, her attention wandering over his bare body. Satisfaction rippled through him when he detected a glimmer of interested appreciation in her inspection. Her gaze dropped to his smallclothes, to where his obvious arousal strained against the cotton fabric.

His face burning, he jerked on his breeches to cover himself. "I do beg your pardon."

Alarm crossed her face. "Where are the boys?" She sat up. "What if that man went after them next?"

"They are well." He reached for his shirt. "They are safe with Miller."

She clutched the bed linens to her chest. "How can you be certain?"

"I had Fletcher check on them." He pulled his white linen shirt over his head. "Miller is with the boys in the nursery and has strict instructions not to let them out of his sight."

She watched him don his waistcoat. "I was on my way to the nursery to be with them before that man told me Peter was in danger."

"We are going to find this William person and get to the bottom of this."

"You found me before it was too late." A small smile tilted her lips. "Coming to my rescue once again."

He shrugged into his jacket, determined to look decent before the doctor arrived. "I'm thankful I arrived in time."

"As am I." She ran a hand through her hair, pushing a dark tendril away from her face. "Why did you come? Has there been a new development in the investigation?"

"No, nothing like that." He hesitated, not caring to discuss his lingering injury with anyone. "I came to avail myself of Thea's ice."

"For your foot?"

"Yes. Ice helps relieve the discomfort." He never thought he'd be grateful for his injury, but without it and his need of ice to ease his pain, Lilliana might have died.

He paused before continuing. "I also want to apologize for my impertinent question about issues of great privacy to you. And to assure you I do not doubt your word."

"Thank you," she said quietly.

He rubbed the back of his neck. "And I apologize again for any offense I caused in relation to—" he gestured toward the bed.

She smiled. "You saved my life. I should thank you, not censure you."

"Nonsense." He bristled. "I did what anyone else in my place would do."

"And I did not take offense to—" She gestured in the general direction of his person.

He grimaced. "It's unseemly."

"It's human, and I am not innocent to the physical impulses of men," she said, her voice gentle. "Besides, you only offered proof of what you yourself have already said."

Confusion crossed his face. "And what is that?"

A knowing gleam entered her beautiful eyes. "That you are not indifferent to my, as you termed it, charms."

They were interrupted by a knock on the door and the arrival of the doctor. Atlas stepped out while the doctor examined Lilliana and learned from Fletcher that William was nowhere to be found. After asking the butler to send for Endicott at Bow Street, he went out back to examine the garden and path leading to the icehouse.

The bolt on the icehouse door could not have been thrown by accident. The only way to get locked inside was if someone bolted the door from the outside. He came back into the house to find that Endicott had already arrived and was interviewing Fletcher and Miller.

"Mr. Catesby." The runner looked up from his notebook. "I hear it was a near thing for Mrs. Warwick this evening."

"I'll say." Lilliana drifted down the stairs in a white dressing gown that enhanced the pallor of her fine skin. "Someone tried to kill me."

"Why are you out of bed?" Atlas strode to the foot of the stairs, watching as she descended with the breezy fabric of her dressing gown floating behind her. "You should be resting."

Before today, he had never seen her hair down. It was black as coal, highlighting her flawless porcelain skin, and glistened like the night sea. "As if I could sleep. The doctor says I am fine, albeit very fortunate to have escaped any lastin effects from being locked in the icehouse." She reached the landing and turned to the runner. "What do you make of it, Mr. Endicott?"

"Before I draw any conclusions, I should very much like to hear your version of events, yours and Mr. Catesby's."

"Why don't we do it over a drink?" Atlas led the way to the parlor. "I could certainly use one."

While Atlas poured the brandy, Lilliana told the runner how she came to be locked in the icehouse. "He left me there on purpose," she said in conclusion.

Endicott looked up from his note-taking. "Can you be absolutely certain?"

Her expression firmed. "Yes. He even bade me to go farther inside the icehouse, away from the door." She hugged herself against the memory. "When I turned to tell him Peter wasn't there, he slammed the door and slid the bolt into place."

Endicott scribbled in his notebook. "Fletcher tells me William is one of the newer footmen, only been here a few months. His room in the attic servants' quarters has been completely cleaned out. He's taken his things and vanished."

Atlas's pulse thundered in his head. "You have to bloody well find him."

"And so we will." Endicott looked up, speaking in his usual affable manner. "My men are out looking for him as we speak. In time, we'll run him to ground."

"First Godfrey and now me." Lilliana's fine-boned hands fisted and unfisted the skirt of her dressing gown. "Who would want to do away with us both?"

Atlas pressed a glass of brandy into her hands. "Who benefits if both you and Godfrey are out of the picture?"

She closed her eyes and sipped from her brandy before opening them again. "I do not know. Everything passes to the children."

Endicott chewed on the end of his pencil, his expression thoughtful. "We cannot automatically assume this attempt on Mrs. Warwick's life is related to her husband's murder."

She regarded him with surprise. "Surely you do not think it was a coincidence."

"It seems unlikely," he allowed. "However, if we make assumptions without concrete proof, we risk missing clues that would lead us to the true culprit."

"Lilliana?" Thea stood on the threshold, her face wrought with concern. "Fletcher says you were locked in the icehouse. Are you well?"

Lilliana nodded. "Yes, supremely so, especially when one considers what could have happened."

Atlas exhaled. "I got to her in time after William locked her in the icehouse."

Thea's face froze. "William, my new footman? Surely he didn't leave her there deliberately."

"Most deliberately, I'm afraid," Lilliana said.

Thea blinked. "But why?"

Atlas shifted, restless. "That's what we'd all like to know."

"He was most likely hired by someone else." Endicott turned to a blank page in his notebook. "What can you tell us about your former employee?"

Thea regarded him with a blank expression on her face. "Who?"

"This William fellow," the runner said. "I think we can safely assume he has no intention of returning."

Thea's face blanked. "I know nothing about him. He's only been here a few months. And Fletcher and the housekeeper handle all the hiring." It was no surprise to Atlas that Thea, as engrossed as she was in her math studies, knew little about the newer servants.

"No matter." Endicott closed his notebook. "We are looking into it and should turn him up soon. I'll see myself out. In the meantime, I will have one of my men stand guard outside as a precaution."

Atlas stifled a curse. He needed to find whoever was trying to harm Lilliana. And he couldn't shake the sense that, in order to do so, he would need to find Godfrey Warwick's killer.

He'd almost reached home after leaving Lilliana and Thea when he realized he'd missed the appointment he'd set days ago with Kirby Nash.

He wanted to get a better sense of the tailor, and having a few tailcoats made by the man would afford him that opportunity. He got to the shop on Pall Mall just as one of Nash's clerks was closing up for the evening, but the shop attendant recognized him.

"Everyone else has gone home, but Mr. Nash is still inside," the clerk told him as he unlocked the door to let Atlas in. "He said he wasn't leaving just yet, that he'd wait a little while longer for you."

Atlas thought it odd that Nash would remain behind, waiting for him, while sending everyone else at the shop home. He stepped inside, and the clerk locked the door behind him and went on his way. The shop floor was dark, with only a few lanterns burning. "Mr. Nash?"

Silence met his inquiry. Perhaps the tailor was waiting for him in the back room. Atlas had already seen his books and maps, which meant Nash had nothing to hide on that account. But an awareness that all was not as it should be prickled his neck. He purposely lightened his footfalls, muting his approach. If someone was lying in wait for him, Atlas would be the one to take the assailant by surprise and not the other way around.

The door to Nash's private back room was ajar, and a guttural groan sounded from within. As he drew nearer, Atlas caught sight of the man locked in a passionate embrace. His amour's face and most of her body were obscured as Nash pressed her smaller form up against the bookshelves with his. The tailor's paramour ran her gloved hands hungrily over the man's body, down his back, and over his buttocks to the place where their hips ground together.

Nash groaned. "I have to have you now."

Just as Atlas was about to quietly retreat and leave them to their privacy, Nash turned his head, and the flushed, amorous face of the Duke of Somerville came into view.

Chapter Twenty

Somerville ran a tender hand through Nash's dark hair with its unusual streak of gray. "I've missed you."

Shock rendered Atlas momentarily immobile. It was one second, maybe two, but it was long enough for Somerville to sense his presence. The duke's soft, passion-hazed gaze landed on him and settled there, uncomprehending for a moment, before realization, then alarm, sharpened in his soft-brown eyes.

Atlas's heart hammered. It was folly to leave. His presence had been noted, and there was certainly no unseeing what he'd just witnessed. It was too late to pretend he hadn't. From his place just outside the door, he turned, giving them his back and a modicum of privacy to put themselves to rights.

It was a minute or two before the duke summoned him. "You may as well join us, Catesby." His voice was calm, almost relaxed.

Atlas pivoted and walked inside. The lovers were far apart now—Nash at the opposite end of the room pouring drinks, the duke settled in a comfortable leather seat near the hearth, giving no indication of distress, even though they all knew buggery was punishable by death.

The duke tracked his movements with a keen gaze. "Please sit."

Still numb from the shock, Atlas lowered himself on the green leather sofa. He knew such men existed, of course, but to witness their intimate interaction was something else entirely. "Forgive the interruption," he managed to say. "Nash's man unlocked the door and directed me back. He was under the impression Nash was alone."

The duke rested his elbows on the armrests and steepled his fingers under his chin. "I entered through the back. He would not have known I was here."

Nash came over to hand the duke a splash of brandy. Somerville's hard gaze softened as he accepted the glass, his fingers brushing Nash's for a brief moment. "My thanks."

The expression of tenderness on the duke's face astonished Atlas. He had always assumed buggery to be motivated purely by lust, by physical impulses, but he detected something more intimate in the interactions between these two men.

"Brandy?" Nash's face was a mask of inscrutability as he extended the glass to Atlas, but the slight tremble in his hand betrayed his nerves.

"Thank you." Accepting the drink, he took a long swallow to settle his own nerves. His mind reeled from what he'd just discovered. The idea that the duke could be a molly seemed incomprehensible. Atlas barely noticed when Nash slid into a spot at the opposite end of the sofa.

The duke sipped his brandy. "Naturally, you will be well compensated to disregard what you have seen this evening."

Atlas held his gaze. "That will not be necessary."

Nash moved restlessly. The duke leaned back in his chair, crossing one ankle over his knee, his posture utterly relaxed. "Very well. What will your silence require?"

"What I have seen this evening is no one's business, least of all mine." Indeed, he'd prefer to wipe the past five minutes from his memory—if only that were possible.

Somerville studied him. "I fear I don't exactly take your meaning."

"This goes no further." Atlas glanced at Nash, then immediately looked away. "I swear on my honor that I will not breathe a word of it to anyone."

Somerville and Nash exchanged a look before the duke spoke again. "That is all you have to say on the matter?"

He inclined his head. "I cannot conceive of what else there is to say, except to add that I deeply regret the intrusion." Beside him, Nash released a harsh breath.

Somerville sipped his brandy. "Charlton speaks highly of you. He says you are a man of your word."

"I am."

"Then I shall consider the matter closed."

Atlas looked into Nash's ashen face. "This is the secret that Warwick discovered, isn't it? The reason he was extorting money from you."

Somerville answered for him. "Yes, he found us here, much in same way you did this evening."

Nash was agitated. "I locked the door this time. No one should have been able to enter."

"Your man recognized me. He let me pass because he thought you were expecting me." But even as he said the words, Atlas realized Nash had used the pretense of waiting for him as an excuse to remain behind at the shop for a secret assignation with the duke.

"Yes, I had expected you earlier," Nash said tightly. "But the shop is closed. I had locked up for the night."

"It is all right, Kirby." The duke's words were gentle. "Do not reproach yourself." He looked at Atlas. "Now that there is no longer any reason to dissemble, you understand that Mr. Nash has an alibi for the evening of Warwick's murder."

"He was with you."

"Yes, in my bedchamber, all night. I assure you I would have known if Kirby had left." Intimacy wrapped around the way the duke's lips framed his lover's name.

"You intended to pay to keep Warwick quiet."

"Yes, but in the end, it didn't come to that. He died before the first payment was delivered."

"You must have worried that he couldn't be trusted to keep his mouth shut."

"Not at all." The duke took a leisurely sip of his brandy. "Men like Warwick are motivated by greed. As long as I kept the funds coming, I knew the haberdasher would rather cut out his tongue than risk losing the income I was prepared to provide."

"I see." Atlas rose to his feet, eager to escape the uneasy tension hovering in the air. "Thank you for the brandy. I'll see myself out."

He hastened through the dark shop and stepped outside, pulling the door shut behind him. Fog blanketed the ground, but he barely noticed as he turned automatically toward Bond Street.

The duke and Kirby Nash. The very idea astounded. He forced the more salacious aspects of this evening's revelations from his thoughts. Once he did, the list of possible suspects in Warwick's murder reshuffled in his mind for the second time that day. The duke might think he'd saved his lover by giving him an alibi, but Somerville had also revealed something far more damning; both he and Nash had a compelling reason to want Warwick dead. The murdered man had discovered their deepest secret, one that could send them both to the gallows.

He could not think of a more powerful motive for murder.

* * *

He was surprised to hear whistling coming from his bedchamber when he reached home. The clean scents of beeswax and lemon greeted him the moment he entered his apartments, and he noted that the gleaming floors had been freshly polished since that morning. He found Jamie in his bedchamber putting away immaculately laundered cravats and snowy linen shirts, all of which had been expertly pressed.

"Don't tell me you've perfected the art of laundry after just three days away," he said to the boy.

"No, sir, these were cleaned and pressed by his lordship's staff." Jamie walked into the dressing room to put away a pile of cravats, calling out to Atlas in a muffled voice. "I'm to arrange them for you before returning to Curzon Street to continue my training."

Atlas surveyed his bedchamber, taking note of the shiny surfaces and crisp, clean bed linens. "I see Charlton is determined to see to my comforts while you are away."

Jamie reappeared. "Yes, sir, and Mrs. Garroway, the earl's cook, sent supper. It's still warm, and there's some sweet rolls that will keep until morning for breakfast."

Hunger yawned in his stomach, reminding him he had not eaten since that morning. He wandered out to the sitting room and sat at the small table, pulling away the linen cloth covering the food tray Jamie had set out.

The aroma of pigeon pie and rich, succulent lamb filled his nostrils. Atlas was beginning to see he'd be well looked after during Jamie's training. The boy appeared with a bottle of wine and poured as Atlas tucked into the generous cut of lamb.

"There's plenty," he said between bites. "You are welcome to share the meal with me."

"Thank you, sir, but no thank you." Jamie's posture—straight-spined with shoulders back—had never seemed so perfect.

"Why not?" He eyed the boy. "Surely you are hungry. You are always ready to eat."

"It wouldn't be proper, sir. My role is to see to my gentleman's every need, to make certain he wants for nothing." Jamie's scrawny chest puffed up with pride. "No proper valet would take a meal with his master."

"I see," Atlas said with some amusement. "And are valets meant to attend table at meals as well?"

Jamie inclined his chin. "Yes, sir. If there is no footman, it is my place to serve at table." Atlas bottomed out his wine, which Jamie promptly refilled. "My role is to see to it that your day goes smoothly from the moment you awaken until you retire in the evening."

Atlas took another healthy swallow of wine. Weariness tugged at him. "I certainly would have welcomed a more tranquil day than the one I experienced today."

Jamie eyed him sympathetically. "Is it trouble with the investigation then?" Atlas briefly recounted the attempt on Lilliana's life. Jamie's eyes widened. "Why would anyone want to kill Mrs. Warwick? Has it anything to do with Mr. Warwick's murder?"

"I'm not certain what to think." The terrible image of Lilliana lying cold and motionless replayed in his mind. "The way Warwick was killed suggests it was more a crime of passion than a well-thought-out murder, while the attempt on Mrs. Warwick's life appears to have been planned well in advance."

Jamie nodded. "I don't know why anyone would want to do away with Mrs. Warwick, but I am not surprised about her husband. He was a nasty one, was Mr. Warwick. He could rile up an angel. Why, he even drove poor Miss Verity to tears, and she being so gentle and delicate-like."

"Verity?" Atlas's forkful of pigeon pie paused in midair. "Are you speaking of John Warwick's wife?"

"The very same, and she was overset after their meeting."

"What?" Atlas put his fork down. "When did this meeting take place?"

"Maybe one month before he died."

"Was Miss Lilliana present?"

"No, Miss Verity came when Miss Lilliana was out with the boys."

"Do you have any notion of what was discussed?"

Jamie shook his head. "They walked too far into the garden to be overheard."

Interesting, that. Perhaps the youthful love affair between the two had not ended after all. John Warwick did not seem the murderous type, but what if he'd discovered his wife was having an affair? And Verity was dead too. John could have done away with both of them in a jealous rage. "Did Godfrey and Verity often meet in private?"

"No, never, not that any of the servants saw."

"So this visit was unusual."

"Yes, we all remarked upon it. Nothing improper took place, because they stayed in plain sight where we could all see them. But the staff did think it was strange that they would go for a walk together."

"How do you know he upset her?"

"We couldn't hear much, but at the end of their conversation, Mr. Godfrey raised his voice and laughed. He said he would finally beat Master John where it mattered most because his child would inherit everything after John died."

"Meaning Godfrey's son, Peter, because John and his wife had no children?"

He nodded. "Everyone knows Peter is Master John's heir. Miss Verity rushed away, and when she passed me, I saw she was crying." Jamie shook his head. "It was wrong of Mr. Warwick to remind Miss Verity of her childless state. Everyone knew how much she wanted children."

"Did Godfrey often entertain female visitors?"

"Not that I ever saw. He never stayed in Slough for long when he visited. He came Saturday afternoons and would leave Monday morning."

Which wouldn't leave much time for Godfrey to conduct an illicit affair with his brother's wife. So why had Verity gone to see Godfrey, and what had he said to upset her?

He wasn't sure whether the encounter had any bearing on Godfrey's death, but he thought another visit to John Warwick might be in order.

The following day was Tuesday, and in the morning, after enjoying the sweet buns Charlton's cook had sent over, Atlas set out for Slough to see Felix Bole and, hopefully, John Warwick. The ride to Slough would take two hours, and he expected to be back in Town well before dark.

Although Bole, the magistrate, had returned from holiday, he was not at home when Atlas called, but he finally managed to track Godfrey Warwick's friend down at the local church across the village green, where he was attending a committee meeting. Inside, the old stone church, which was likely built during medieval times, showed its age in the uneven slate floors and high stone bases supporting hefty oak posts. During a break in the meeting, Atlas took the opportunity to approach the man.

"Mr. Catesby." Bole's unkempt sandy brows lifted. "Back in our fair county, I see. Have you made any progress in the investigation?"

"I've learned a great deal, but I do not know how much any of it pertains to Mr. Warwick's death." He paused, carefully watching for the man's reaction. "For example, I did learn that you and Mr. Warwick were not on speaking terms when he died."

Bole's expression did not change, but he turned to walk toward the back of the chamber, separating them from the others milling about, allowing for some privacy. "Godfrey was not an easy man. He was always in a confrontation with someone."

"I am interested in what led to your disagreement."

Facing him, Bole kept his voice low. "Not too long ago, unsavory rumors began to circulate about me."

"What sorts of rumors?"

"That I accepted money for corrupted services in relation to my magisterial duties," he said indignantly. "I learned that it was Godfrey who was spreading them."

"Warwick accused you of bribery?"

"Not directly. I also learned that he had made overtures to certain people, which left no doubt at all that he was attempting to sully my reputation so he could steal my situation. Naturally, I confronted him on the matter, and that led to our argument."

"Godfrey wanted to be a magistrate?" Such an aspiration would not be outside the norm. Traditionally, landed gentry filled the role, but of late, more and more professional-class people such as Bole were assuming the duty.

Bole sneered. "I don't know how he expected to fulfill the role when the haberdashery kept him from the village most days of the week."

"Why do you think he wanted to be magistrate?"

"I expect it's because John Warwick used to be a magistrate, and Godfrey never liked to be outdone by his brother."

Atlas couldn't help but wonder whether that resentment had worsened when Godfrey had lost the woman he'd wanted to marry to his older, wealthier brother.

"Were you aware that Godfrey had hoped to marry Verity Warwick before she wed John?"

"Of course. You'd be pressed to find anyone in the village who was here at the time who didn't know it."

"I imagine Godfrey didn't take the loss too well."

"He resented being beaten by his brother more than anything else. Later, he said losing Verity had been a stroke of luck since she turned out to be barren."

"He didn't retain any tender feelings for her at all?"

Bole guffawed. "I don't think Godfrey was capable of tender feelings. He didn't miss a chance to gloat to his brother about how Lilliana had borne him two sons while John remained childless."

"And becoming a magistrate would be another way for Godfrey to match and possibly beat John."

"I suppose."

Atlas studied the man. Slough was about a two-hour ride from London, but the journey could be made in an hour with a strong, healthy mount. It would have been possible for Bole to slip into Town, kill Warwick, and return home well before the sun rose. "May I inquire as to where you were when he died?"

Bole's gaze remained strong and steady. He answered the question confidently, as if he'd been waiting to be asked. "Here with Mrs. Bole, all tucked in and asleep like decent country folk. We don't keep those city hours you Londoners prefer. There was a steady drizzle outside, not the fairest weather."

"Hardly a drizzle." Atlas frowned. "It was storming that evening."

Bole gave him a funny look. "Perhaps in London, but there was no storm here, just a gentle patter on the roof, as it were." Their discussion was cut short when an older bearded man called the meeting back to order.

"In any case, I did not kill my friend because he coveted my job." Bole glanced over to where the men were reassembling. "I had no reason to. He would not have prevailed."

"How can you be so certain?"

"John's good opinion is valued in this county, and he would not have supported Godfrey's ambitions in that direction."

"Why not?"

"Mr. Bole." The bearded man called from the committee table. "Will you join us? We are reconvening."

"Yes, yes, of course." He hurried to rejoin the meeting without giving Atlas another look.

Chapter Twenty-One

After talking to Bole, Atlas sought out John Warwick, who received him in the same parlor as the last time they'd met.

Despite its cheerful decoration of creams and red velvets, the portrait of Verity Warwick loomed over the room, the black drape over it a somber reminder that this house, and the husband she'd left behind, remained in mourning.

"To what do I owe this return visit?" Warwick gestured for Atlas to take a seat, the strain of his recent losses evident in the deep grooves tracking across his forehead. "Lilliana and the boys are well, I trust."

"Only by the grace of God."

"What do you mean?"

"A footman led Mrs. Warwick to the icehouse and locked her inside, presumably leaving her for dead."

He gasped. "An accident, surely."

"That appears unlikely. The icehouse door was bolted from the outside."

"Where is this footman?" His voice trembled with anger. "I hope he has been properly dealt with."

"Bow Street is looking for him as we speak. Hopefully, they'll run him to ground soon." Atlas took the chair John had offered. "The reason I am in Slough is because I was visiting Felix Bole. I learned he had a dispute with your brother and was curious to know what it was about."

"I presume he told you about this magistrate business." John leaned heavily back in his chair. Even the slightest movement seemed cumbersome for him. "It was not one of my brother's finest hours."

"How serious a threat was Godfrey to Bole's magisterial role?"

"Our family is old and well-known. We are the largest landholder in this area. Godfrey could have presented a viable challenge."

"Bole intimated that you did not support your brother's magisterial ambitions."

He dipped his chin. "That is true. A local magistrate needs to be present, and Godfrey was away from Slough most of the week. The community would not have been well served."

"Your brother could not have been pleased with your lack of support."

"He was angry, but my position had no bearing on the matter." He paused to cough lightly into his fist. "Godfrey had made the right friends, and the position was as good as his."

"It was?" Atlas leaned forward. "Did Bole know?"

"Yes."

And yet Bole had purposely led him to believe otherwise. "When did he find out?"

"Shortly before Godfrey died, the Sunday before, I believe."

"Bole learned he was about to lose his magisterial position two days before Godfrey was killed?"

His brow furrowed. "I hadn't thought of it that way before."

"I gather Bole takes the role of magistrate very seriously."

"Very. I suppose he feels it lends him consequence. He would not have reacted well upon learning he'd lost the position."

Atlas met Warwick's gaze. Fine lines webbed out from the man's eyes. "Do you think he would be angry enough to turn violent?"

"If you are asking whether I think Bole is capable of killing my brother, the answer is, I don't know. He is not known to be a violent man, but my brother had a talent for bringing out the worst in people."

Had he also brought out the worst in Verity Warwick? He cleared his throat, hesitant to raise a sensitive topic. "There is another question I have regarding your late wife."

Confusion flickered in John's eyes. "Yes?"

"I understand your wife visited Godfrey at his home, and whatever was said between them upset her greatly."

John became more alert. He straightened, leaning slightly forward. "When was this?"

"About one month before your wife succumbed to her illness."

"I see." His expression turned thoughtful. "How do you know Verity was upset by the encounter?"

"The staff witnessed the exchange but were too far away to hear what was said. However, Mrs. Warwick left in tears."

Something Atlas couldn't quite identify flashed across John's face but was quickly veiled. "I'm afraid I can be of no help," he said stiffly. "I had no idea at all that Verity went to see Godfrey."

"They were close once."

His expression turned cold, distant. "Very long ago, yes. But that is an old story. Whatever Verity went to see Godfrey about, I can assure you, with complete confidence, there was nothing illicit or dishonorable about it."

Atlas could see he would learn no more from John Warwick. He rose and took his leave. As he departed, John Warwick's housekeeper—a tall, buxom woman with round, dark eyes—rushed out after him. "Mr. Catesby, isn't it?"

He paused. "Yes?"

She pressed a basket of food into his hand. He was just about to politely refuse it when she identified herself. "I am Mrs. Sutton, Jamie's mum."

Suddenly, her face seemed more familiar to him. His baby-faced valet had his mother's eyes. "I thank you, Mrs. Sutton. Perhaps I will share it with your son."

She shone with pride. "I appreciate all you've done for my boy. You gave him a place when he had no letters of reference."

"Mrs. Lilliana Warwick spoke very highly of him."

"I know he needs training, but you won't find a more loyal, hardworking valet."

"Yes, I am beginning to see that." He hesitated, wondering whether Mrs. Sutton might provide some insight into the goings-on in John Warwick's household.

"I've just come from seeing Mr. Warwick," he said. "He seems to be suffering greatly from the loss of his wife."

"And of his brother," she said. "He has been most aggrieved since Mr. Godfrey Warwick died. It has surprised us how hard he has taken his brother's death."

"He has truly mourned him, then?"

She nodded. "Very deeply." Compassion settled in the lines of her face. "But it was his wife's death he took the hardest. He closed himself up in his study for days. We worried for him."

"I understand he was very fond of his wife."

"I never saw a couple more devoted to each other."

"Even though she once wanted to marry Godfrey?"

She waved her hand. "Foolish, youthful nonsense. She loved Mr. John and no other. And he her. He never reproached Miss Verity for being unable to bear him children. He loved her that much. Imagine how Mr. Godfrey would have treated a wife who couldn't have children."

"Abominably, I expect." The man had treated Lilliana despicably, despite her having given him two fine sons.

"Mr. John was even more destroyed after the medical examiner delivered the results of his wife's autopsy."

"Autopsy?" His head swung around, his attention piqued. "I thought Mrs. Warwick died of scarlet fever. Why would the medical examiner be involved?"

"I cannot say, but Mr. Warwick was beyond despair once he heard the results of the postmortem."

"How do you mean?"

"He took to drink like I'd never seen before. He didn't eat. He insisted the draperies remain closed in honor of his mourning, even the ones that don't face out the front of the house."

Atlas's mind churned. Why would a postmortem be necessary, unless someone suspected foul play in Verity Warwick's death? He could see no other reason for one otherwise. "Where can I find this medical examiner?"

"Old Benedict Dixon? He's over in the village, but he's a bit of a recluse. I don't expect he'll be of the mind to speak to a stranger."

He thanked her and took his leave. Recluse or not, he had every intention of speaking with Benedict Dixon to learn what exactly had caused Verity Warwick's death.

After inquiring in the village, he tracked the medical examiner down to a modest cottage with heavy timber framing located next to the butchery. He knocked repeatedly at the weathered wooden front door, but no one responded, even though he could detect the shuffle of people moving around inside. He stepped back, peering up at the mullioned windows, contemplating calling out to see if someone might be persuaded to open the door.

"You may as well give up." A husky man of middle age in a bloodstained apron ventured out of the butcher shop. "You could knock all day, and he still won't open the door."

"Why is that?" Atlas asked. "I mean him no harm."

The butcher shrugged. "You're a stranger, and old Benedict don't care for strangers. He doesn't think much of people in general. That one likes to keep to himself."

"I see." He stared up at the house, eager to speak with Dixon. Why had Verity Warwick needed an autopsy, and what had that postmortem revealed? He suspected his questions would remain unanswered, at least for today.

"Thank you for your time." He tipped his hat to the butcher. "Good day."

* * *

"Benedict Dixon?" Lilliana said the following morning. "He's rather sweet."

"He is?" Atlas stared at her. They were in Thea's breakfast room, where his sister was at the table scribbling her usual mathematic gibberish. Charlton had come with him to check in on Lilliana, and Atlas was pleased to find her looking well and taking tea with his sister.

"I have heard Dixon is a recluse who doesn't care for people," he said to her. "He wouldn't come to the door when I knocked."

Charlton adjusted his pristine white cuff. "He probably finds you considerably less charming than Mrs. Warwick." As was his habit, the earl had immediately settled himself in the most spacious chair in the room. Atlas noticed he was wearing one of his somber new jackets, this one in a fine navy color.

Lilliana set her saucer down. "I'll go to Slough with you. Mr. Dixon won't turn me away."

"I cannot ask that of you." Atlas shook his head. "Discussing a postmortem will be most unpleasant."

"No more unpleasant than being sold at auction, the death of my husband, or being locked in an icehouse," she said dryly. "I suspect I shall be able to survive an interview with the medical examiner."

"Of course you will." Thea looked up from where she was working on her equations. "Pray don't be a jackanapes, Atlas."

He stiffened. "I am merely trying to protect Mrs. Warwick from further unpleasantness. She has been through quite enough."

"Hmmm." Skepticism hummed in Thea's throat. "How goes the investigation otherwise? Have you developed any possible suspects?"

"A few. Godfrey Warwick was not a popular man." He reached for a bread-and-butter sandwich from a platter Miller had brought in with the tea. "For one thing, he was out to steal his closest friend's occupation, and he'd pretty much succeeded right before he was killed."

Lilliana leaned forward. "Do you speak of Mr. Bole?"

"Yes, it seems Godfrey wanted to be a magistrate, and Bole learned he'd succeeded two days before Godfrey was killed."

Charlton sipped his tea. "Sounds like Warwick's death was very convenient timing for this Bole fellow."

"Very," Thea agreed. "I suppose Mr. Bole gets to keep on being the magistrate now that his usurper is dead?"

Atlas nodded. "And then there is Nash, the tailor. We know Godfrey was trying to extort quite a bit of money from him."

"Because the man reads books and attempts to better himself?" Thea shook her head. "That hardly seems like something that should be hidden."

"Agreed." Atlas did not share the true reason for the extortion. And he neglected to mention that Somerville was also a viable suspect.

"Anyone else?" Charlton asked.

He reached for another sandwich. He wasn't convinced John Warwick could be excluded as a suspect, but he did not say so aloud. "Nothing beyond pure conjecture."

Thea studied Charlton. "Are you attending a funeral?"

"Me?" The earl flattened one hand against his chest. "No. Why?"

"Because you are usually outfitted like a peacock. This"—she waved a hand toward his navy coat—"is quite a departure from your normal flamboyant state."

"I'm flattered you noticed." Charlton brushed a hand over the lapel of his new tailcoat. "Shall I take that as a compliment?"

But Thea, having already lost interest in him, focused her attention on her brother. "What will you do next?"

"Next," Lilliana interjected, "we go to Slough and speak to Benedict Dixon."

"If you're certain—" Atlas began to say.

"I am." Challenge sparked in her eyes. "Don't you dare object."

Atlas swallowed the last of his sandwich. "I wouldn't dream of it."

The sound of Fletcher clearing his throat sounded from the corridor just before the butler himself appeared. "Mr. Endicott is calling, madam."

The runner's portly frame appeared behind the butler's slim form. "Thank you, Eddie. Don't trouble yourself anymore. I can show myself out when we're through here."

When the butler stiffened, Atlas mouthed, "Eddie?" as a silent question to his sister. Amusement stamped Thea's face as her brows rose in response.

The butler turned to the runner, his neck flushed a bright red. "It is Edward, Edward Fletcher," he said loudly. "Just Mr. Fletcher or Fletcher to you, sir."

"As you say." Endicott clapped the man's shoulder in a friendly gesture. "Very good, Mr. Fletcher, very good, indeed."

Fletcher stared at the beefy hand clamped on his shoulder, as if unsure of how to react to the runner's casual amiability.

Thea came to his rescue. "That will be all, Fletcher." Closing the book in front of her, she turned her attention to the new arrival. "To what do we owe this visit, Mr. Endicott? Dare we hope you have news?" A grateful-looking Fletcher discreetly melted away while the runner stepped farther into the room.

"Yes, indeed." He smiled blithely. "We have found William."

Lilliana came up out of her chair. "The footman who locked me in the icehouse?"

"Who put him up to it?" Atlas also surged to his feet, a renewed upwelling of anger churning inside him at the whoreson who'd tried to hurt Lilliana. "Did he say?"

"He professes not to know." The runner pulled a notebook from his pocket and flipped through it until he reached the page he'd been searching for. "Says he was approached by a—as he put it—swell who paid him very handsomely to lock Mrs. Warwick in the icehouse."

Charlton leaned forward, his face alight with interest. "The culprit behind the attempt on Mrs. Warwick's life is a gentleman?"

The runner dipped his chin. "So it would appear. William described him as a well-dressed gentleman. Unfortunately, it was dark, and William says he didn't get a good look at the man."

Lilliana put a hand to her chest. "And I was definitely this man's intended target?"

"Most definitely." Endicott nodded. "According to William, the gentleman identified you by name and also described your physical characteristics."

Thea crossed her arms over her chest. "Did this man say why he wanted to harm Mrs. Warwick?"

"I'm afraid not."

"That's it?" Atlas struggled to contain his temper. "What else did William tell you about the man?"

"He could not describe him except to say he is of average height. However, he did say the man was wearing a large gold-and-ruby ring."

The breath left Atlas's chest. "A ruby ring, you say?"

"Yes." The runner studied him. "Why? Are you acquainted with a man who wears a large ruby ring?"

"The man Warwick had a physical altercation with at the shop shortly before he was killed, the well-dressed gentleman, wore a ruby-and-gold ring."

"He did?" Lilliana stared at him. "How do you know that?"

"The clerk at the haberdashery, Stillwell, told me about it."

Endicott scribbled in his notebook. "But the clerk could not describe this man."

Atlas cursed silently to himself. "Unfortunately, no. He claims he never got a good look at him."

"Just so." The runner stuffed his notebook in his pocket. "I think I will go and have another chat with young Mr. Stillwell."

Atlas saw him out. "What do you make of all this?"

The runner placed his rumpled hat on his head. "It seems there is more to Mr. Warwick's death than a dispute over his wife."

Atlas regarded him with surprise. "Are you saying I am no longer your primary suspect?"

Amusement wrinkled Endicott's forehead. "Do not look so shocked, Mr. Catesby. I go where the evidence takes me. And at the moment, it leads away from you."

Atlas stared after the man as he took his leave. Endicott's about-face did take him aback. He'd have thought the investigator would be too proud to admit he'd been mistaken in his certainty that Atlas had killed Warwick in a fit of anger. Still pondering this latest development, he returned to the others.

Lilliana sank back into her chair when she spotted him. "Why would someone want to harm me?"

Atlas pinched the bridge of his nose. "Since this man was seen at the haberdashery before your husband was killed, it would appear the two cases are connected."

Charlton cocked his head. "You believe Warwick's killer is behind the attempt on Lilliana?"

"I cannot say for certain, but Endicott now seems to believe it could be so," Atlas said. "It stands to reason that if we identify Warwick's killer, we are likely to find the man who attempted to harm Mrs. Warwick."

And he was going to run the bastard to ground before he came after Lilliana again.

Chapter Twenty-Two

They set out for Slough the following day, arriving in the early afternoon. The door to Benedict Dixon's house was answered on the first knock by a housekeeper who promptly invited them inside. A gray-bearded man in his late sixties rushed forward over rough hemlock floors to greet them.

"My dear lady," he said to Lilliana. "To what do I owe this delightful visit?" Dixon was surprisingly tall, full-bodied, and bald on top with longish, unkempt hair around the sides in a style reminiscent of the one worn by the American Benjamin Franklin.

"Mr. Dixon, may I present Mr. Catesby?" Her smile was gracious. "He is investigating Mr. Warwick's death and would like to ask you a few questions."

Dixon's brow knit. "But how can I be of service? I didn't perform the postmortem on your late husband."

Atlas removed his hat. "No, but you did examine Mrs. Verity Warwick."

Dixon crossed large arms over his chest. "How does that signify?"

"In all probability, it doesn't." Lilliana laid a gentle hand on Dixon's arm. "However, if Verity was murdered, it might have a bearing on the case."

"She was not murdered, I can assure you," he said decisively. "Beyond that, the matter is a private one. Her husband has suffered greatly."

Lilliana nodded. "Of course he has." Her voice was rich with sympathy. "And whatever you share with us will be kept in the strictest confidence." When Dixon cast a gimlet eye at Atlas, she continued, "Please. Someone has made an attempt on my life as well, but Mr. Catesby came to my rescue. We must explore every avenue to find the person behind Godfrey's death and the attempt on my life."

Dixon exhaled. "Very well. I cannot see how the two can possibly be related, but do come into the parlor, where we can talk privately." He led them to a small room dominated by a large hearth. A basket of fruit and a cup of tea sat on the lone small round table next to a straw-backed chair before the fire.

"Oh, no," Lilliana said with some dismay. "We've interrupted your teatime."

Dixon brushed aside her concern, and once they were settled, he said, "As I stated, Mrs. Verity Warwick was not murdered."

"Why conduct a postmortem then?" Atlas asked. "I thought she died of scarlet fever."

"She had some of the symptoms of that disease—chills and abdominal pain—but she did not die of scarlet fever."

"What did kill her?" Lilliana asked.

"Are you certain she wasn't murdered?" Dread washed over Atlas. What if some bedlamite was out killing Warwicks?

"Not deliberately, but I believe one could make a case for murder."

Lilliana blanched. "How so?"

"The reason I conducted the postmortem was at John Warwick's request." Dixon cleared his throat. "Something his wife told him shortly before she died prompted him to charge me with examining the body."

Atlas leaned forward. "And what did you find?"

Dixon's expression was grave. "I found her womb to be in a very disorganized state."

"Her womb?" Lilliana asked.

He nodded. "The inflammation and gangrene made it difficult to detect the severity of the violence done to the poor lady."

"Violence?" Atlas was confused. "Was she stabbed?"

"No, she was given a potion to bring on a miscarriage."

"A miscarriage?" Lilliana exclaimed. "Verity was with child?"

"Yes, and she went to see a midwife who gave her a potion and then subjected her to a barbaric procedure involving a feather quill and a piece of wire." He shook his head with obvious disgust. "It was butchery, pure and simple."

Surprise reverberated through Atlas. "You're saying Verity Warwick was the victim of a—" He paused, hesitant to mention an indelicate matter in Lilliana's presence.

The medical examiner had no such reservations. "A botched abortion. Yes."

Shock stamped Lilliana's fine-boned features. "Verity would *never* do such a terrible thing." Her voice shook with indignation.

"She was desperate for a baby. She would never have agreed to something so awful."

"Perhaps she was too old to have a child?" Atlas asked. "Was there a risk to her health?"

"She was nearing forty," Dixon answered. "An advanced age for childbirth, to be sure, but there are many women who successfully bear children at that age."

Several thoughts shuffled through Atlas's mind. Why had Verity Warwick chosen to abort a much-longed-for child? Had she done it to spite her husband, to deny him an heir, for some unknown reason? He recalled John saying he would have forgiven his wife anything. Had he been talking about the abortion or something else?

"How did Warwick react when he heard the results of your examination?" he asked the medical examiner.

"Is it possible you could be mistaken about what ailed Verity?" Lilliana inquired.

"No, and indeed my finding seemed to confirm what John already suspected. He was torn up with grief about it. I've never seen a man more devastated."

"But how could John think that of Verity?" Lilliana was obviously shaken.

"Who was the midwife Verity went to see?" Atlas wanted to know.

Dixon shrugged. "I have no notion. None at all."

After a few more questions, they thanked Dixon and made their good-byes. By the time they reached the carriage, Lilliana seemed to have recovered herself. "There is only one midwife in Slough," she said, "and that's Maud Honeywell, so we may as well start with her."

He helped her up. "Then we must go and see her, but unfortunately, it will not be today because we have an engagement to keep."

She looked frustrated. "Charlton's dinner party."

"If we mean to attend, we have to leave Slough now."

He could see she wanted to protest, but he also knew she was too well mannered to miss the earl's gathering after having promised to attend. "Very well. But we must return to talk with Maud tomorrow."

"Absolutely." He climbed into the curricle and set a fast pace for London in order to avoid being late for Charlton's dinner party.

* * *

The earl lived in a palatial town house on Curzon Street built in the neoclassical style. Atlas was shown through large mahogany double doors to an opulent drawing room dominated by large Greek columns.

He was surprised to find the Duke of Somerville and his former guardian, Cyril Eggleston, among the guests in attendance. Somerville acknowledged him with a formal courtesy that revealed nothing of their previous uncomfortable encounter in Nash's private back room.

"I thought you said this was an intimate affair," Atlas said to Charlton once they retreated to a corner of the massive chamber.

"It is." Charlton adjusted the cuffs of his snowy shirt. He was dressed once again in somber colors, all black except for his stark white cravat and cuffs. "I count Somerville a friend, as you well know, and Eggleston, well, he manages to insert himself when he can. As you know, he is loath to relinquish his hold on the duke."

"I doubt Lilliana will want to be seen in company." He remembered the way the duke had stared at Lilliana at the park. It was obvious now that Somerville wasn't her lover, given that Atlas had learned the duke's tastes ran in an entirely different direction. So what was the connection? She shared a surname with the duke's butler, but he couldn't imagine her emerging from the servant class. She appeared too refined for that. "She is in mourning."

"This is a small, private supper. It will be to Mrs. Warwick's advantage for it to be known she was the guest of an earl and in company with the Duke of Somerville."

Atlas studied his friend. "You're attempting to make her acceptable in society."

Charlton's smile was smug. "In the event you do decide to wed her, which I suspect you would like to do the moment she is out of mourning, her path toward respectability will have already been established."

"Society can hang, for all I care." He helped himself to brandy from a footman circulating the room with refreshments on a silver tray. "Also, you presume far too much."

"Do I?" Charlton's blue gaze flickered over him. "I suspect not. Can you tell me you have not seriously considered wedding the lovely Mrs. Warwick?"

"I have considered it," he admitted, taking a healthy gulp of his drink. "But the lady is not amenable."

Charlton's forehead lifted. "Why ever not? It would be an excellent match for her, the widow of a tradesman, to marry the brother and son of a baron, especially one with such old and distinguished family lines."

"Perhaps noble bloodlines do not hold the same degree of importance for her as they do for you."

"I cannot imagine it. Especially as such a connection would clearly be advantageous for her children." He tapped his chin with his forefinger. "Although they are tainted by their unfortunate father's involvement in trade, the Warwicks are landed gentry, and as such, the children's future status in society is not completely without hope."

Atlas stared into his glass. "Be that as it may, she means to leave London once Warwick's killer is found."

"And go where?"

"Far away." A weight settled in his chest. He would miss her when she was gone. But he'd also be well into his next voyage by then, and hopefully the maudlin sentiments that seemed to have him in their grips these days would be all but forgotten. "She intends to go to a place where no one has heard of how that degenerate husband of hers sold her on the street like a common whore."

A frown marred the earl's perfect features. "What an unfortunate twist. Mrs. Palmer will be most disappointed. I expect she's already taken it upon herself to book the wedding at St. George's."

Atlas was silent for a moment. Mention of Thea made him recall her words about his lacking aim or direction. He'd initially disregarded her comments, but as much as he'd like to forget them, they'd made an impression. "Charlton?"

"Yes."

"What Thea said the other day, about my being adrift, do you agree with her?"

An awkward beat followed. "My dear fellow, far be it from me to tell anyone how to live their life. We all muddle along as best we can."

Atlas shifted. "That's not an answer," he pressed.

Charlton pursed his lips as if debating what to say. "You do seem restless," he finally responded. "You always have done, ever since Cambridge. It is as if you are searching for something but aren't quite certain what that something is. Perhaps you expect to find it somewhere along on your travels."

Atlas blinked. Charlton had obviously given the matter some thought before now. "When did you become such a philosopher?"

Charlton looked toward the massive double doors. "Ah, here are Mrs. Warwick and Thea now."

Atlas followed thc direction of his friend's gaze, and his breath caught. Lilliana was resplendent in a black lace evening gown layered over white silk. The round neckline showed her ivory skin and the long, graceful column of her neck to excellent advantage. She made him forget all about Thea and Charlton's dubious analysis of him. Charlton went toward the two women.

"Welcome to my home, Mrs. Palmer, Mrs. Warwick."

"My goodness." Thea ran an approving look over Charlton's muted clothing as Atlas came up beside him. "I almost didn't spot you among your guests."

Charlton smiled broadly. "I've decided to relegate orange and red to the back of my dressing room, for the moment at least. I must say, you two ladies look ravishing this evening."

"You certainly do." Atlas's attention was fully focused on Lilliana.

A delicate blush washed over her angled cheekbones. "Thank you."

"Yes, thank you." Sarcastic amusement tinged Thea's voice. "I doubt you could tell me what color my gown is."

Atlas tore his attention away from Lilliana to look at his sister's gown. "Blue, of course."

"Yes, of course." She shook her head before scanning the room. "Goodness, what's Somerville doing here?"

A sound of distress erupted from Lilliana's throat. She'd gone pale as parchment, her mouth open in distress as she stared at across the room. Atlas followed her gaze, with a very good idea of who he would find at the other end of it.

The duke, still standing next to Eggleston, seemed moved as well, but it was happiness, and not distress, that showed on his face. He took a step toward her. "Roslyn?" Astonishment, followed by a look of pure joy, illuminated his face. "Rosie, it is you. I feared I was conjuring images in my mind when I saw you in the park."

Shaking her head in jerky movements, she took a quick backward step and almost tripped over her gown. Atlas caught her elbow to steady her. "No," she exhaled the word. She was shaking, and it took Atlas a moment to recognize her reaction as pure, icy fear.

By God. What had Somerville done to her? Atlas stepped closer, shielding her. "Do not be afraid," he said quietly. "I won't let anyone hurt you."

She stared at him as if he didn't understand anything, which at the moment, he didn't. Somerville didn't strike him as a cruel or unsavory character, but Lilliana's reaction told him all he needed to know about the man.

"Rosie, it's me, Matthew." The duke approached her, a welcoming smile wreathing his face. "I've looked everywhere for you."

Her eyes glistened before she jerked her elbow away from Atlas and spun around, dashing out the mahogany double doors and vanishing around the first turn. Atlas followed her with the duke on his heels.

"Rosie!" the duke called.

Atlas halted and spun around, purposely blocking the duke's path. "She clearly does not wish to be in your company."

Somerville flushed and tried to step around Atlas's brawny frame, his gaze fixed on the corridor Lilliana had dashed down. "See here, Catesby, this is none of your concern."

Atlas stepped in his path. "I disagree."

Eggleston came out of the drawing room. "Your Grace, you are causing a scene."

"I don't give a damn," Somerville snarled. "It's Roslyn." He pointed in the general direction where Lilliana had vanished. "Didn't you see her?"

Avoiding the duke's gaze, the older man shifted from one foot to the other. "She has obviously chosen a different life for herself."

"But why did she run away?" Confusion filled his voice. "The three of us were all we had left." He turned back to Atlas with a menacing glare. "Get out of my way. I mean to go and find my sister."

CHAPTER TWENTY-THREE

"Your sister?" Atlas stared at the duke. "The devil you say." The words came out like a growl. "Her name is Mrs. Lilliana Warwick."

The massive double doors to the parlor closed behind them. Someone giving them privacy.

"Her name"—Somerville punctuated each word with the full weight of his ducal authority—"is Lady. Roslyn. Lilliana. Sterling."

"How can that be?" Atlas narrowed his eyes. "Everyone knows Lady Roslyn is living in Scotland with her sister, Lady Serena, now the Countess of Dunston."

"Wrong." Somerville lowered his voice. "My sister has been missing for ten years. Eggleston put it about that she'd gone to live with our sister."

Eggleston dipped his chin in agreement. "Quite right. It was my duty as guardian to save the family name from scandal and taint. Then as now." He placed a hand on the duke's sleeve. "Your Grace, perhaps it is best to let her vanish again.

Think of the scandal. She was never a biddable girl. Lord only knows what manner of mischief she's involved herself in all these years."

Somerville shrugged the man's hand off. "That will be all, Eggleston." He spoke with steely courtesy.

"Your Grace—"

The duke's expression hardened. "Leave us. Now."

It appeared that Eggleston wanted to continue to protest, but finally he bowed his head and retreated to the drawing room. The duke turned his attention back to Atlas.

"What business do you have with my sister?"

Atlas's gut twisted. Whatever hopes he'd briefly harbored of taking Lilliana—Roslyn—to wife were effectively dashed by this revelation. She was the daughter and sister of the Dukes of Somerville, one of the highest dukedoms in the land. She'd never been beneath him. In reality it was he, the youngest son of an only recently titled baron, who was no match at all for her. "Why did she run? What did you do to her?"

Rage blazed in Somerville's eyes. "What exactly are you accusing me of, Catesby?" He stepped closer, lowering his voice. "She vanished when I was ten-and-five. Are you intimating that I am the reason she ran away?"

Atlas didn't know what to believe. "I only know what I saw. She ran from you. It did not appear to be the touching family reunion that you perceive it to be."

Somerville exhaled. "I cannot understand it. We're barely ten months apart in age. We were always as close as a brother and sister can be, especially after Serena—our older sister—married and moved to Scotland."

"Let me go and find her," Atlas said. "And then perhaps we can sort all of this out."

"I will do no such thing." Somerville spoke with indignation. "What exactly is the nature of your relationship with my sister?"

"Rest assured I have only her best interests at heart." For now, it was best to avoid the details of how they'd met. "The rest I will leave for Lilliana to share with you." Without awaiting a response, Atlas pivoted and went in search of Lilliana. Behind him, he heard the duke call out. "You there, where does this corridor lead?" Atlas grimaced. Somerville obviously wasn't content to wait while Atlas sought Lilliana out. Be that as it may, Atlas intended to locate her first.

He succeeded, finding her on the upper level of Charlton's massive, two-story library. The room was decorated in wood tones with bookcases lining every wall, a huge fire roaring in the hearth at one end of the chamber. Atlas made his way up to her, his hand running along the dark wood bannister perched atop elaborate scrolled iron balusters.

When he reached the landing, she watched him approach. "I thought this house was big enough to get lost in."

He smiled a little. "Fortunately, Charlton's servants are not so discreet that they could not point me in the right direction."

She was curled up on a window seat, her arms around her tucked knees, the skirt of her gown pulled over them, guarding her modesty. His throat tightened. He'd never seen her look so vulnerable. Even when that brute Warwick had sold her in the yard, she'd worn her dignity like a suit of armor. Now she allowed herself to be laid bare before him. "So," she said, "you know the truth about me."

There was so much he didn't know about this woman he'd thought to wed. "Lilliana Hastings?"

She acknowledged the irony in his voice. "I had to come up with an assumed name rather quickly when the runner asked for my family name."

"That is why you used the butler's surname."

"I did not think Hastings would mind. I suppose you spoke with Somerville."

"To your brother?" He took a seat next to her. "Yes. And, briefly, to your guardian."

She released a shaky breath. "I suppose there's no escaping him now."

He clenched his fist at the thought of Somerville hurting his sister. "He cannot harm you any longer."

"If only that were true."

"I will help you leave this place and disappear somewhere in the countryside with the boys." He spoke with urgency. "No one need ever find you."

"Ever the gallant." She smiled, sad and wistful. "Always coming to my rescue."

"I won't let Somerville get within a horse's length of you."

"He was always such a sweet boy and very protective after our parents died, although we both had a naughty side. Unlike my sister, Serena, who always followed the rules."

He blinked, puzzled by the fondness that shone in her eyes when she spoke of her brother. "I am confused. You weren't running from you brother?"

"Mattie? Not exactly. I just don't know who he is anymore." Her face darkened. "Mattie was away at school. He couldn't help me, and Serena had just married and moved to Scotland. I was alone with him."

A cold knot formed in his stomach. "Alone, you mean, with your guardian—with Eggleston."

"Yes."

Fury tunneled through him when he recalled she hadn't bled on her wedding night. "Did he force you?"

"He tried." She swallowed. "He . . . touched me . . . and forced me to touch him . . . in ways . . . and in places that he shouldn't have. When I resisted and said I would tell my aunt, my father's widowed sister, he threatened to lock me away in a hospital for bedlamites where no one could find me. I had no one to turn to." She angrily swiped away a tear, as though frustrated with herself for showing any emotion. "I would lock the door to my bedchamber against him. But then he had the lock removed."

He gritted his teeth. "Is that when you left?"

She nodded. "My maid helped me. I dressed in servants' clothing, and she got her cousin to take me to Town. I was going to try to find my aunt, but she was abroad. Her house was closed when I arrived. I had no idea where to go, and then I saw the haberdashery."

"Warwick's place."

"Yes, I remembered going there with my mother when I was a little girl. Godfrey was kind to me then. He always gave me a sweetmeat." Atlas could well imagine the avaricious shopkeeper indulging the young daughter of the renowned Duchess of Somerville, his wealthy and celebrated patron. "I went in and asked if he was looking for a shop girl. He didn't recognize me. He hired me, and I had been there less than a month when Godfrey offered marriage. I was willing to do almost anything to get away from London. I lived in fear that Eggleston would find me and lock me away in some asylum where Mattie and Serena would never be able to find me."

"So you wed Warwick."

"Yes, and he took me to live in Slough."

Many of the questions he had about her past began to resolve in his mind. "I suppose the jewelry Warwick sold was yours, gems worthy of a duke's daughter."

Her eyes widened. "How did you know about the jewels?"

"I learned about them during the course of the investigation."

"Yet you never asked me about them."

"I supposed you would tell me anything you wanted me to know." He paused. "The love letter that Godfrey found among your things. Was that perchance a missive from your brother?"

"You know about that too?" She rose and went to the railing before turning around to look at him. "Yes, it was a letter Matthew sent me shortly before I ran away. It was all I had left of him." She took a deep breath. "It added to Godfrey's anger. When he didn't find blatant evidence of my maidenhood, he was convinced there had been another man. I didn't defend myself against his accusations. I was so young and inexperienced that I wasn't certain whether or not Eggleston's actions had truly robbed me of my innocence."

Atlas swallowed a curse. The suggestion that Eggleston's abuse might have been that invasive of her body made him want to run the bastard through with a saber. "When we came to London, why did you not go to Somerville and tell him the truth, now that he has come of age?"

"He was so young when I left. I knew Eggleston would have spent the last ten years poisoning him against me. I had no idea what kind of man he had become." She leaned back against the railing, her hands resting on either side of her hips. "And when I saw Matthew in the park with Eggleston by his side, I knew I couldn't risk going back."

"I think you underestimate your brother."

"Do I?" She sighed. "The men in my life have not always given me cause to trust them. I feared Eggleston would find a way to lock me away and separate me from my boys."

Atlas surged to his feet. "Stay here. I'll send Thea to you and see that you are taken home."

"Where are you going?"

"To take care of Eggleston," he called over his shoulder as he ran down the stairs.

"Atlas," she called to him from over the railing. "Stop. It's over."

"No, it's not. But it will be soon."

An inferno raged inside of Atlas as he stormed through the mansion's endless corridors before finally reaching the drawing room. He zeroed in on Eggleston, who stood whispering in the duke's ear. He strode straight to him, drawing off his white kid leather glove as he did so.

"Atlas," Thea called from behind him. "Is Lilliana all right?"

He barely heard her. He halted before Eggleston and slapped the man hard across the cheek with his glove. "Hampstead Heath at dawn. Name your second, Eggleston."

Eggleston's eyes went wide. A collective gasp sounded throughout the room.

Somerville stepped forward. "What is this about, Catesby?"

He did not take his eyes from Eggleston's pale face. "My official letter of challenge will arrive at Somerville House tomorrow."

Charlton was suddenly by his side. "Surely, we can resolve this matter as gentlemen."

"No, we cannot."

Eggleston coughed. "Come now, Catesby." His voice shook. "I have no idea what is the matter with you—"

"Your very presence offends me." He came closer until he was practically nose-to-nose with the bastard. "And I will not be satisfied until I have dealt with you in the manner you deserve."

Eggleston's face turned an unhealthy shade of gray. "Whatever I have done to cause offense, I apologize."

Atlas stared him down. "I do not accept." He wasn't letting the whoreson off that easily.

"Whatever is the matter?" Charlton asked.

"Yes, do tell." Malice swirled in Eggleston's eyes. "What exactly is the offense I am accused of? I should like everyone in this chamber to hear of it."

"You little bastard." After all he had done to Lilliana, the swine now intended to sully her name. Atlas whispered furiously in the older man's ear. "Did you think you could take indecent liberties with a young girl, your own ward, who you were charged with protecting and nurturing, and not pay the price for it?"

Somerville's face flushed. "What are you speaking of, Catesby?" He stared at his former guardian, a look of disbelief on his face. "And where is my sister?"

"In the library. I think she would welcome your presence there."

Chapter Twenty-Four

"Well." Charlton handed Atlas a drink. "You certainly know how to break up a perfectly good party."

They were in the earl's drawing room along with Thea, who was pacing back and forth. Somerville remained closeted in the library with Lilliana. Eggleston, at least, had had the good judgment to depart quickly after the scene with Atlas.

"Although," the earl continued, "this supper that never happened will be notorious once word gets out that you issued a challenge here this evening."

Atlas took a sip and grimaced. "This is whiskey."

"I thought the occasion called for something stronger." Charlton settled himself in an overstuffed chair and looked over toward Thea. "Perhaps you'd care to sit, Mrs. Palmer, before you tread a hole in my Axminster."

She rounded on him, her expression fierce. "This is not a laughing matter. Atlas, that big jackanapes over there, could be dead by the day after tomorrow at this time."

"Nonsense." Atlas took another taste of whiskey, savoring the smoky, spicy flavor. "I'm an excellent shot."

"Why are you doing this?" She came to stand over him with her arms crossed over her chest. "What did Eggleston do to Lilliana?"

Atlas examined the amber liquid in his glass. "This has nothing to do with Mrs. Warwick," he said, unwilling to subject her reputation to the taint of yet another scandal. "It is a private matter between gentlemen and shall be settled as such."

She stared down at him. "You're a terrible liar." She pivoted to Charlton. "You're supposed to be his friend. Talk him out of it."

Charlton placed his drink on the table beside him. "That would be rather difficult, as I have already agreed to be his second."

"You've what?" Outrage contorted her usually pleasing features. An angry Thea was a formidable sight, one that any sane man would try to avoid. "I should have known. You're an even bigger idiot than he is."

"Why am I the bigger idiot," Charlton asked, "when your brother is the one who will be on the business end of a pistol?"

"Because cooler heads are supposed to prevail," she snapped. Thea resumed her pacing. "A duel! It's dangerous and ridiculous. I'll never understand why men are such imbeciles."

"Ladies have been known to duel as well," Charlton protested.

"I should like to see that." The warmth of the whiskey floated through Atlas. "It's said they do so in a state of partial dishabille," he said, referring to the rumored practice of females dueling while topless.

The two men exchanged a knowing grin. Thea threw up her hands. "I give up on the both of you. Acting like randy boys barely out of the schoolroom when there are lives at stake." She marched out of the drawing room while calling for her wrap.

Atlas bottomed out his whiskey. What Thea failed to grasp was that it was precisely because lives were at stake that he turned to humor to ease the tension.

"I will do my best to try to settle this matter without violence," Charlton said. In his capacity as Atlas's second, it was his duty to determine whether an actual duel could be avoided.

"Don't you dare. The duel goes forward."

"I somehow suspected that would be your answer." His expression became more somber. "As bad as all that, was it? What he did to her."

Atlas clenched his teeth. "Let's just say a bullet wound is the very least of what he deserves."

"Excuse me, gentlemen." Somerville entered the room and turned to Charlton. "Would you mind? I need a word alone with Catesby."

"Not at all." Charlton rose and sauntered in the direction of the double doors that led to the dining room. "I think I'll have a bite to eat. It would be a shame for all of Cook's efforts to go to waste."

The pocket doors slid open as he approached, no doubt thanks to an alert footman stationed on the other side of them. Charlton turned to face the men. "Do join me, gentlemen, if you care to once you've had your talk." He reached out and pulled the sliding doors shut, disappearing behind them and leaving Atlas and the duke to their privacy.

"Mrs. Warwick?" Atlas looked to Somerville. "You spoke with her."

"Yes, she has just gone home with your sister." Somerville's expression was strained. "It seems I owe you my thanks."

"I don't see why."

"For coming to Roslyn's rescue when she was alone and subject to the whims of that vile husband of hers."

"I did what any gentleman would do in the same situation."

The duke's face flushed. "When I think of how she suffered, how she felt she could not come to me . . ."

"Both of you were practically children when she left. The only person to blame here is Eggleston."

The duke settled heavily into the chair Charlton had just abandoned. "About that."

"The duel goes forward," he said. "The bastard deserves to have his day of reckoning."

"I agree. But I am Roslyn's brother—I am the man who should have the privilege of protecting her honor. Even if I am a little late in taking up that duty."

"That's ridiculous. You're a duke, and I'm an entirely disposable fourth son. Besides, you have no heir as of yet."

"An heir?" he said wryly. "You comprehend enough about me to know it is unlikely that I will ever beget a son."

Atlas lapsed into silence for a moment. It had not occurred to him that Somerville only bedded men. "I suspect others in your situation have managed it before."

"It is dishonest." His mouth twisted with distaste. "I could not do that to any woman I respected enough to take to wife."

"I would think there are many women willing to tolerate such an arrangement in exchange for the opportunity to be your duchess."

Somerville gave him a pointed look. "And why would I want such a woman to be the mother of my children?"

"Charlton mentioned recently that you intended to take a wife in a year or so. Was that designed to keep the gossips at bay?"

"In part. I used to think I would eventually marry, but that was before I met Kirby. Now I know I could not do that to him."

The frank admission startled Atlas, who still found the notion of romantic love between two men to be extraordinary. "You care for Nash."

"That surprises you?" The duke's brows rose. "You think our kind isn't capable of true attachment?"

"What of the artist you've put up in the house in Kensington?" he asked with genuine curiosity. "Everyone presumes she is your mistress."

Somerville shrugged. "I have never lied about Marian. I am a patron of the arts who admires and supports her work. It is not my concern if society chooses to attach an unsavory taint to our association."

"One that happens to protect your reputation."

"Nash and I . . . since I met him sixteen months ago . . . there have been no others." Atlas rubbed his chin, still attempting to comprehend the full extent of Somerville's unusual attachment to Nash. He wondered whether the duke loved his paramour enough to kill for him.

"In any case," Somerville continued, "it is my place to defend my sister's honor."

"Lilliana and the boys have little enough family as it is. It would destroy your sister if she were to lose you in a duel fought over her."

Somerville cocked his head. "What are you to my sister that you would risk your life to protect her honor?"

Atlas came to his feet. "As I said, I am merely acting as any gentleman would. I am famished." He headed toward the dining room. "Deal with your former guardian how you see fit, but I do not intend to withdraw my challenge."

* * *

That evening, Atlas drew a lungful of air through the hookah hose and exhaled long and slow, watching as the sweet, redolent smoke swirled into the air. Fresh from a hot bath, he'd slipped into a comfortable burgundy silk banyan he'd picked up in Lyon years before. After dismissing Jamie for the evening, he'd settled into a stuffed chair with his thoughts.

Lilliana, the daughter of a duke. It made perfect sense once he considered the proud way she carried herself or the manner in which she could spear a man with a look when she was displeased. Of course she was highborn. He'd suspected it from the first, only he'd never imagined how lofty that birth might be. An insistent rap at the door interrupted his musings.

"Who the devil?" Setting down the hookah hose, he pushed out of his chair and paddled barefoot through the front hall, wondering who could be calling at this late hour. As he pulled the door open, the rich scent of tobacco drifted up the stairs from the shop down below.

A feminine figure cloaked in black stood on the landing. Although a hooded cape cast her face in shadows, he immediately recognized his visitor.

"What are you doing here?" he hissed, pulling her into his front hall and closing the door behind her. "What if someone sees you?"

Lilliana threw back the hood in a defiant gesture, revealing her face and flashing golden-copper eyes. "Then so be it." Despite the bold words, her bravado seemed to falter slightly when she registered his state of complete dishabille. Her gaze widened as it swept from the scowl on his face to the open neck of his dressing gown that exposed part of his chest, then down to his bare feet.

He tugged his banyan more tightly around him, a poor attempt to make himself decent in the presence of a lady. "This is the home of a bachelor. You should not be here."

Her nostrils flared. "And you should not be contemplating meeting Eggleston at Hampstead Heath."

Ah, so that is why she'd come. "It is a matter of honor," he said, leading the way into his sitting room. He watched her take in the room's bright colors. Her survey paused momentarily to rest on the lit coals glowing in a little round saucer perched at the top of his hookah.

"If you've come to try to dissuade me," he said, "you have risked your reputation for naught."

"Someone needs to talk some sense into you." She pulled off her cape and draped it over one of his stuffed chairs. "It seems my brother and your sister both failed."

"This is a matter between gentlemen."

"Don't do that. Don't you dare pretend this has nothing to do with me." Emotion clogged her voice. "I grow tired of men telling me I don't have a say about what goes on around me. This has everything to do with me. Pray do not insult me by telling me not to worry my pretty little head about it." She stopped, seeming surprised by her own outburst, and he watched as she drew a deep breath to gather herself.

"Lilliana . . . or should I call you Lady Roslyn now?"

"It won't make a whit of difference what you call me if something happens to you." She crossed her arms tight across her chest. "This compulsion of yours to rescue women in distress has gone too far. I will not have your blood on my hands."

His jaw went rigid. "I would not wish that upon anyone," he said softly. "It is a terrible burden to feel responsible for someone's death."

"Do you—? Whose?" She could barely form the question.

He forced the words out. "I had a sister once who was badly used by her husband."

"Phoebe."

"Yes." He tried to ignore the pain coiling in his chest like a cobra readying to strike. "He abused her badly, and she did not survive it."

Her breath caught. "Surely, you cannot mean—?"

"That he killed her? I believe so, yes, but it was ruled an accident."

"I am sorry."

He avoided looking at her. "I was in the house when it happened. I had been staying with them." His hands gripped the back of the chair, his fingers white from the exertion. "I did not protect her, my own sister."

"When did this happen?"

"Phoebe died in eighty-eight."

"Eighty-eight?" He could see her adding up the years. "That's twenty-one years ago. You were how old?"

"I was eleven. Phoebe was three-and-twenty and my parents' firstborn. They were never the same after she died."

"You were eleven, just a boy. No one would have expected you to defend your sister against a grown man."

"They were arguing. I tried to stay in my bedchamber whenever he yelled at her. And then there was a terrible silence. I'll never forget it." He swallowed, his throat aching. "She'd fallen down the stairs. Her body was twisted in such an unnatural way that I knew she was gone."

"How awful." She put a hand to her throat. "For a young boy to witness such a thing."

"Vessey, her husband, was at the top of the stairs looking down at her. When he saw me, he claimed that she'd fallen, that she was stupid and clumsy, but I knew he had pushed her. And he knew that I knew and that I wouldn't do anything about it."

"You couldn't do anything about it because you were just a *boy*." She grabbed his arm, as though tugging on it would shake some sense into him. "Meeting Eggleston at dawn will not right the injustice done to your sister."

"No, but it will avenge the wrong done to you."

"I have survived what Eggleston did to me. I am not like Phoebe. I am alive, and I intend to live a full life. A happy life with my children. But I cannot do so if something happens to you."

He pressed a hand against the amulet hanging from the chain around his neck. It felt cool against his skin. "In Carthage, they believe this will protect me against harm."

She blinked, looking at the hand-shaped amulet with an eye at the center of its palm. "What is it?"

"It's called a hamsa. Carthaginians believe it protects against the evil eye."

"I don't even know where that is." She took a deep breath and then released it. "All I know is that in England, being on the receiving end of a pistol can result in death. I wouldn't be able to bear it. Please don't go through with the duel."

He winced at the sight of a single tear rolling down her smooth cheek. He moved closer and cradled her jaw in his hand, using the callused pad of his thumb to swipe away the tear. "Shhh, Lily, all will be well."

"Avenging me, however gallant, will not bring your sister back." Her voice trembled. "Nor will it right the wrong that was done to her. But you could get yourself killed—" Her voice broke.

"Don't cry." He drew her into his embrace. She was soft and warm against him. "Please."

She surprised him by wrapping her arms around his waist and laying her head against his partially bare chest. He inhaled the scent of her. Jasmine and cloves. "I am safe and reunited with my brother. He plans to cast Eggleston out. It is enough." She pulled back and stared into his eyes. "Please let it be. For me."

"Lily." He lowered his face and touched his lips to hers. He brushed his mouth against hers once, then twice, and she surprised him again by parting her lips. He kissed her sweetly, gentling the passion he felt for her.

She wrapped her arms around his neck and pressed herself closer to him. He widened his mouth over hers, deepening the kiss, brushing his tongue against hers. Stunned by the sensation and need swamping his body, he pulled away before he lost his mind and dragged her off to his bedchamber. "Very well." His voice was hoarse. "You win."

Her delicate cheeks were flushed with color, her breaths coming short and quick. "I do?"

"Yes, I will allow Charlton to negotiate a way for Eggleston to decline."

She put a hand on his arm. "Thank you."

He moved away. "You have what you came for." He put his back to her. "You should leave now before we do something we both will regret later."

"I'm not certain I would regret it," she said softly.

His entire body stiffened. He forced himself not to turn around. "Nor I." The words were gentle. "Please go now. I gather you have someone outside waiting to take you back to Thea's."

"Yes, her coachman." He turned back to her as she reached for her cape. He helped her put it on. "Lily," she said.

"I beg your pardon?"

"You asked what you should call me." She smiled, and he felt it in his gut. "No one has ever called me Lily, but I should like for you to when we are in private."

He walked her to the door, certain he would never be alone with her again, but he did not say so. "Good evening, Lily." He opened the door and gently ushered her out, closing the door behind her with a gentle click.

He listened to the soft tread of her footsteps as she went down the stairs, then crossed over to the window overlooking the street in time to see Thea's coachman help her into the carriage. While he watched, she paused for a moment to look up toward his window over the tobacconist's shop. His heart beating quickly, he stepped away and stayed out of view until he heard the carriage pull away.

Chapter Twenty-Five

"Atlas. There you are." Charlton stood in shirtsleeves behind the massive desk in his study. The room was decorated in soft wood tones and massive stuffed furniture—the creature comforts the earl so enjoyed. "I'm almost done here."

"Done with what?"

"Cleaning the dueling pistols ahead of your dawn engagement with Eggleston." He held one pistol up, examining the walnut and brass design with its delicate inlays of brass wire. "You need to test its weight, to become accustomed to the feel of the weapon against your palm."

Atlas exhaled heavily through his nostrils. "That won't be necessary."

Charlton selected a rod from the mahogany gun box lined with red velvet and inserted it into the pistol's long barrel. "What won't be necessary?"

"The dueling pistols." He had difficulty forcing the next words out. "As my second, I want you to seek a reconciliation."

"A reconciliation?" Charlton's attention shifted from the Holster pistol to Atlas's face. "I beg your pardon?"

"You heard me," Atlas said gruffly. He paced away, his blood boiling at the idea of allowing Eggleston to escape retribution.

"Yes, but there must be a problem with my ears because I cannot believe what I am hearing." He replaced the pistol in its mahogany box. "Just yesterday, you said nothing would stop you from shooting the man."

"I said nothing would stop me from satisfying my honor," he corrected.

Charlton reached for a linen cloth on the desk and wiped his hands. "Which in this case meant shooting Eggleston between the eyes."

"It is a second's role to attempt a reconciliation," Atlas said tightly. "I am authorizing you to do so."

Charlton studied him with his head tilted to the side. "And what, may I ask, brought on this sudden attack of equanimity?"

He avoided his friend's gaze. "Cooler heads have prevailed."

"Your temper never cools on its own. I wonder who has wrought this miraculous change on you when Somerville, Thea, and I all failed."

"Must you talk so much?" Atlas said irritably.

"Yes, I rather think that I must." Charlton smirked. "I can think of only one person who might be able to influence you away from doing violence to Eggleston."

There was no use in denying Lilliana's role. "Mrs. Warwick convinced me a duel would be ill-advised." Regret swamped him for having given her his word to stop the duel. But once he'd lost himself to the sweet press of her mouth and once he'd tasted passion from her lips, he'd have done anything at all for her. He'd have run naked through Mayfair if she'd asked.

He'd overstepped with the kiss. Although it had been a mistake, he did not regret it. Now that he knew who she really was—a duke's daughter so far above his touch that it was laughable—he did not expect to enjoy any further intimacies with her, especially with her brother already taking steps to restore her to her rightful place in society.

The West End was buzzing with news that the Duke of Somerville not only had thrown his former guardian out on his arse but had also given him the cut direct. Eggleston was ruined. No one in decent society would accept him after his very public and very dramatic falling out with the powerful Duke of Somerville.

"The lovely Mrs. Warwick convinced you, did she?" He could hear the laughter in Charlton's voice. "I will not ask what means of persuasion she employed."

"Watch yourself." Atlas gritted his teeth. "You are speaking of a lady."

"And well I know it," he said lightly. "And you are a healthy young man."

Atlas struggled to keep his temper under control. "You've had your fun, Charlton. Perhaps now you can trouble yourself to arrange a meeting with Eggleston's second."

"You are in luck, my friend." Charlton closed and latched the gun box. "They are in the drawing room awaiting our pleasure. I sent a note around to Bond Street not an hour ago."

"I did not receive it."

"Possibly because you came here of your own volition before my missive arrived at your apartments."

"What are we waiting for?" Atlas strode for the door. "Let's get this disagreeable business over with."

When they reached the drawing room, they found a pinch-faced Eggleston standing by the window, playing with the gold ring on his fourth finger, repeatedly sliding it up and then back into place. His second, Guy Blackwood, with whom Atlas was only slightly acquainted, sat in one of Charlton's straight-backed green velvet chairs.

Blackwood rose and greeted them when they entered. All four men took their seats, Eggleston and Blackwood sitting across from Atlas and Charlton. A pale, perspiring Eggleston continued to fiddle with his ring. It was a swivel bezel ring, with an optional alternate design facing down on the finger, which could be turned upward to provide a different look.

Impotent rage swamped Atlas. He clamped down hard on his chair's armrests, battling the urge to launch himself at the whoreson and pummel him senseless.

Blackwood spoke first. "It is my hope that we can settle this unfortunate matter with an apology."

"Mr. Catesby is amenable to that," Charlton said.

Eggleston's head shot up. "He is?"

The earl didn't spare a glance for Eggleston. He kept his focus on Blackwood. "Tempers have settled, and Mr. Catesby will accept an apology. However, he has a condition."

"And what is that?" Blackwood asked.

"Eggleston is to leave London, completely withdraw from society, and never return. If he agrees, Mr. Catesby will consider this matter settled."

Eggleston's face paled. His position was everything to him. Even though the duke had cut him, Eggleston still seemed to harbor hope of working his way back into society. He dropped the ring he'd been fiddling with. "The devil you say!"

Blackwood looked at Atlas. "And that will satisfy, Mr. Catesby?"

Atlas didn't hear him. A sharp buzzing filled his ears as he stared at Eggleston's ring on the Axminster carpet. The swivel ring's alternate underside design was apparent, its bright-red ruby gemstone shining against the rug's intricate golden designs.

"You bastard." Fury clouded his vision. "You're the one who tried to kill her." He launched himself at Eggleston, the momentum toppling the man's chair backward with a hard thud. Once on the floor, Eggleston tried to scramble away, but it was hopeless. Mindless with violent anger, Atlas was already on top of him, raining down heavy, punishing blows.

He heard the satisfying crack of bone and Eggleston moaning beneath him. Someone behind him implored Atlas to stop before he killed the man. He registered nothing but the desire to do intense violence to the man who'd not only abused Lilliana but also tried to kill her.

Then several hands—Charlton's footmen—were pulling him off Eggleston and physically restraining him until he began to regain some of his composure. Eggleston's still body and bloodied face came into focus. Blackwood stared at Atlas with a horrified expression on his ashen face. Even Charlton appeared uncharacteristically somber.

"Get the doctor," the earl ordered. "And send someone to Bow Street for Ambrose Endicott. Tell him we've found the killer he's looking for."

* * *

"Yes, that's him." William, Thea's former footman, pointed at Eggleston. "He's the gent who paid me to lock Mrs. Warwick in the icehouse."

Endicott nodded to the two runners flanking the footman. "That'll be all." They led William out of the drawing room. A couple of hours had passed since Charlton had sent for Endicott, and the doctor had attended to Eggleston, who now sported two black eyes and a broken nose in addition to a big lip.

"It's a damned lie!" Eggleston winced, gingerly touching the open cut on his swollen lip. "Surely you're not going to take the word of someone of the lower classes over the word of a gentleman."

"I am inclined to," Atlas said.

"Me too," Charlton added.

The runner wedged his considerable girth into one of the straight-backed chairs. "Tell us, Mr. Eggleston, why you wanted Lady Roslyn dead."

"She's nothing but a lying strumpet who enjoyed lifting her skirts for anything in breeches." He spat the venomous words. "She ran away because I tried to put a stop to her lewd and indecent behavior."

Anger and indignation flared in Atlas's chest, and he started to rise. Charlton, who stood behind him, laid a heavy hand on each shoulder, momentarily impeding him. "I would suggest you tell the truth," he said to Eggleston. "Before Catesby here decides to break both of your arms in addition to your unfortunate nose."

"Besides"—Endicott laced his beefy fingers together and rested them atop his distended belly—"the clerk at the haberdashery has identified you as the man who argued with Mr. Warwick shortly before his death. What I don't understand is why you wanted to kill Mr. Warwick and his wife."

Eggleston's eyes widened. "I didn't kill Warwick. You cannot attach that murder to me."

"We can try." Atlas ran a light finger over his lacerated knuckles, which still throbbed from the beating he'd given the man. "And it would give me great pleasure to do so."

Eggleston was momentarily silent. "I wanted to frighten Lady Roslyn, not kill her."

Endicott gave him one of his friendly smiles. "Which is why you arranged to have her locked in the icehouse," he prompted.

"Precisely. If she were allowed to return to society, I knew she would make false accusations that would poison His Grace against me. I have devoted my life to the dukedom. I wasn't going to let a hysterical, unstable woman given to mendacity blacken my name and take everything from me."

Atlas gripped the armrests, willing himself to be calm. Eggleston was a lying bastard, but Atlas managed to hold his tongue so that the runner could continue the interview.

Eggleston took a deep breath. "I paid William to lock Lady Roslyn in the icehouse to scare her. I fully expected someone from the household to discover her before any real harm came to her. You cannot prove that I intended to kill His Grace's sister any more than you can prove I killed that Warwick fellow."

"Why did you argue with Warwick?" the runner asked. "His clerk witnessed the altercation."

"He broke our deal."

Endicott pulled out his notebook. "What deal was that?"

"Shortly after she ran away, I tracked Roslyn down to where she was working at the haberdashery. She didn't see me, but Warwick did, and we struck a deal. For a price, he would marry her and move her far away to the country and never bring her back to Town."

"Did Warwick know he was marrying the sister of the Duke of Somerville?" Charlton asked.

"No." Eggleston shook his head. "He had no idea why I wanted her gone, and once he got his money, he didn't much care."

"And then, ten years on, you saw her again in Hyde Park and realized Warwick had broken the deal to keep her away from Town," Atlas said.

"I knew she'd returned to Town well before that."

Atlas shifted. "How did you know that?"

"I've checked in on her occasionally since she married Warwick. I didn't want any surprises from that quarter. One evening, shortly after she returned, I visited Warwick at his apartments above the haberdashery and reminded him of our bargain."

Endicott retrieved a pencil from his jacket pocket. "And what happened?"

"He said he would take care of it, but then, I saw her a fortnight later in the park." Anger gleamed in his eyes. "I went to

Warwick and accused him of breaking our agreement, and he said that retrieving her was proving much more difficult than he'd expected because Catesby here and his sister were sheltering her."

"And then what happened?" the runner asked.

"He demanded more money, which angered me, but I eventually agreed to pay him to get Roslyn away from London."

The runner scribbled in his notebook. "Are you saying you struck a new deal with Mr. Warwick?"

"Yes. I saw the exchange as well worth it. I needed Warwick alive to stop Lady Roslyn from ruining my life." He exhaled. "I'm the last person in the world who would have wanted Godfrey Warwick dead."

* * *

"Well, now we know why Godfrey wanted me back so desperately," Lilliana said.

Atlas had stopped by his sister's after leaving Charlton's to find Somerville visiting with Lilliana. It would take getting used to, the idea that Lilliana Warwick, the widow of a tradesman, was in fact Lady Roslyn Sterling, sister of a duke, scion of two of the *ton*'s shiniest lights who'd been tragically lost at the height of their glory.

"He wanted me back because he'd been paid handsomely," she said.

Atlas could barely conceive of it. Any man who required payment to be with Lilliana was an idiot. He'd have given his right arm to be with her. "And after Warwick was killed," he added, "Eggleston became so desperate that he hired William to make certain you didn't reunite with Somerville."

"Do you believe him?" the duke asked. "Do you believe Eggleston didn't kill the haberdasher?"

"I am inclined to." Atlas suppressed a smile at His Grace's snobbish attitude toward Godfrey Warwick, which was particularly ironic in light of the duke's own affaire d'amour with a tradesman; he seriously doubted Somerville would ever refer to Nash as "the tailor."

Lilliana paced away from them. "I agree. He doesn't appear to have a motive to kill Godfrey." She turned back. "Which means we keep looking."

The duke raised an imperious brow. "We?"

A lesser woman might have cowered beneath the weight of his ducal displeasure, but Lilliana merely shrugged. "We need to speak to the midwife in Slough, and that's not something Atlas can do without me."

Atlas blinked. "The situation has changed." A duke's sister could not very well go gallivanting across the countryside in search of a killer.

"How so?" He read the challenge in the way she crossed her arms over her chest. "I am the same woman I was yesterday morning."

Perhaps, but he viewed her differently now. "I thought you might be occupied with reacquainting yourself with your brother."

Somerville steepled his fingers under his chin. "Not to mention Aunt Olympia. She and our cousins will be most eager to see you again."

Joy lit her eyes. "Aunt Olympia is our only family besides our sister Serena," she said to Atlas. "We spent a great deal of time with her and her five daughters when my parents were alive."

“Perhaps Catesby here is correct,” her brother said. “Perhaps it is best to leave the investigation to the runners.”

“No, Mattie—”

“Call me Matthew, please.” Somerville looked pained. “We are no longer children.”

“Exactly. I am not a child, nor an innocent miss.” Steel coated her words. “I am a widow and, as such, have more license than an unmarried young girl. I intend to enjoy my freedom.”

It occurred to Atlas that Lilliana and Somerville were very much alike, with that regal bearing and sometimes-imperious attitude. He imagined any future disagreements between them would be epic ones.

Somerville held up his hands in surrender. “Very well. Do as you please.”

She smiled. “I intend to.” Turning to Atlas, she said, “I want to speak to Maud to learn more about Verity’s situation. I doubt she will tell you anything if I am not present.”

He couldn’t disagree. They made plans to return to Slough the following day.

Chapter Twenty-Six

"Do you know this midwife well?"

Lilliana nodded. "Maud Honeywell delivered both of my children, and I count her a friend."

Atlas directed the horses around a sizeable hole in the road. "And yet she might very well be responsible for Verity's death."

"I cannot imagine it." She paused. "I just remembered Maud said the strangest thing the last time we saw each other."

"About what?"

"She implied that Verity was not as loyal to her husband as he was to her."

Although he had begun to suspect as much, this was the first confirmation he'd heard that Verity Warwick might not have been utterly devoted to John Warwick. "When was this?"

"When I went to close up the house and prepare it for rental after Godfrey's death."

"What prompted this midwife to question Verity's allegiance to her husband?" Atlas asked, even though he thought he had a fairly good notion. The revelation that Verity had sought an abortion only served to reinforce his suspicions.

"She seemed to think Verity didn't want John's child, but I don't believe that. Verity wanted children desperately."

"Did the midwife elaborate further?"

"No, and I did not press her. I just remember thinking how odd her comments were. They did not fit with anything I remember about Verity."

She was quiet for the remainder of their journey, appearing to be lost in thought, speaking only when needed to direct him to Maud Honeywell's ivy-covered thatched cottage. They arrived to find the midwife, a petite woman with generous curves, at home and very welcoming.

"Mrs. Warwick! How good of you to call." Pleasure lit the woman's round face before her curious gaze bounced to Atlas and then back to Lilliana. "How are the children? I'll wager they've grown a great deal since I last saw them."

"Indeed. You wouldn't believe how tall Peter has gotten." Lilliana hugged the other woman. Atlas noted how open and relaxed she seemed with the midwife. "Maud, this is my friend Mr. Catesby. He is helping to investigate Godfrey's death."

"Is he now?" The midwife pushed open her front door and led them into a tidy cottage with white plaster walls and beamed ceilings. "You may as well come in for tea. I've some fresh biscuits that will go down nicely with it."

Once they were settled at the round table before the hearth with their refreshments, Maud said, "I don't know how I can be of help, but I am happy to try."

Atlas sat back, content to let Lilliana take the lead, which she immediately did. "We recently spoke with Benedict Dixon, who told us the postmortem showed Verity had a certain procedure. Were you aware of that?"

Maud grimaced. "Yes."

Lilliana swallowed. "Did you perform the procedure?"

Maud reared back. "Of course not! I do not kill babes. I help bring them into the world."

"I see." Lilliana released a heavy exhale. "I didn't think you could do such a thing."

Atlas learned forward in his chair. "Yet you were aware that she'd undergone the procedure."

Maud nodded. "She came to me afterward. She was in great pain and hoped I could offer her some relief."

"And could you?" Atlas asked.

"Not really." She shook her head sadly. "Her womb had been terribly abused, and I suspected an infection had set in. The truth is Verity was beyond help by the time she came to see me."

"But why would Verity want to rid herself of the baby?" Lilliana asked. "Did she tell you?" Atlas had a pretty good sense of why and wasn't surprised when the midwife confirmed his suspicions.

"The child wasn't John's."

Lilliana emitted a sound of utter disbelief. "No!"

"I could scarcely believe it myself." The midwife reached for a biscuit and broke it in two. "By then, the guilt at having been unfaithful was consuming her."

Lilliana still appeared stunned by the revelation. "When you said Verity was not as devoted to John as he was to her, this is what you meant."

"By all accounts, John Warwick wanted a child very badly," Atlas said to the midwife. "Why not pass the child off as his? It's not as if it hasn't been done before."

"She considered it." Maud sipped her tea. "But the true father refused to stand down. He was interested in being a part of the child's life."

"Which meant John would eventually have to learn the truth," Lilliana said.

"Exactly." Maud bit into a biscuit. "And Verity was determined that John never learn the truth. She was desperate not to hurt him."

"Who was the man?" Atlas asked. "Who was the father of Verity's child?"

"She never said." She sipped her tea. "Her husband came to see me after he learned the results of the autopsy. He was stunned his wife had had an abortion. The poor man couldn't make sense of it."

Atlas stood up. "Why don't you stay and visit with Mrs. Honeywell while I attend to a quick errand?"

"That would be grand." Maud patted Lilliana's hand. "It's been far too long since we've been able to visit over a cup of tea."

"Indeed." Lilliana came to her feet. "I'll just walk Mr. Catesby out." She was quiet until they stepped out of the front door. "You are going to see John."

"Yes. I do not think he would appreciate you being there when I ask him about his wife's infidelity."

"Nor do I wish to be there. What bearing do you think this has on the investigation?"

He didn't want to hurt her but felt he had no choice but to share his suspicions. "If your late husband was Verity's lover, that would have given John Warwick a strong motive for murder."

She showed no sign of being shocked. The possibility must have occurred to her as well. "An affair. I cannot conceive of it. Godfrey might have been capable of such duplicity, but Verity was not."

"We do not always know people as well as we think."

"Something is missing here." She looked out, unseeing, into the cornfields beyond the cottage. "I knew Verity quite well for ten years. She was like an older sister to me. She was not capable of that kind of disloyalty."

"To you or to John?"

"To both, but mostly to John. She loved him unreservedly." She shook her head. "We're still missing a key part of the puzzle. I'm certain of it."

When he called at John Warwick's white stucco manor house, Atlas was directed back to the garden, where the man in question closed the open book on his lap when he spotted Atlas coming down the path.

"Mr. Catesby." Warwick sat in a green wooden chair among the flowers—bunches of Sweet Williams in a variety of pinks and reds and sumptuous, plump peonies that lent a cheery note to an otherwise grim tableau. Warwick's cheeks were more sunken than Atlas remembered, and his clothes hung loosely on his frame. There could be no doubt the man's health was in decline. He seemed to be slowly wasting away.

"I apologize for calling unexpectedly."

"It is no bother. I am taking advantage of one of our rare sunny days. My wife enjoyed the sun. Sitting out here makes me think of her." He looked up at Atlas, using his hand to shield his eyes from the sun. "What brings you here? Has there been another turn in the investigation?"

He leaned against the stone retaining wall. "Something like that."

"And you've come to ask me about it."

"Yes."

"If you had waited, you could have saved yourself the trip out to Slough because I will be in Town tomorrow to visit the boys and arrange the sale of the haberdashery. But as long as you are here, you might as well ask your questions."

He hesitated. "They are of a delicate nature."

"Allow me to make it easier for you. I know you went to see Dixon."

"He told you?"

"Yes, he told me about that first visit, when you went alone, without Lilliana."

"But he never came to the door."

"He wanted to guard my privacy, which I appreciated. However, I asked him to speak to you and to tell you what you wanted to know."

"That your wife had an abortion and that's what killed her."

A slight grimace marred John's weary face. "Yes, she suffered terribly for it."

"Excuse me for being somewhat confused," Atlas said. "Why would you consent to the medical examiner sharing such personal matters with me?"

"You are pursuing my brother's murderer, and he must be brought to justice. If you believe these lines of questioning will bring you closer to learning who killed my brother, then so be it."

"Very well." He forced out the next question. "Who was your wife having an affair with?"

The puckered lines around Warwick's mouth deepened. "She was not having an affair. She was a good and honest woman."

"Yet the babe she carried was not yours."

John's eyes were ice. "She'd been forced."

Atlas straightened, his heart thumping. "By whom?"

"She never said. I didn't even know she'd been raped until she lay dying." He exhaled, a rattling, shuddering sound. "By then, she could barely get any words out."

"Where and when did this rape occur?"

"I've no idea. She wasn't able to tell me. She was too far gone." Warwick dragged both hands down his face. "I think of it often. Did it happen while she walked home from the village? She used to love to go for long walks. Did it happen in the wood?" He dropped his face into his hands. "I'll never know."

"I'm sorry."

"As am I," Warwick said. "In the end, it seems all we have left are our regrets."

Atlas left the man there in the garden, torturing himself with thoughts of his beloved wife and the attack by an unknown assailant that had eventually taken her from him.

* * *

"Poor Verity," Lilliana said. "How awful for her."

Atlas set the horses in the direction of London. "Do you believe she was forced?"

"Of course." She drew back to look at him seated beside her in the curricle. "I told you she wasn't the sort to conduct an illicit affair."

"An abortion seems particularly extreme and dangerous."

"She must have felt she had no choice. I cannot imagine what it would be like to raise a child that resulted from a rape."

"I imagine it would be very difficult."

She gave a small laugh devoid of mirth. "Godfrey would have taken her pregnancy very hard."

"How do you mean?"

"In those last few weeks before . . . the inn . . . whenever we were with Verity and John, he would often mention how his child would inherit everything after John died. He was so smug and self-satisfied."

Atlas shook his head. The man had truly been a varmint. "He would speak in such a reprehensible manner in front of John and Verity?"

"Yes. His comments were like daggers in poor Verity's heart. She would grow pale and tremble. Sometimes she would leave the room in tears. He was awful to her, constantly reminding her of her failing as a wife for not having given John an heir."

"She would have been pregnant at the time."

"Yes, I suppose."

"There were certainly many people who had a motive to kill your husband. Verity would be an ideal suspect if she hadn't died first."

"Have we hit a dead end?" she asked.

"No . . . maybe."

"What is it?"

He paused. "I feel like you had the right of it when you said we are missing a key to the puzzle."

"Which means we still need to find it."

"Yes, and when we do, we will find Warwick's killer."

* * *

Atlas awoke the following morning to find Jamie had returned. He heard the valet moving around in the front rooms.

"Are you back for good then?" he asked with a yawn, pulling on his banyan as he walked into the sitting room.

"Indeed, sir." He was setting the table with fine china and gleaming silver. Quite fancy for Atlas's little bachelor establishment. "Are you ready for your meal?"

"Has Charlton's cook sent yet another feast fit for a prince?"

"Yes, sir. She knows how well you like kidney pie. Cook sent that along with baked eggs and honey cake. And I brought some coffee from the shop a few doors down."

"Perfect. I'll start with that." He eyed Jamie's attire more closely, noting the expensive black trousers and pristine white linen shirt topped with an exquisite cream waistcoat. "New clothes?"

"Yes, sir." Jamie straightened his waistcoat. "A valet must always be impeccably dressed."

"I shudder to think how much I am going to owe Charlton."

"Nothing at all, sir." He poured the coffee into the saucer. The resulting steam that rose suggested the libation was still hot. "A valet usually receives his master's hand-me-downs. This is clothing the earl no longer needs, and his valet was kind enough to pass these pieces on to me."

He wondered whether a valet was supposed to be better turned out than his employer. "I hope you're not expecting anything so fine from me." He accepted the hot drink Jamie held out to him and went to sit at the game table. The Gainsborough was almost complete, the perfect picture coming into focus. He picked up a piece and tried it where he thought it might fit. It didn't. As he tried again in a different section, he thought over what he'd learned the day before.

Except for the sounds of his sipping the hot coffee and moving the puzzle pieces around, all was quiet, which allowed his thoughts to settle as the information he'd gathered began to fall together in his mind.

Something didn't quite fit. He thought back to the evening of the murder, when a horrible storm had raged outside. His mind moved to Verity, who had told Maud that the man who'd fathered her child had wanted to be a part of the child's life. Such a man did not sound like a rapist. Unless—

He shot up from his chair. "That's it."

Jamie reappeared instantly. "Sir?"

Atlas strode to the bedchamber. "Help me get dressed. I must get to my sister's house as quickly as possible."

Chapter Twenty-Seven

Less than an hour later, Atlas pushed open the door to Thea's breakfast room. "Where is everyone?"

She turned from her chalkboard, a smudge of white on her chin. "Must you barge in so early in the day? Really, Atlas, one would think you were raised by savages."

"Where are Lilliana and the boys?" he demanded.

She studied his face. "They've gone to the park with their guardian. The boys wanted to show Mr. Warwick how well they can bowl hoops."

Cursing, Atlas spun on his heel and practically ran for the front door. His sister dashed after him. "What is amiss? Are they in danger?"

"Possibly." He threw open the front door and charged in the direction of the park with Thea on his heels. They hadn't gone far before he spotted them walking toward him. Lilliana strolled alongside Warwick, who carried young Robin in his arms while Peter rolled his hoop along the sidewalk. Clara, the boys' nurse, trailed behind the group. Street carts and carriages rumbled by in the muddy street.

Tension coiled in Atlas's gut. He needed to get Lilliana and the boys away from Warwick before confronting the man.

Lilliana spotted them first. "Thea, Mr. Catesby." Her face lit up. "This is an unexpected surprise."

"Mr. Catesby!" Peter ran up to him, eagerness and excitement written all over his face. Atlas had not seen the boys for a while, in keeping with their mother's wishes that he keep his distance. "I was showing Uncle how well I bowl hoops. Want to see?"

He forced a relaxed tone. "I should very much like to see that, Peter." His gaze moved to Lilliana and settled on Warwick. "Good day. Enjoying the fine weather?"

"Very much," Warwick replied in the same courteous tone, yet there was no ignoring the tension that strummed between them.

"Me too." Robin squirmed in John's arms. "I'll show you, too, how I can bowl hoops. Down."

Warwick tightened his hold on the boy. "Not now, Robin. Stay with Uncle." His gaze fastened on Atlas as he withdrew something from his pocket—a sweet treat for the boy, who settled immediately, sucking contentedly.

Robin's attention was diverted by livestock in the street. He pointed. "Look at the cows."

A man drove the livestock past them, no doubt headed for market somewhere. The stench of animal dung hung heavy in the air. A man driving a cart cursed at the drover for blocking the street before wedging his cart around the animals and being on his way.

"Come to have a word with me, have you?" Warwick asked Atlas.

"Yes." He saw no reason to deny it. Warwick wouldn't believe any attempt on his part to dissemble.

Lilliana looked from one man to the other. "About what?"

Atlas kept his attention on the other man. "Put the boy down and let them be on their way with their mother."

Warwick edged closer to the street. "Robin is content enough in my arms." The young boy was still staring at the passing animals.

Lilliana stiffened. "What is going on between the two of you?"

Thea turned to Clara. "Take the boys and return to the house now."

"Yes, Mrs. Palmer." The nurse moved toward John. "It is time for the young master's nap."

John stepped away. "No need. I'll keep him with me." Clara looked to Thea for guidance.

"Go on with Peter," Thea said. The nurse ushered the older boy away.

Warwick stared at Atlas. "You've finally put it all together, have you?" He shifted the boy in his arms, resettling his weight. "How did you manage it?"

"Now is not the time to discuss this."

"I don't believe we'll have another chance. How did you realize?"

"You helped me with some of it." Atlas contemplated whether he could lunge at the man and pull Robin from his arms without endangering the boy. "The rest I worked out on my own."

The drover and his animals were well past them now and had turned a corner. The traffic on the street began to speed up. Robin yawned and rubbed his eyes. He laid his head on his uncle's shoulder.

"Which part was that?" Warwick asked.

"It did not storm in Slough the night your brother died."

Warwick's brow wrinkled. "I don't follow."

"You said you did not leave your house that evening because there was a terrible storm outside, but Bole said there was only a gentle patter on the roof."

Warwick's attention turned to the boy who'd fallen asleep in his arms. He used the pad of his thumb to gently wipe a smudge from Robin's cheek. "How does that signify?"

"There was a terrible storm here in London. It rained all night. The only way you could have known that is if you'd come to London yourself that evening."

All color leached from Lilliana's face. She reached for her son. "John, give Robin to me."

Warwick ignored the request. "He was a vile man."

"John." Lilliana pleaded with him, a panicked tremble shaking her voice. "Let me have my son. I beg of you."

He acted as if he hadn't heard her. "Tell me your theory, Catesby."

"You came to see your brother, to kill him, to make him pay for what he'd done to your wife."

"No, you are wrong. I did not come to London to murder Godfrey. I came with the intention of trying to talk some sense into him." He absentmindedly stroked Robin's back. "I'd learned he intended to charge you with criminal conversation. It was abominable. Lilliana did not deserve that. I was aghast that he intended to shame the mother of his children in that way."

Lilliana stepped in front of him and reached for her son. "Give him to me."

To Atlas's extreme relief, John relented, allowing Lilliana to take her child. Once she had ahold of her son, she moved quickly away from John, toward Thea. "Please take him home."

Thea took the sleeping child and settled him in her arms. "Are you certain you don't want to come with me?"

"Quite certain."

Thea turned to go. "Have a care," she said softly to her brother before she walked away with the child in her arms.

Warwick didn't seem to notice. He appeared too wrapped up in remembering the last evening of Godfrey Warwick's life. "My brother laughed and said that considering that fact that I couldn't even control who my own wife laid with, I had no business trying to tell him how to conduct his marriage. That's when I knew he was the one who had raped her."

The pieces began to fall into place. The midwife had said the father of Verity's child wanted to be part of the baby's life. "When she found out she was pregnant, she did want to pass the child off as yours, but Godfrey wouldn't allow that."

John nodded, his eyes going to the rumbling traffic in the street. "That is what the argument in the garden was about. Godfrey told me she'd begged him not to say anything, but he told her he would make sure I knew it was his child I was raising."

Lilliana paled. "When Godfrey kept mentioning how his child would inherit everything, he wasn't talking about Peter, was he?"

"No, he was referring to the babe he'd put in her belly. By force." John's expression was hard, angry. "He enjoyed tormenting her."

Atlas moved closer. Just one more step, and he'd be able to grab ahold of John. "Did he admit to raping her and getting her with child?"

A coach and four came charging down Great Russell Street, going far too fast for a street where families with children lived. "He said she enjoyed it. That he was disappointed she'd died because he had looked forward to watching us raise his child, all the while with me knowing he'd cuckolded me." His tone was flat, emotionless. "He hated me."

Atlas edged nearer. "He hated you because you'd always gotten everything he'd ever wanted—the land, the house, and the woman he'd intended to marry."

"I lost my mind when he began to describe the attack in vivid detail." He shifted closer to the street. The rustle and roar of the approaching coach and four, the clopping of the horses' hooves, grew louder. John raised his voice to be heard over the approaching traffic. "I grabbed the candle holder and swung it as hard as I could at his belly. Anything to shut him up."

"It was an accident," Lilliana said urgently. "You can tell the runner that. The authorities will understand. You did not mean to kill him."

"Oh, in that moment, I certainly wanted him dead." He looked toward the busy street. "And now I must pay for my crime."

John's diminishing health began to make sense. It wasn't illness that consumed him—it was guilt. "You wanted me to discover that it was you," Atlas said. "That's why you allowed the medical examiner to share the results of the postmortem with me."

He nodded. "I am a murderer and must be punished as such."

"Not if you didn't intend to kill Godfrey." Lilliana held out a calming hand. "He provoked you, and you reacted in anger. Come back to the house with me, John. The boys are waiting for you."

"No, they do not need for all of society to know their uncle killed their father." He smiled, the expression eerie and distant, as if he'd already escaped the bonds of earth. "It is better for it to be known that a tragic accident took me."

The coach and four bore down on them. John leapt into the street before Atlas could stop him.

"No!" Lilliana screamed and instinctively lunged after him. Atlas grabbed her and pulled her into his arms, turning to shield her from the gruesome sight in the street as the four perfectly matched gray-dappled mares reared and whinnied and trampled John Warwick to death.

* * *

They buried him a few days later in the same churchyard where his wife and brother had so recently been laid to rest. The service was crowded, with many expressing dismay at having lost such a fine man to a tragic carriage accident. Unlike his brother, John Warwick had been well regarded in the county and would be missed.

He left a will bequeathing everything to Peter and Robin. Although Peter received the house, John left a respectable inheritance of land and funds for Robin, the younger brother.

Endicott attended the burial. "I wonder," the runner said to Atlas as they left the churchyard, "what would drive a man to take his own life."

"I wouldn't know," Atlas replied in a mild, almost disinterested manner. "It is a terrible tragedy that befell John Warwick, falling into the street that way."

"It is the strangest thing. We have a witness who says he leapt in front of the carriage." Endicott clasped his hands behind his back. "I interviewed John Warwick on two occasions, and his health had declined markedly. In retrospect, it was almost as if guilt literally ate away at him."

"Surely your witness is unreliable. The sister of the Duke of Somerville says his death was an accident. As do I." Atlas looked straight ahead as they walked. "If anyone were to surmise that John Warwick killed himself, or that he had a hand in his brother's death, it would leave a terrible stain on Mrs. Warwick and the children, who have already endured far too much hardship and loss."

Endicott stopped and peered at him with intelligent black eyes among the fleshy folds of his face. "If I had the proof, I would name John Warwick as the killer and close this case." He shrugged his hefty shoulders. "Unfortunately, I do not have sufficient evidence. Consequently, the murder of Godfrey Warwick will likely remain unsolved."

Atlas held out his hand. He'd come to respect the man's intelligence and dedication to duty. "Until we meet again, Endicott. Hopefully under more pleasant circumstances."

The runner gave a hearty handshake. "I look forward to it, Mr. Catesby."

"As do I," Atlas said, realizing—to his surprise—that he might actually mean it.

* * *

"Must you be so damned stubborn?" The Duke of Somerville fixed Atlas with an icy glare.

"Yes, I'm afraid I must." They were in the front hall of Somerville House, where Atlas prepared to take his leave. The duke had summoned him to his palatial home bordering Hyde Park to discuss rewarding him for repeatedly coming to Lilliana's aid. Atlas had been insulted by the very suggestion.

He took in the splendor of the place. This is where Lilliana had grown up, and it was now her home again. He hadn't seen her or the boys since they'd moved in with Somerville a sennight ago.

"I only wish to give you a small token of my appreciation," Somerville intoned.

"I told you he wouldn't take it." A smiling Lilliana appeared from behind the statue. He was rather fond of that off-kilter smile of hers, the only imperfection he could find in an otherwise impossibly elegant woman. "Hello, Atlas."

"My lady." He bowed, his heart contracting at the sight of her. She was finely dressed in a shimmering blue gown with jewels dripping from her ears and neck. He was glad to see she'd shed the color of mourning, at least while at home. Seeing her here in her girlhood abode, completely at ease with her brother, the duke, made him keenly aware of the mammoth chasm between them.

"Why haven't you come to call?" she admonished. "The boys are keen to show you how well they can bowl hoops now."

"Yes," the duke said. "I fear I am atrocious at it."

"Will you stay for supper?" she asked, her expression hopeful. "My cousins are coming. It will be my first time seeing them again."

"I wouldn't want to intrude."

The duke scoffed. "It is no intrusion. We are entertaining my aunt and her five daughters. You would at least help to balance our numbers."

Seeing no reason to prolong the inevitable, Atlas began to decline just as the footman opened the front door and a crowd of swishing gowns and chattering voices filled the space.

"My cousins have arrived," the duke said. "Save yourself. I only wish that I could." He turned to his aunt and cousins, greeting them with courtly flair.

Atlas looked at Lilliana. "I must go. This is a family affair."

She paused, a hint of uncertainty in her beautiful eyes. "You'll call on me soon, won't you?"

He smiled, but before he could respond, her cousins enveloped her, and she was swept away in a cloud of silk, laughter, and perfume. Turning to leave, he placed his hat on his head, content to have had a hand in returning Lily to her world, one to which he would never belong.

It was past time for him to resume his own life anyway. Cousin George's frigate had finally pulled into port. When it set sail again in a few weeks, he intended to be on board, bound for his next adventure.

The footman dressed in sumptuous gold-and-black livery drew open the door, and Atlas stepped outside, breathing in the cool late-autumn air. It would not be long now before winter's frost set in. A carriage clattered by, and somewhere far off, the forlorn call of a clarinet filtered through the Mayfair darkness.

Pulling his greatcoat closed to ward off the chill, Atlas bounded down the stairs and went into the night.

Acknowledgments

England during the Regency was a place of contrasts. The formal Regency lasted from 1811—when mad King George III was deemed unfit and his son was named Prince Regent to rule in his place—until George III's death in 1820.

Unofficially, this distinctive period in English history, a time when art, architecture, style, and literature flourished, lasted from 1795 until 1837, when Queen Victoria ascended the throne. I wanted my protagonist, Atlas Catesby, to move in this world because it was a time of extremes: of elegance and extravagance, as well as crime and poverty.

I owe a great debt to my friend Megann Yaqub, mystery reader extraordinaire, for the numerous hours she spent brainstorming this story with me, mostly over the phone, although we did sneak in some lunches along the way. Joanna Shupe, JB Schroeder, and Tina Kashian read the manuscript and offered critical suggestions. Michele Mannon can also always be counted on for writerly support and lots of laughs. I'm so grateful for all of my writer friends who make up the Violet Femmes at NJRW.

In her elegant, gracious, and tenacious way, my agent, Kevan Lyon, pushed me to make this manuscript memorable, and then my outstanding editor, Faith Black Ross, made it shine even more. My thanks to everyone at Crooked Lane Books, including Lori Palmer, who gave me a gorgeous cover.

My husband, Taoufiq, was the first and most ardent supporter of my writing, and my boys, Zach and Laith, make everything worthwhile.

But my sincerest appreciation of all goes to you, the reader, for spending this time in Atlas's world. I hope you've enjoyed it!